AMAZON BURNING

A James Acton Thriller

By
J. Robert Kennedy

James Acton Thrillers
The Protocol
Brass Monkey
Broken Dove
The Templar's Relic
Flags of Sin
The Arab Fall
The Circle of Eight
The Venice Code
Pompeii's Ghosts
Amazon Burning

Detective Shakespeare Mysteries
Depraved Difference
Tick Tock
The Redeemer

Special Agent Dylan Kane Thrillers
Rogue Operator
Containment Failure
Cold Warriors

Zander Varga, Vampire Detective
The Turned

AMAZON BURNING

A James Acton Thriller

J. ROBERT KENNEDY

ISBN-10: 1500778397

ISBN-13: 978-1500778392

First Edition

10 9 8 7 6 5 4 3 2 1

For the best friend I ever had, Paul Conway.

You are missed.

AMAZON BURNING

A James Acton Thriller

"There are many humorous things in the world; among them, the white man's notion that he is less savage than the other savages."

Mark Twain, Following the Equator: A Journey Around the World

"You can't measure the mutual affection of two human beings by the number of words they exchange."

Milan Kundera

PREFACE

Imagine a small town in the middle of the desert in Nevada. It has no roads leading in or out, and never has. The people have lived there for as long as anyone can remember, happily, peacefully, at one with each other and their land. No planes fly over it, no tourists stumble upon it and only the occasional explorer or adventurer has even been near it. It is isolated and unknown to the outside world. The outside world as much a mystery to it, as it is to the outside world.

Then imagine one day it was gone, its population wiped out because under the town, there was something a previously unknown town wanted, and they were in the way.

Who would know? Who would weep for them?

Though fictional, this scenario is happening today, in the real world. On July 3rd 2014 it was reported that a previously uncontacted tribe had emerged from the Amazon Rainforest in Brazil, near the Peruvian border. The tribe, to this point able to live in peace far from Western civilization, had been forced ever closer to other tribes by illegal logging in Peru. As their traditional lands were destroyed, they eventually had no choice but to make contact with another tribe who they knew had relations with the "white man".

International treaties protect these uncontacted tribes, once thought to be so desperately primitive that we would actively seek them out and "rescue" them from their misery, inviting them into the bottom rungs of Western society. Modern thinking has evolved to the point where we now leave them alone. Many are aware of us, but chose not to contact us, and still others are not. Brazil estimates there are 77 uncontacted tribes in their territory, with another 15 in Peru and still more in other Amazonian

1

countries. Dozens more have been located through aerial surveys in New Guinea and the Andaman Islands off India, and still more are thought to live in Malaysia and central Africa.

Though these tribes may appear primitive to us, who are we to say our lives are any better than theirs? They live, they work, they laugh, they love. They have friends, families, homes and communities. They have purpose and they have problems.

So how are they different from us?

In one fundamental way. They cannot harm us, but with our technology, with our greed and ambivalence, we can wipe them out in a single stroke.

But when it happens, and it does, who would know that one more uncontacted tribe had disappeared when no one remains to sing their songs and tell their stories, including the final story, of when the white man came.

Northern Amazon
54 Cycles after the Year of the Screaming Eagle
Fifth Day of the Third Moon

Tuk blushed.

Quickly looking away, he pretended he hadn't been staring at TikTik, instead following the track of an imaginary bird in the sky. Out of the corner of his eye he glanced back in her direction and saw her smiling at him as she brushed her future mate's grandmother's hair.

She's so beautiful.

His heart sank as he saw Bruk sneak up behind her then roar as he wrapped his arms around her and lifted her off the ground. She giggled in glee, a shy kiss exchanged before Grandmother snapped at them to settle down and wait for the mating ceremony otherwise they'd be cursed with ugly children.

Another peck was exchanged behind the old grandmother's back before TikTik returned to her ministrations, Bruk receding into the forest, spear in hand, probably off to slay something for dinner big enough to feed most of the small tribe.

And it ate him up inside.

You're pathetic.

And he was. Among the men he was the slightest, the weakest. His voice was high and lacked any of the confidence the others had.

He was a woman with a penis.

And you'll never get a mate like TikTik.

His face fell with his shoulders as he shuffled into the forest leaving the village clearing behind him, the sounds of life and laughter quickly fading, replaced with the constant cry of the jungle. The creatures they shared their home with were well known to him, one of his many intellectual talents the ability from a young age to distinguish the sound of every creature in the forest.

His father, the greatest hunter he had ever known, had taught him how to track and Tuk had become exceptional at it. Unfortunately he didn't possess the strength to throw the spear to take down the prey he found. He could aim and hit a target with ease, it was piercing the skin deep enough that was the problem.

A tremendous disappointment to his father.

As he quietly walked through the forest, his bare feet enjoying the coolness of the damp morning ground, he heard a wild boar squeal in the distance and knew Bruk had found his next kill.

And his heart felt a twinge of regret for the poor, helpless creature. And perhaps that was it, that was why he could never throw hard enough. Perhaps it was that these creatures who would be their dinner were as helpless as he was. Weak in the face of the mighty hunters of the tribe, like he was. Perhaps they were his kindred spirits.

He gently pushed aside a large, lazy snake with his spear as it dangled in front of him, eyeballing him. Even his slight state would present a challenge to this particular creature, but he knew some of the bigger ones could swallow him whole with ease.

The thought terrified him.

As a child he had seen a yakumama snake devour a boar then regurgitate the still live creature as if toying with it, only to swallow it down again moments later, the look in its eyes one of pure evil. It was to be respected, and avoided. Rarely would the tribe tackle such a creature, though there had been times when one would get a taste for man and they, along with some of the other tribes in the area would cooperate to hunt it down and kill it.

The feast would be glorious, though he always wondered if they were indirectly eating their fellow tribesmen.

He shivered.

Maybe I should see how she is doing?

The thought of his future mate warmed him and brought a smile to his face. He would be marrying from outside the tribe, which was encouraged whenever possible. She was no TikTik, but was beautiful in her own unique way, and in time he knew they would both grow to love each other the way he secretly loved the forbidden TikTik.

A scream from the other side of the village had him frozen in place as he turned his head, cocking an ear as the sounds of the forest changed.

Another scream.

A man's scream.

Bruk!

And it was fear, not anger. Tuk could honestly say he had never heard Bruk ever express fear, and it sent a chill down his spine like he had never experienced before. His instinct was to run the other way, to escape whatever had terrified this great warrior, but he resisted the urge. His mother was still in the village.

And TikTik.

More screams, then strange cracking sounds and shouts, voices he didn't recognize, words that were foreign to him. He readied his spear and rushed back toward the village, the thoughts of another tribe attacking his small family filling him with rage. TikTik screamed, her voice so beautifully distinctive he'd recognize it anywhere, then his mother's. A beast roared, trees snapped, and still he ran toward the horror, determined to help his family and friends.

And the woman who would be Bruk's mate.

The roar of the beast was louder now and continuous. He had never heard such a creature before, its sound so loud and long, he wondered when it would need to pause for breath. Trees continued to be felled by the beast, it clearly massive if it were able to take down so many so quickly.

He was almost at the clearing where his village had sat for as long as he had been alive. Their numbers were small now, only half a dozen huts enough to contain all thirty of their clan. Over the years many girls had been born, more than boys, and then several boys had died in a tragic incident with a wild boar. With the tradition among the local tribes of the man finding a mate from another tribe, and bringing her back to live with the male's tribe, their numbers had dwindled, the girls taking mates and leaving, and not very many men reaching mating age to bring a spouse home. They were few, and eventually they would all be gone, leaving their tribe a mere memory to be lost as the forest reclaimed what was rightfully Hers.

Perhaps my new mate and I can delay that for another generation.

He tore past the ring of trees around the clearing and dropped to his stomach instantly, scurrying back into the cover of the forest as his jaw dropped and his already racing heart threatened to burst from his chest. The roaring beast, quieter now but still growling, sat near the edge of the trees on the other side of the clearing. Creatures, all black with faces as smooth as a still pond were pouring into the village, short spears not much longer than a man's arm held in their hands. It was as if pure black Panthers had learned to stand on their hind legs.

Then his heart leapt into his throat and he slowly slid farther back into the jungle as he realized what he was seeing. It was an abomination, a legend told to frighten children and respect the forest.

He had never actually dreamed they were real.

The Panther People.

6

He had heard of the tribe that had long ago killed the regal creatures and worn their skins, disrespecting their kills, failing to honor the Mother for Her sacrifice.

And they had paid a horrible price.

The black panthers had entered the village and consumed them all, and as a reward from the Mother, been given the powers of man.

It was a story told to children to prepare them for their first hunt, and to warn them of the dangers of disrespecting the forest, the Mother. All life was sacred, and all life served its purpose. If it were necessary to kill to feed or protect oneself, the Mother understood. To kill for pleasure? That was a sin punishable by banishment or worse—though he thought death would be preferable to banishment from the tribe.

He loved his tribe, his family, his friends.

For he had friends. Even the great Bruk was his friend. None of the tribe faulted him for his lack of ability as a hunter, none of them teased him. It was simply accepted as a fact, and he helped in other ways, usually as a tracker for the hunters, or as a trader with nearby tribes since they found him unintimidating.

And as he watched the Panther People round up his tribe, tears rolled down his cheeks as he sat by helpless, cursing himself for not having the soul of a warrior like Bruk.

It was then that he saw two of the Panther People pull a body into the center of the village and dump it on the ground.

Bruk!

TikTik screamed, rushing toward him but was struck down as one of the creatures pointed at her. She fell to the ground, shaking horribly, then was still. Dead.

He cried out in rage, jumping to his feet and hurtling his spear through the air. His aim was true, hitting the creature in the chest, but his weapon bounced off the thick black skin harmlessly.

Then the creature pointed at him.

Tuk realized the horrible mistake he had made and spun, racing into the trees as cracking sounds erupted from their attackers and the trees around him began to erupt, splinters bursting from the mighty trunks as he fled the only home he had ever known.

As he swiftly cut a path silently through the trees, his mind unable to comprehend what had just happened, the sounds began to fade into the distance and he slowed to catch his breath.

What am I supposed to do?

He realized he needed help, he needed the other tribes to help fight the Panther People, but he also knew they would probably be too scared to fight, instead more likely to flee their own villages.

Then he realized what he had to do.

He had to ask the Woman of Light for help. He knew she had special powers, and he knew she would help him. She was one of the Spirit People, and had let herself be taken.

And after the Cleansing Ritual, he would be ready to present her to the tribe.

As his mate.

He closed his eyes as he remembered their first successful communication. Her voice, so different from those of the women of his tribe, had said his name with little effort.

"Tuk?" she had repeated, and he had nodded fervently, so happy she had said it, the sound of her voice filling him with a rapturous wonder, this creature a woman like no other. He had urged her to say it again and again until she had laughed at his excitement, a wondrous sound that echoed through the forest, bringing it to life as the creatures around them had shared in their joy.

Then she had taught him her name.

It had been hard to say, but she had been patient, and after an annoying length of time he had finally mastered it.

And he said it now, filling himself with warmth and love as he set off to ask for help from his future mate.

"Lau-ra-pal-mer."

Rio Negro, Northern Amazon, Brazil
Present Day

Professor James Acton lay in a hammock, it swaying gently as the quiet put-put of the engine guided them to the farthest reaches of the Amazon River. A bottle of water balanced on his stomach, rising and falling with each breath, his face one of contentment as he simply listened to the jungle around him, a never ending cacophony of sound that at first was overwhelming, but after two weeks was now oddly soothing. He knew he'd miss it when they went back home.

Sitting in a lounge chair on the other side of the deck was his wife, Professor Laura Palmer. They had married not even two months before, finally managing to find time to gather their closest friends and family, and not have some terrorist group or ancient cult interfere with their plans.

It had been wonderful.

Laura had been stunning in her dress, a simple yet elegant affair that he had no doubt cost a fortune, but not audaciously so. His wife was rich, unbelievably rich. Though both archeology professors on opposite sides of "the pond"—both making modest salaries as such—her late brother had been an Internet pioneer, divesting himself of his company before the bubble burst, leaving him with hundreds of millions of dollars, and leaving it to her when he had been killed on a dig in Syria.

He had no idea she was rich when he first met her several years ago, and when he had found out she was "well off", he had no clue just how much so for some time. Their first meeting was anything but romantic, but when he had caught his first real sight of her, standing in front of her classroom, lecturing her students at University College London, he had felt a flutter.

It had been love at first sight, though it took a few more looks to realize it, what with half the city trying to kill or capture him.

They had fallen in love, she secretly confessing to having a bit of a crush on him for years, following his work from afar after reading a spread done on him in National Geographic. He had been flattered, and somewhat embarrassed to have to admit he had never heard of her before he had found that damned crystal skull and discovering she was considered the expert in them.

It was during that first day together that they met Detective Chief Inspector Hugh Reading, who occupied a second hammock at the far end of the rear deck. Mosquito netting covered the entire deck, the bugs far too thick at times to make their journey enjoyable if left exposed. They were designed to be raised and lowered, but had been lowered most of the time, Acton now firm in his belief that Reading simply wasn't an outdoorsy type.

Happy Hugh, Happy Cruise.

Laura had coined the phrase, much to Reading's annoyance. The aging ex-cop, now an INTERPOL Special Agent, had become a loyal friend, helping them out over the years on many occasions, and though they rarely saw each other, they often talked on the phone, Acton now considering Reading one of his best friends. Laura adored the man as well, and Acton was certain Reading thought of her like a daughter, though he'd never admit it—it would mean he'd have to admit he was old enough to be her father.

After honeymooning in South Africa—a ten day safari the highlight—Laura had surprised him with four all access passes to the World Cup in Brazil. He had to admit he wasn't a soccer—football!—fan, though he had slowly begun to develop an appreciation for the sport since Laura and Reading would talk about it non-stop when they were together, and he had been forced to watch umpteen matches on the "telly" as they called it, and on a few occasions had actually seen the games live, Laura getting the three of them tickets to see her favorite, Manchester United.

At times the game was so slow it reminded him of a particular Simpsons episode, leaving him wishing a soccer riot would break out, but usually the games were actually exciting, though low scoring. After seeing a few games he could see why the crowd would go nuts when a goal was finally scored.

Boredom relieved?

The World Cup had been fantastic, and not the fiasco he had feared might happen. He had been disappointed for his British friends on how their team had done, but was happy to have watched several of the US team's better performances. He turned his head to look at the possessor of the fourth ticket—his best friend and confidante, Gregory Milton. Milton had been his best friend since college, and had been his boss for over five years—and it hadn't affected their friendship in the least. During the crystal skull business Milton had taken a bullet in an assassination attempt but luckily survived, relegated to a wheelchair he had been told he'd never leave.

They were wrong.

Determination, hard work, and a loving support network had him now walking, though for short distances. The poor bastard had toughed it out through the entire wedding, keeping his promise to himself that there wouldn't be a single picture of him in his wheelchair. It still brought tears to Acton's eyes when he thought of the text message his friend had sent when he thought he was dying.

And it had been days before he had discovered his friend was actually alive, saved by an off-duty ER surgeon who had stopped for gas at the same station.

Milton sat in his chair, his head lolled back as he gently snored, his Kindle sitting in his lap, his once skinny legs now healthy and propped up on a stool.

This is the life.

Four friends, together, cruising up one of the source tributaries of the world's mightiest river in its biggest rain forest, in silence. No need to talk, just enjoying each other's company, a mix of classical guitar playing through an iPod docking station nearby, the volume low so the sounds of Mother Nature surrounding them could still be heard.

Reading swatted at a bug on his arm and muttered a curse about one of the bastards getting through. Acton took a swig from his water bottle as his friend swung his legs to the floor then stretched with a groan that could wake the dead, the forest protesting at the disturbance. Transferring to a chair, Reading looked over at Acton.

"You seem pleased with yourself," he observed.

Acton chuckled, swinging out of the hammock a little more elegantly than his friend, then walking over to give Laura a peck. He sat beside her, taking her hand in his. "Just enjoying the company," he said, squeezing Laura's hand.

Milton stirred, bolting upright in his chair before gaining his bearings. "What did I miss?"

Laura shook her head. "Nada, just a bunch of lazy folks doing and saying nothing."

Acton decided to have a little fun with Reading. "You know, I was doing some checking and if I'm not mistaken, England has never won the World Cup."

Reading's eyes widened and his chest expanded as he leaned forward, his finger raising to jab his point home. "I don't know where you get your bloody facts, but we won in 1966, on home soil!"

Laura squeezed Acton's hand, already realizing what was about to happen. "1966? You mean the one where the Soviet referee gave you that goal that never actually went in?"

Acton had to bite his tongue to prevent himself from smiling as Reading jumped to his feet. "That was a goal! Everyone knows that was a goal! Only the damned Germans say it wasn't, and that's because they lost!"

"Are you sure?" Acton waved his iPad as if it were the key piece of evidence in a murder trial. "On here it shows how it was impossible for the ball to have actually gone in. They say it bounced on the line and back out."

Reading walked over and snatched the iPad away, turning back to his chair as Acton and Milton exchanged grins. "I saw that bloody match and I know it was a goal. Whoever is feeding you these lies is a bloody Hun!" He paused. "Sorry, that was uncalled for. But whoever they are, they are bloody anti-British!"

His fingers flew over the iPad and he held it up triumphantly, a clip of the 1966 World Cup final against Germany playing. "Look at that, it clearly goes over the line!"

Laura leaned forward, gasping. "Hugh! Do you realize how much that costs to download from here! That's tethered to the satellite phone!"

Reading blanched, his jaw dropping, clearly aghast. His finger flew at the pause button.

"It's still downloading, Hugh!" exclaimed Milton as he leaned forward, joining in on the fun.

Acton pointed at the iPad. "You have to close the browser window!"

"How the bloody hell do I do that?"

"My God, that must be, what, a thousand dollars already?" Milton bit down on his thumb as he exchanged glances with Acton and Laura.

"There!" cried Reading triumphantly as he simply turned off the device, his face red. He looked at Laura. "I'm so sorry, I had no idea—"

The three of them burst out laughing and Reading realized he'd been had. Acton rose and took the iPad, grabbing his friend's shoulder and shaking him. "I'm sorry, Hugh, that was just too damned easy!"

"Fowk off!" muttered Reading under his breath as he shook his head. Acton returned to his chair as Reading calmed himself slightly. "Okay, you got me. So how much did that cost, anyhow?"

"Oh, Greg's about right," replied Laura. "Probably about a grand." Reading's jaw dropped again but before he could say anything Laura waved her hand to dismiss any apology. "And I don't care. James watched Netflix last night. It probably cost us ten times that."

Acton suddenly felt the same guilt and shame his friend had moments before. He turned to Laura. "My God, Laura. I'm sorry. It didn't even occur to me!"

"Love, if it mattered, I'd have said something. I just want us all to be happy, and God knows we can afford it."

Acton shook his head, still feeling guilty. He smiled at her slightly. "At least I selected lo-def! I bet Hugh didn't!" He spun his head at Reading, his eyes glaring at him. "J'accuse!"

"Don't try that Frenchie shit on me, old boy. Besides, I wouldn't know lo-def from low-jack. It's all bloody Greek to me."

Acton took Laura's hand in his, kissing her wedding ring and winking at her. "I guess we'll never know if England really should have won that soccer match."

"Football!" cried Reading and Laura at the same time.

They all roared in laughter, their happiness carrying across the water, when Reading pointed. "Hallo! What's this? Looks like a good place to hole up for the night."

Acton looked to where his friend was pointing to see a shallow inlet with a clearing on the shore. Reading was right, it was perfect.

Laura shouted for the captain of their boat, Fabricio, who appeared moments later. "Yes, senhora?"

She pointed at the inlet. "What do you think?"

15

Fabricio looked and smiled. "Perfeito!" He disappeared, shouting orders, and the boat slowly turned toward its resting place for the night.

Acton turned toward Reading. "So, when are the FIFA Oscars announced."

"Huh?"

"For all those dives the players take during the match."

Reading shook his head. "Bloody Americans. Just wait until I start in on baseball and see how you feel."

"Bring it on!" Acton suddenly stopped, the smile disappearing from his face. "What's that?"

Northern Amazon
First day of the Third Moon
Three days before the attack

Tuk's shoulders heaved, the heaviness in his heart overwhelming. The woman he loved barely knew he existed, so much so she was pledged to another man. A man who was his friend. A man he had envied his entire life, and now even more so that he had captured the heart of the beautiful TikTik.

TikTik!

He screamed her name in his head, his eyes closed as he pictured her smile. To say she barely knew he existed wasn't fair. She knew him—she knew him well. After all, their tribe barely numbered thirty so it interacted closely with the neighboring tribes, hers only an hour's walk away. They had grown up together, played together, and because of his slight size, he hadn't roughhoused with the boys as much, instead preferring the company of the girls.

I'm a woman with a penis!

It was his own insult to himself—he was his worst tormentor. Some from the other tribes would tease him, especially when he was younger, but now that he was a man and dealing mostly with adults, the teasing was mostly gone, unless the alcohol started to flow, then the teasing began anew. He would usually make an excuse and leave beforehand, returning to his village should there still be enough light, or to his guest quarters, pretending to sleep, instead wincing with each barb at his expense as it sliced through the laughter and darkness, the truly vicious insults delivered at an ever increasing volume.

Too often he cried himself to sleep.

He was so lonely it hurt, and he knew his face revealed his pain every time his mother looked at him. His father had died years before saving a young hunter from a charging boar, and it had opened a void in his life, his father his constant companion. His friend Pol had filled that void, an older boy who took him under his wing, and in time a friendship developed that was so close the two became each other's confidants, no secret too great that wouldn't be shared.

Even his longing for TikTik.

Pol had always been there for him, day in and day out, filling the void. When he needed someone to listen, Pol was there, when he needed advice, Pol would oblige. If he just needed to sit in silence, but with a companion, his friend was there.

And now he wasn't.

He had become sick a few weeks ago and no one knew of what. A vicious cough turned into fever, shaking and sweating. Eventually he had begun to see things, to imagine people and creatures around him, and in a moment of lucidity had called out for Tuk, but Tuk had been at the next village trading, assured by their medicine man there was no hope of ever speaking to Pol again.

But he had been wrong.

And Tuk blamed himself for missing his one last opportunity to say goodbye to his friend, and it broke his heart every time he thought of his friend calling for him, and he not there to answer, to take his hand in his and just let him know he wasn't alone, and that he was loved.

Tuk wiped the tears away from his face with the back of his hand and looked up as a sound carried over the waters of Mother's River. It was a three day's hike from his village, and he had only seen it once before when he was younger, but when Pol had passed, he had run away lest anyone see his tears, and after much indecision, eventually decided to visit Mother's River. The last time had been with his father shortly before he had died, and now he sat on the very spot where he had once relaxed with his father as he told tales of strange people and stranger boats that carried them. His father had never seen them himself, but the stories were passed on during visits from tribes that lived closer to the great river.

The Spirit People.

And there was one thing they all agreed upon.

Never approach these strange creatures, and never be seen by them.

Lest death befall you.

It was believed they were from the next life, the one after this, when the great Mother reclaimed her children and rewarded them with everlasting life. Some believed that was a life of joy on the Mother River, others believed it was in the sky at the firesides that twinkled in the night. Tuk wasn't sure what to believe, but he did believe in prudence.

He rose slightly and stepped back into the forest, abandoning his perch at the side a small inlet of calm water and pleasant shade. The cool breeze that had at one moment helped keep the bugs away now carried curious smells, and sounds that continued to get louder.

Laughter.

Several people were talking and laughing, their voices carrying across the water, and as his curiosity overcame his fear, he edged forward, peering around a large tree as the oddest looking boat he had ever seen came around a bend in the river. It was massive, at least the length of five men if not ten. And tall, rising out of the water higher than the tallest building in their village.

It was completely white, as white as the eyes in his head, and seemed to be moving without any sign of oars, the only way he knew to propel a boat, though he was no expert, his own tribe rarely venturing this far.

19

He heard a woman's laugh, it so casual and genuine, it lifted his soured spirits. He peered across the water and finally caught sight of the source of such a beautiful sound.

A woman whiter than any he had ever seen.

And more uniquely beautiful than he could have ever dreamed.

And in that very instance, he knew he had to possess her.

Somebody on the boat yelled and pointed to his position. Tuk's heart leapt into his throat and he plunged back in the woods as the boat turned toward him.

Rio Negro, Northern Amazon, Brazil
Present Day

"What is it?" asked Laura as they jumped to their feet, all eyes on the shore.

"I saw someone, or at least I think I did." Acton had to admit he wasn't sure. It was more of a shape, small, slight, sort of reddish brown. As soon as he had pointed it had disappeared. "It must have been an animal."

"Are you sure?" Reading sounded concerned. "Perhaps we should find another place to weigh anchor."

Acton shook his head, motioning toward the western horizon. "The sun's low already. The chances of us finding another location like this are slim to none before nightfall, then we're stuck in the middle of the river. I'd rather get off the boat and set up camp where we can stretch our legs."

Reading frowned but acquiesced. Acton suppressed his smile, knowing damned well that Reading would enjoy any excuse to stay onboard, the eight legged and no legged creatures he hated in far too great abundance on land for his liking. Even Acton had to admit to a little bit of trepidation, the insects large, numerous and exotic in appearance.

Especially when they were sitting on your chest staring at you when you woke up, and you could physically feel them walking away.

That was the first night and from then on he made certain the tent was sealed up tight every instant it was ashore. There had been no more bedtime surprises, but many campfire ones. He was loving the trip, of that there was no doubt, but he had to confess he was looking forward to getting home and back into his comfortable bed.

Or Laura's.

They still hadn't settled on living arrangements, though there hadn't been much time since the wedding. After their two week honeymoon, they had split some time between his house and her flat, then came to Brazil for most of June, and then straight to this cruise.

Thank God it's summer break!

The subject had been avoided the entire time, and Acton wasn't sure if it was intentional or not. All he knew was that it would need to be settled soon, since this little trip was over in four days, the Venezuelan-Colombian border less than half a day away at which point they would turn around, return to Manaus and take Laura's private jet home.

Home.

Part of him wondered why they needed to change anything. It had worked out well so far. They split their time between London and Maryland, Peru and Egypt. It kept things exciting.

But it's not a marriage.

The boat pulled up to the shore, its shallow draft hull allowing them to get within a few feet. A ramp was thrown down and several of the crew quickly tied the boat to nearby trees, the anchor dropped. The clearing and nearby forest were inspected and the all-clear given. Acton was off first, Laura second with Reading and Milton taking up the rear. Acton placed Milton's chair near the shore, pushing it down to make sure it was stable, then he and Reading helped him into his seat, the most comfortable on the boat. The crew of six had the clearing free of debris, a fire pit dug and ringed with rocks, then tents set up within less than half an hour.

Acton had to admit they had skills.

They had boarded the Juliana at the end of the main tour that most tourists took out of Manaus, a city buried in the heart of the Amazon Rainforest at the mouth of the Rio Negro where it emptied into the mighty Amazon River. This smaller, more maneuverable boat had taken them where few had gone before, deep into the jungle where their guides assured them tribes never before seen by modern man still lived to this day.

How exciting would that be?

To discover a tribe never before seen by "modern man". To communicate with them, to learn their ways and culture. To destroy their entire belief system by exposing them to modern technology.

He sighed.

They need to be left alone.

He would happily settle for seeing them from a distance, undisturbed, going about their daily lives as they had for thousands of years. And the thought reminded him of what he had seen from the boat. He walked over to the tree where he was sure he had seen something and examined the area, the only light now from the flickering fire ten feet away. He debated getting his flashlight but decided against it when the cook announced dinner.

I'm sure it was nothing.

But something made the hair on the back of his neck stand up as he turned, a feeling of forewarning he had felt too many times just before something took a turn for the worse. He eyed Laura, who smiled at him and patted a clear spot beside her on the ground.

Perhaps we should *sleep on the boat tonight.*

Northern Amazon
First day of the Third Moon
Three days before the attack

Tuk watched the man from his perch not twenty paces away. He was tall, taller than any man he had seen before. And there was another older man who appeared even taller. In fact all the pale ones were tall, including the woman.

They must be from a mighty clan of warriors!

The man turned away and Tuk shifted, a loose branch rustling slightly. The man froze, and Tuk could tell he was resisting the urge to turn around. Tuk prepared himself, ready to disappear deeper into the forest should it become necessary, but after only a few moments the man resumed walking toward the fire where a darker skinned man was preparing what Tuk assumed was food, the few wafts of it that had drifted his way delicious.

You better keep that fire fed, otherwise you'll have uninvited company.

Every carnivore within half a day's travel would be smelling this feast, the wind blowing inland. It would shift soon, out over the river, but these strange people didn't seem to understand the ways of the Mother. He said a silent prayer for their safety. Fools didn't deserve to die at Her hand, these people clearly not of this land.

But where are they from?

They wore strange things on their bodies, covering up most of their skin. In the tribes he had been exposed to, nothing more than a loin cloth was used to cover the private areas, and some tribes didn't even bother with that. He reached down and felt his own cloth covering his manhood then tried to imagine what it would feel like to have his entire body confined by animal skins.

What a waste!

Like the stories from when he was younger.

The Panther People.

They had disrespected the mother, killing the stately creatures for their skins, abandoning the rest of the carcasses, all so they could adorn themselves in their shiny, black furs.

Disgusting.

But the Mother had her revenge on the tribe, the result an abomination, a fiction to scare respect of the Mother into the children of the tribe.

Or was it a fiction? These people were clearly wasteful, adorning themselves in unnecessary skins just like the Panther People.

As he sat watching these strange people eat around the fire, he wondered what the Mother thought of their coverings. Would She disapprove? Would She demand punishment? If She did, he hoped She would spare the woman. Tuk couldn't tear his eyes off her, her appearance unlike anything he had ever seen. It was so exotic, he wasn't certain it was beauty or novelty that attracted him. TikTik was beautiful, of that there was no doubt. In her entire tribe she was considered the most beautiful of them all, and Bruk, her betrothed, the most handsome in his.

Tuk was far from the top.

In fact, if there were a list, he would be at the bottom, he was certain.

His pain overwhelmed him again and he felt his eyes burn with the memory of Pol. Pol should be here with him now, sharing in this fascinating experience. These pale people were so different, he knew the stories he would tell of this encounter would never be believed. In fact, he was so certain they would never be believed, he debated whether or not he should even bother mentioning it when he returned home.

He couldn't bear to not be believed. His word was all he had, his looks, strength, and skill as a hunter not virtues anyone except his mother recognized, and even she, he knew, was only humoring him.

He blinked away the tears and glared instead at the man who was clearly the woman's mate. As the fire lit her impossibly pale face and her light, reddish hair, he felt his chest tighten with excitement, his loins stir against their leather encasement.

A woman of light!

It was as if she were the sun itself, the radiance of the Mother trapped inside this creature, its light escaping every pore, creating the white skin and light hair so strange to him.

She was a creation of the Mother, delivered to him in his moment of need, to fill the void left by the loss of his friend, and to be his companion, at his side, for life evermore, TikTik forever out of his reach.

But there was only one problem.

The nine men between him and her.

Rio Negro, Northern Amazon, Brazil
Present Day

Laura sat, rocking side to side, her arms folded, her beloved James tucked in behind her, his arms wrapped around hers as he matched her to and fro motion. Fabricio was playing the Portuguese guitar, its teardrop shape and twelve strings producing a uniquely beautiful sound. He and a few of the crew sang traditional Brazilian folk songs, the Portuguese lyrics completely foreign to her, but the beauty and warmth they represented not.

She was feeling a little warm, the couple of glasses of wine starting to kick in, her eyes were beginning to droop. Reading was already dropping his chin onto his chest then waking up instantly from the surprise as he tried to stay awake. Milton had already gone to bed on the boat, his back sore and not up for sleeping in a tent tonight.

She worried about him, wondering if he had taken on too much by coming on this trip. She hadn't worried about him at the World Cup. There they were in civilization. If something happened he could get to a hospital with ease, and be flown back to the States in a few hours should it be necessary.

But here, in the middle of the jungle?

If something were to truly go wrong, they were a two to three day journey back to the tiny bit of civilization that had been gouged out of the center of the rainforest, where he would still have to be flown out of to get real care. Her private jet would be there waiting for them in three days when their journey was scheduled to be finished, but part of her was wondering if they should call things short and head home in the morning. The rest of their journey was only vanity, to be able to say they made it all the way to the border, but there was little if anything significant to see by way of unique features between here and there.

"I was thinking…" she began.

"What?" James' voice was a whisper, the music still playing, the crew enjoying the entertainment as much as them, the rule on the trip—no alcohol. She was thankful for that, though felt a little guilty for having some herself. It was her experience however that too much alcohol amongst the hired help could lead to problems, and she had made it a rule whenever possible to have a dry policy for them. That was one of the reasons she actually liked working in Muslim countries since they were dry by law for the most part, so alcohol wasn't as much of a concern. It still was, just not as much, the hypocrisy of the true believer something shared the world over.

"Perhaps tomorrow morning we should head back."

She felt him nod into her shoulder. "I was thinking the same thing."

Her eyebrows climbed her forehead slightly as she turned her head to look at him. "Really?"

He looked at the boat then at Reading. "I think Greg's back is bothering him more than he's letting on—"

"That's exactly what I was thinking. He's not protesting people helping him anymore."

"Yeah, and that tells me he's in pain."

"Then it's settled?"

"What's settled?" asked Reading, his eyes semi-open.

"We'll head back first thing in the morning," replied Laura.

"Sounds like a fantastic idea to me," said Reading through a stifled yawn. "I think Greg's back is bothering him."

Laura felt James chuckle behind her as they both realized all three of them had come to the same conclusion. It made her feel warm inside that the four of them were in such good tune with each other that they could pick up on these things. She just felt bad that Milton didn't feel comfortable enough to say something. Then again she knew men, and their pride would prevent them from admitting anything but the very worst, especially if they knew their troubles would affect the entire group.

"So do we," she said, raising her finger to get Fabricio's attention.

"Yes, senhora?"

"First thing in the morning we'll head back rather than continue on." She smiled. "And don't worry, you'll still get paid for the full journey."

The man beamed as he began to strum again. "Thank you, senhora!" He relayed the news to the crew in Portuguese and smiles abounded as the men realized they'd get at least an extra day's pay for no work. If everything continued to go well, the tip she intended to lay on each of them would make their year.

"Bed time?" suggested James, to which Reading grunted his wholehearted agreement, immediately struggling to his feet with some windmilling of his arms that had Laura concerned for a few moments. Balanced, their friend said his goodnights and climbed into his tent, bitching and moaning the entire time until he was finally settled.

James stood and pulled her to her feet. "Goodnight, everyone!" she said, smiling to the crew who all chimed in goodheartedly.

"Don't go to bed early on our account!" added James. There was some laughter as Fabricio translated. Laura unzipped the tent and climbed in, James directly behind her who zipped it up immediately and began a critter inspection with his flashlight. "All clear!"

She quickly changed, careful to have the light in front of her so her silhouette wouldn't provide a show to the crew, James the only one getting to enjoy the view, which from the grin on his face he certainly seemed to be.

"See something you like?" she asked as her eyes drifted down. A bulge in his shorts was the response.

He stripped out of his clothes and turned the light off as he embraced her. His hands explored her body as hers did his, a growing urgency in his demands sending her heart racing as he ground into her, revealing just how turned on he was. Their tongues tasted each other, exploring the other's mouth as her moans grew in intensity and she felt her own furnace of desire blaze with an intensity only James could produce.

He lowered her to the ground, their sleeping bag providing a little bit of comfort, but she didn't care. She wanted him, she needed him, and as she stifled her moans by locking onto his mouth even harder, she could care less about the crew twenty feet away still singing, or Hugh in the next tent already snoring.

All she wanted was James inside her, right here, right now.

She groaned when he obliged, her bliss only beginning.

Jealousy raged through Tuk's heart as he heard the moans not ten paces away. At the shore the dark men continued to sing, something being passed around now that looked like it held some sort of liquid, the jar unlike anything he had ever seen. In the firelight it was as if you could see through the clay, but he was certain it was simply his eyes playing tricks on him.

A jar made of water!

It was folly.

But he paid them little mind. It was the Woman of Light that he cared about, and that man who was clearly her mate was now making love to the woman who was the solution to his problems.

He didn't care though. Once his plan was complete, the man would be gone, never to bother them again, and he alone would possess her. She would learn his ways, she would be cleansed of her current mate's impurities, and she would join the tribe as his mate.

And TikTik will be so jealous! And Bruk envious.

It made him feel good. To know that *he* would be the one envied, that *he* would be the one admired for the first time in his life had his heart racing in anticipation. As the sounds continued from the covering they were sleeping under he could hear how happy she was and began to feel a twinge of regret at the idea of taking her from the others.

Then he suddenly realized who these pale people were.

The Spirit People!

As he continued to watch he realized the stories were true, that it was indeed the Spirit People who lived on the Mother River. He had heard of spirits that walked amongst man because they chose to, and he realized now that if she were indeed one of the Spirit People, then there was no way he would be able to take her unless she was willing to be taken.

He scratched under his arm, waiting patiently for the group to sleep. It didn't take long for the water-jar to apparently empty and all but one of the dark men to board their boat, the other left to stoke the fire then apparently stand guard. He was fast asleep under a tree, a head covering hiding his face, an oddly shaped spear resting on his lap.

The tent quieted down and the snoring of the man spirit soon could be heard. The Woman of Light exited their shelter then walked toward the boat, disappearing inside for a few minutes.

This was his chance.

Snoring continued from the two shelters and the guard against the tree. He crept forward, readying his blowpipe, inserting a carefully chosen dart. The last thing he wanted was to kill her, if that were even possible—kill a spirit? Perhaps a medicine man could, but not him, a mere man.

The Woman of Light walked down from the boat and onto the shore. She approached her shelter, a smile on her face, and again Tuk felt a twinge of regret.

She will only let you take her if she is willing.

He raised his blowpipe and took a deep breath. Taking aim, he placed his lips over the end of the tube then with a sudden exhalation, launched the laced dart toward the spirit. She grabbed her neck, wincing, then immediately began to wobble, her knees losing control.

Tuk leapt from the underbrush he had been using as cover and in an instant was in front of her. Her eyes bulged with fear, and a strange word came out of her mouth, louder than he had been expecting. The guard stirred, his head covering falling off its perch and onto his lap as the man woke.

Tuk had no time. He bent over and lifted the Woman of Light at the hip, tossing her over his back as he spun and rushed into the forest, his experienced feet carrying him swiftly away from the camp. A loud cracking sound erupted behind him and he heard something hit a tree nearby followed by shouting, first by who he assumed was the guard, then soon by several others.

But he had her.

He had his spirit, in his arms.

Which meant she had gone with him willingly.

And he had found his mate.

Acton bolted upright, wired, listening for what had woken him. He looked for Laura but she wasn't beside him, sending his heart immediately racing. He knew something was wrong. A gunshot rang out and he leapt forward, grabbing for his clothes with one hand as he unzipped the tent with the other. Rolling out onto the ground he heard Reading to his right.

"What the bloody hell is going on?" he roared as he burst from his tent. Shouts from the boat grew louder as more people woke up.

"Laura!" he yelled as he struggled into his underwear then shorts, not giving a damn if anyone saw his nakedness. Reading was now on his feet, looking in the direction their guard was pointing. Nothing but unintelligible Portuguese was making it out of their protector's mouth, but it was evident as Acton shoved his hiking boots on that he was terrified.

"Laura!" he yelled again as Reading joined him.

"Is she missing?" he asked.

"I don't know. She's not in the tent and she's not answering." He looked at the boat and saw Fabricio rushing down the ramp, gun in hand. "What's going on?" He spotted Milton on the deck. "Greg, check to see if Laura is on the boat, maybe the bathroom!"

Milton nodded and disappeared. Fabricio spoke to the panicked guard for a moment then ran over, pointing into the forest. "He say a native took the woman!"

"What?" Acton felt faint and he dropped to a knee, Reading thankfully taking over.

"Is he sure?" demanded the law enforcement officer.

Fabricio's head bobbed rapidly.

"How many?"

"He say only one."

"When?"

"Just now, just before he shot the gun."

Acton shoved himself back to his feet. "Then they haven't gone far, especially if she's resisting."

"Silence!" yelled Reading, and they all listened for her shouts, but there were none. The guard came forward with the other men from the boat, all armed, saying something in Portuguese to his captain. Fabricio questioned him again and the man repeated his answer. Fabricio turned to Acton.

"He say she knocked out somehow. The man carry her over his shoulder."

"She's not here!" announced Milton from the boat.

"She's been taken by a native!" yelled Acton.

"What?"

The confusion was evident in Milton's voice but Acton didn't have time to deal with it. He pointed at Fabricio. "We need flashlights, guns and your best trackers."

"Flashlights and guns we have, but none of us is trackers." He pointed into the jungle. "And to go in there at night, it is suicide!"

Acton grabbed at his hair in frustration, the time ticking by painfully evident as with each second she was another step away. He turned to Milton. "Get me the spare satellite phone, iPad, manual charger, Taser, Glock, five mags, and food and water for three days."

"I'll go help him," said Reading, rushing toward the boat.

Acton turned to Fabricio. "Can you radio for help?"

"Yes, senhor, but it will take at least three days to arrive."

Acton was pacing in circles, indecision threatening to take over when he stopped and took three deep, slow breaths, his finger held up to silence everyone around him.

He opened his eyes.

"Are there any tribes here that could help us?"

Fabricio shrugged his shoulders. "Perhaps, but we won't find them until morning, and by then I fear it will be too late."

"What do you mean?"

"Whoever took her knows the forest, he will not be found unless he wants to be found."

"Why would he take her?"

Again Fabricio shrugged. "Any reason. He might want wife, trophy, food."

"Food?"

"He might want to eat her."

"There's cannibals here?"

"There are rumors."

Acton growled in frustration as Reading ran down the ramp, two backpacks in hand. He tossed one to Acton. "Everything you asked for is inside."

Acton took a quick look to confirm, then disappeared into his tent, dressing in more appropriate clothes to help protect him from the jungle, then threw a few extra pairs of socks and underwear, along with his utility knife, in the bag. He reemerged with Reading preparing to leave, Milton struggling to join them.

"What can I do?" he asked.

"Stay on that boat and make sure they don't leave. Try to radio for help and tell them cost is of no consequence. See if they can fly in a search team, task a goddamned satellite if you have to." He pointed to the satellite phone in Milton's hand. "Keep that on you at all times, and charged. We'll check in every hour if we can. Don't call us just in case we need radio silence."

Milton nodded, gripping their lifeline in both hands.

Acton turned to Fabricio. "From this point on you are all being paid triple." He pointed at Milton. "He's in charge. You do as he says. In the morning I want you to try and contact a local tribe to see if they can help."

Fabricio looked terrified at the prospect but nodded, greed overcoming fear.

"Are any of your men willing to come with us?"

Fabricio translated and the other five men stepped back slightly, looking away.

Cowards!

"Very well. You'll hear from us in an hour."

He turned toward Reading who was already pointing at the ground. "I see footprints here."

Acton stepped out of the light of the fire and into the inky black of the forest.

"Let's go get her back."

Northern Amazon

Three days before the attack

Tuk rushed as quickly as he could, dodging around the trees, his deeply attuned eyes able to see sufficiently. The shouting in the distance had faded to nothing, replaced by the nocturnal creatures of the forest, too many of which were deadly. The safest course of action would be for him to find a place to shelter for the night and begin the return to his village in the morning, but unfortunately that wasn't an option right now—he had to put distance between him and the Spirit People.

He had taken their woman, their only woman. Whether the fact she was the only woman was of significance, he had no idea, however the mere taking of her he was certain was.

But she went willingly!

Surely they would know that? Surely they would realize that he, a mere man, could never take or harm a Spirit Person.

Unless they think you somehow bewitched her.

It was true. They had no way of knowing whether or not he was a medicine man, capable of manipulating the Spirit World. They would probably work under the assumption she had been taken against her will, which meant they would do everything within their power to get her back, or at least ask her if she were here against her will.

His heart warmed with the knowledge that she had left willingly, had allowed his dart, made by man, to penetrate her Spirit World skin, to allow the venom it was laced with to take effect. He had been so shocked it had worked, for a moment he had hesitated before actually carrying through with his plan.

She had been silent since her initial call, a call which had elicited an excited response, of that there was no doubt. Which had him wondering just what she had said. If it was 'goodbye', then why would there be excitement at their camp? If it was 'help me', then why was he able to take her if she, a Spirit Person, was unwilling?

Maybe what affects man affects Spirit People as well, if they are willing to be treated as equals?

The thought excited him. It meant the dart had knocked her out as it would a human, and it gave him even more reason to believe she was here willingly. And if things affected her the same as any other woman, should she be willing, then she would be capable of loving him, of mating with him, and of being mother to his children.

He pressed on, more certain now than ever he had made the right choice, and his life was about to finally turn around.

Acton had adjusted the flashlight to give as wide a beam as possible, as had Reading, but it was slow going. Extremely slow. And it was frustrating him to the point where he was almost of no use.

They had no idea where they were going.

He stopped, holding out an arm for Reading whose labored breathing was evident to Acton, despite his friend's attempts to disguise it. Acton aimed his light at the ground. "We could be going in circles for all we know."

"Or in a straight line but in the wrong direction," agreed Reading. "This is useless in the dark."

Acton's chest tightened as his friend said what he himself was thinking already. They were liable to get themselves hurt or lost, and be of no use to Laura.

But he had to go on.

38

"Here's what we'll do," he said, shining his light up between the two of them so they could see each other's faces. "You go back to camp, I'm going to continue forward to the north, then swing back south in an arc and see if I can find any trace of them. If I don't, I'll return to the camp by morning, if I do, I'll send you the coordinates and you and the others can join me."

Reading was shaking his head the entire time. "I'm not leaving you out here alone."

Acton put his hand on his friend's shoulder. "Listen, I'll be fine. I've been in jungles before. But I'm worried about Greg. He's weak, and he's going to try to stay awake the entire time. I need you to relieve him so he can get some rest. Also, if those on the boat try anything, two against six is better than one man who can barely walk."

Reading frowned at the sound logic. Acton pulled out the phone and activated the map, showing their location relative to the river. They were painfully close, their progress negligible. Acton pointed to their left. "Straight that way not even half a mile. If you come to the river and don't see the camp, you should be within shouting distance. If not, go south."

"Why south?"

"Because you're right handed."

"So?"

"So, people tend to drift toward their dominant hand. If you go off course, you most likely will go to the right slightly. Compensate by going left when you get to the river."

"And if I drift too far?" asked Reading with a bit of comic attitude.

"Then it's been nice knowing you, I hope you find a nice native woman to settle down with and make a few more babies."

"Ha ha. One marriage in a man's lifetime is enough punishment." He pointed out his bearing. "Half a mile?"

Acton nodded.

"Okay. Stick to the schedule though. Contact me in thirty minutes."

"Will do. Now go."

Reading slapped Acton's shoulder, his face grim, Acton easily able to see this was tearing Reading apart, but they both knew this was the right decision. Milton was weak and only getting weaker, and Reading was slowing Acton down. As he watched his friend depart, he smiled.

"You're drifting!"

"Fowk off!" came the reply as he disappeared into the trees. When the dancing of Reading's flashlight finally disappeared, Acton struck out directly north, his flashlight examining the ground closely as he made a point to slow himself down, but he soon realized it was useless. He'd have as much luck spinning on his heel with his eyes closed and arm outstretched.

Let nature be your eyes and ears.

It was something he had been told once by a Navajo Indian years ago. He stopped, closed his eyes and tried to control his breathing so as to minimize the sounds coming from him. He took a knee, his own sway as he kept his balance distracting. To his left, toward the river, he could hear the sounds of something moving loudly.

Reading.

Something screamed.

He spun toward the sound, still kneeling, trying to focus on the direction. It wasn't human, it was some sort of animal, probably a primate, but it was a single scream unfortunately not to be repeated. But if he wasn't mistaken, it was directly away from the river, deeper into the rainforest. The vast majority of primates were diurnal, meaning they should be asleep at this time of night. If one were disturbed it would scream just like the scream he had heard.

At least that's what his well-read mind was telling him. The truth was he had no idea, but it was his only hope. Something had disturbed the creature, and he could only hope it wasn't some other animal native to the rainforest.

He headed deeper into the darkness, toward what he hoped might be his stolen love and her abductor, and in the distance behind him he heard a yell from Reading, answered by another, and took comfort that his friend had made it back to safety.

The Woman of Light moaned but Tuk continued forward. He had unfortunately in his haste woken one of the many small primates that they shared the forest with, its protest loud, and if the Spirit People were smart, a beacon as to where he and his future mate were. It was essential he put as much distance between him and the shore, the natural habitat of the Spirit People. He prayed to the Mother that their powers would dwindle to nothing should they get too far away from their home on the mighty river, and maybe by daybreak they would be either too afraid to continue the pursuit, or they would be mere men, mortals like him, with no advantages from the Spirit World.

She moaned again and it was clear the dart was beginning to wear off. He quickly laid her down then propped her up against a tree. He gently smacked her cheek several times and the moaning increased. Suddenly her eyes fluttered open and as she looked at Tuk, she appeared confused then she gasped, shouting out a curious word, the same word he had heard when he took her the first time.

He slapped his hand over her mouth as she was about to scream again.

"You must stay quiet," he said as calmly as he could. "I will not hurt you. Do you understand me?"

Evidently she didn't.

What language do the Spirit People understand?

He knew they spoke to each other in a tongue foreign to him, unlike any he had ever heard, not even from other neighboring tribes, but he had always assumed they would be able to speak all languages.

But what would be the need of that?

They were the Spirit People. They would have no need to communicate with those like him. They looked so different from him, their pale skin, their strange coverings, that to think his people when they died became them was almost unimaginable. It made him wonder whether the stories of what happened after death were even remotely true. If these spirits weren't his dead ancestors, then where did the dead go? Was there even an afterlife?

The very thought filled him with a fear and confusion he had no time for. *No afterlife?* It was crazy, but here he was, the only one of his people he knew to have seen one of the Spirit People so close.

What if the Mother Herself isn't real?

He felt an anger build inside him as he stared at the terrified Woman of Light. *What do you have to be scared of? You who would destroy everything I believe in!* She must have sensed his anger, and he took a deep breath, realizing it wasn't her fault. And was his faith so weak that it would fail within minutes of questions being posed?

He would need to speak to the medicine man, of that there was no doubt. And this one's spirit would need to be cleansed before she could become his mate. Perhaps through their mating, she would learn his language and be able to answer the questions that filled his mind, to assuage the doubts he now had, everything he had believed in his entire life crashing down around him.

But for now he had to get her out of here, her cry most likely heard by her friends.

He had no idea how swiftly the Spirit People could move through the forest, but he had to assume faster than him, at least while still close to the

42

shore. He desperately wanted to ask her, but instead motioned for her to keep quiet. She nodded her head, just as he would if he understood someone, so assumed it meant the same thing.

This is so hard!

They continued forward, this time with her at his side, his hand gripping her arm tightly so she wouldn't try to run away. And she didn't, again reminding him that she had come willingly.

Acton stopped again, listening, but there was no doubt at what he had heard. It was Laura, calling for help. And from the tone, she was scared, and not far. Within earshot in a forest filled with thousands of things to diffuse sound and prevent it from carrying.

She was close.

And alive!

He marked the spot on the GPS where he now stood in case he had to return to it since it gave him a radius for any search in the morning to start from. Running in the direction he thought he had heard her cry, he soon reduced himself to a brisk pace, the root covered ground simply too dangerous to traverse in the dark without eyeballing every foot placement with the flashlight. As he continued forward he dialed the satellite phone.

"Milton here."

"Hi Greg, it's me. Got a pen and paper?"

"Yes."

He gave him the GPS coordinates. "Have any search start from there. I heard her call for help due east of those coordinates. I don't know how far her voice would carry, but I can't see it being more than a mile in this."

"So she's alive."

"She was two minutes ago. Did Hugh make it back?"

"Yeah, he's on the radio now. I think he's trying to reach the British Embassy but isn't having much luck."

"Use the phone."

"We were keeping it clear for your call."

Acton stumbled, almost dropping the phone and realized he needed to take a new bearing. "Listen, contact Rita, and get her on the case. And Terrence."

"Rita? My secretary?"

"You know what she's like."

He heard Milton laugh. "Yeah, she won't quit, that's for sure. And Terrence?"

"Laura's grad student, he worships the ground she walks on. He won't stop at his end either. His number should be in the phone."

"Okay, I'll make those calls right away."

"Good. I'll check back in one hour."

He killed the call and checked the GPS. He was still heading in the right direction, though trending a little to the right, or south. He continued forward, compensating, his bearing on Laura's voice in no way precise. When he had travelled about a mile on the GPS he paused, listening some more.

This is ridiculous! I'm guessing!

If Laura's abductor were carrying her over his back, he couldn't be going very fast. Not at night. Not through a jungle. He didn't care who the person was, they had to be slow. It had been an hour. That left at most a five mile radius from the campsite, probably half that. He was about three miles from the shore now and had kept a decent pace since he had heard Laura's shout, so he should be at least travelling at the same pace, if not making up some time.

But he needed a bearing.

"Laura!" he shouted as loud as he could, the jungle protesting with an eruption of noise.

"James!" came the reply almost immediately. To his left, to the north-east.

And close.

"Laura, it's me!" he shouted. "Just stay alive! Just stay alive and I'll find you!" He knew he was giving away his position, and possibly hastening his opponent's escape, but he had to let her know there was hope. He marked the spot on the GPS again, rushing forward as he dialed the phone.

Voicemail.

Greg must be making those calls still.

He left the coordinates and his new bearing then hung up, trying to keep himself moving forward as quickly as possible without breaking a leg or twisting an ankle. Suddenly he came into a small clearing, a fire smoldering in the center, mere embers now. A shout to his left had him reaching for his gun when he thought better of it, the tip of a spear now pressed against his throat.

Rio Negro, Northern Amazon, Brazil

Reading wanted to slam the radio receiver into the table repeatedly, but realized that would only make him feel better for a few seconds. He turned to Milton who had just hung up the phone.

"I hope you had more luck than I did," said Reading, returning to the rear deck.

Milton shook his head. "I left a message for Rita, my secretary, but it's three in the morning there. We won't get action from her end until at least eight."

"Terrence?"

"Voicemail, but at least he's five hours ahead, so hopefully he can get some action."

Reading sighed. "Just what kind of action are we expecting? It's up to the Brazilians to send a search team, and one is already on the way. Three bloody days away!"

"With a jungle like this, we need dozens if not hundreds of people." Milton shook his head. "She's a needle in a haystack." He noticed a light blinking on the satellite phone and dialed the voicemail. He jotted down some numbers then punched them into the GPS on the iPad. "Jim's heard her again." He handed Reading the tablet computer.

Reading looked at the three marked positions, the first their campsite, the second when Acton had first heard Laura, the third this latest report. This latest report was significant though, since it provided them with a general direction the abductor was heading. "He's heading east-north-east by the looks of it."

This would help narrow down the search area, but only if they could search now, not in three days when any trail would be long cold. He zoomed in on the Google Earth app and found nothing but a thick canopy that no search plane would be able to pierce.

And with the jungle filled with tribes and wildlife, he doubted any type of infrared would help either. They needed boots on the ground. With Laura's money they could bring in people with ease, the problem was getting them here in the middle of nowhere and quickly.

And they needed an experienced tracker. He definitely wasn't it, Milton was a bookworm, and none of the crew seemed to be willing to leave their boat now that the campsite had been compromised.

He didn't blame them, though he doubted there was any more danger. Fabricio had said there was a tribe less than an hour north of here that they might be able to ask for help, but they were very primitive, very scared of white people. They weren't one of the uncontacted tribes that Acton had been telling them about on their voyage up the river, but their contact was minimal. They preferred to keep to themselves, but show them enough respect and they might just help.

Milton was flipping through the numbers stored on the phone when he paused.

"Why would they have a number for Kraft Dinner in here?"

Reading looked up from the iPad. "Huh?" Milton held up the phone, showing the display, too far away for Reading's old eyes to make out. "What are you talking about?"

"It says Kraft Dinner."

"Kraft Dinner? What the hell is that?"

"Pasta and cheese with a chemically induced orange glow?"

Reading grunted. "We call that Kraft Cheesey Pasta. Ours doesn't glow."

"Really? What color is it then?"

"I think we're getting off topic."

Milton flushed slightly. "Sorry, you're right. So back to my original question, why would they have Kraft Dinner in their phone?"

"It has to be some sort of code."

"Initials perhaps?"

"KD?" Reading repeated it several times, unable to think of anyone with a first name starting with the letter K. His eyebrows popped. "Is it Kraft Dinner, or Dinner comma Kraft?"

"The latter, actually."

"So it's DK, not KD." Reading smacked his hands on his knees. "Dylan Kane!"

"You mean—"

Reading held up his finger, cutting Milton off. Dylan Kane was actually CIA Special Agent Dylan Kane, a former student of Acton's who had dropped out of university and joined the army after 9/11. He had excelled, joined the Delta Force, actually training and serving with some of the Bravo Team members they had come to know before being recruited by the CIA. He was secretive, but reliable, having helped his former professor out on occasion, including on their recent trip to Israel.

He might just be the one they needed.

"Are you going to dial it or am I?" he asked.

Milton eyed the phone then shook his head. "You better, you've at least dealt with him. I've only heard about him."

Reading nodded as he rose then took the phone from Milton. He pressed the button, dialing the number, then punched in their number when it picked up, it merely a paging service.

A pager unlike any available to the general public, he was sure.

And waited.

Hai Phong, Vietnam

CIA Special Agent Dylan Kane was in pure ecstasy as Trinh, a stunning Vietnamese masseuse, squeezed and released his tense muscles like only she could. She was the best he had found the world over, and with Trinh, there was never a happy ending.

She was strictly legit.

And worth every damned penny.

And my God, what he'd give for a role in the hammock with her. She was five foot nothing of perfection, her accented English the sexiest he had ever heard. He wondered if her level of attractiveness in his eyes was influenced by the fact she wouldn't sleep with him.

Not for a lack of trying when he had first met her.

"No hanky panky!" she had cried when he had given her the eye that changed most women he met into putty, ready to be manhandled and carnally pleasured.

But not Trinh.

"I married!"

He backed off immediately, never one to interfere in a marriage—unless it was part of the job. As a necessity he had bedded married women, usually to get information from them, or access through them to their husbands. At least one half of the marriage didn't consist of a good person. In the rare case it was the woman, his morals remained intact. In the more common case it was the man, the woman he romanced usually abused or neglected, and he gave them a night or more of escape from their misery, again leaving his morals intact.

What I do for my country!

He moaned as Trinh's elbow dug into his deep tissue.

God I love this woman!

Whenever he was in south-east Asia he made it a point to try and see her at least once. She could go for hours, never taking a break, and when done, he felt like a new man, ready to tackle the world's problems singlehandedly. Which was usually how he had to face them.

"Your husband is a lucky man," he murmured.

"You tell him that!" cried Trinh. "He get jealous I give massage. He say you all expect sex. He say I must be giving!"

Kane realized he might have just opened a can of worms, never knowing Trinh to ever mention her personal life. Or even talk much during a massage. Their relationship, at least five years old, consisted of perhaps a dozen massages a year that lasted two or three hours with few words spoken.

Should I say something?

"It's only because he loves you."

"If he love me, he trust me!" She dug deeper with her elbow and he yelped.

Maybe I should stay out of this.

His phone vibrated on the table beside him. He reached over and saw the priority contact, his eyebrows climbing slightly.

Professor Acton?

"I'm going to have to take this, Trinh," he said, lifting himself off the table, thankful for an excuse to end the massage that felt like it was turning violent against all men.

"Okay, you like I come back tomorrow?" she asked, stepping back and holding up a towel for him.

He took the towel and wrapped it around his waist. "If I'm still here, absolutely. Call the hotel tomorrow around three."

She smiled and looked at the money sitting on the table nearby. He nodded. "Go ahead, you earned it."

"But I not finish."

Kane smiled at her refreshing honesty. "My fault, not yours."

"I do you extra good tomorrow! Extra long!" she smiled, picking up the money, oblivious to how horny her statements made him, or how jealous her husband would be should he hear them out of context.

"Have a good day, Trinh," said Kane as he dialed the number, his call relayed through a private encrypted network he had established for himself years ago. It didn't go through Langley or any other entity. It was his own hardware set up in his own secret location that allowed him to communicate securely and privately with anyone he needed to.

Few had the number.

"Hello?" He didn't recognize the voice. It was a man's, deep, English.

"You called?"

"Oh, hi, Kraft Dinner I presume?"

Kane laughed. "I beg your pardon?"

"Sorry, it's the name in the phone. A code."

Kane shook his head, smiling. "Just call me Dylan. This line is secure. May I presume this is Special Agent Reading?"

"Yes. Hugh."

"How can I help you?"

"Laura Palmer—you remember her?"

"Of course. Professor Acton's wife."

"Oh, you heard?"

"I hear everything."

"Umm, yeah." There was an awkward pause. "Well, she's been abducted."

"Abducted!" Now Reading finally had Kane's attention. "Details."

He was quickly given the rundown of the abduction by a native in the Amazon rainforest, and how Acton had gone out in pursuit. They weren't able to reach anybody for help beyond the locals who were three days away.

"And now Jim's missed his hourly check-in. I think something might have happened to him as well. Is there anything you can do to help?"

"I'll call you back in an hour."

"Thank you."

He ended the call and began dialing another number through his secure network.

"Mr. White."

"Is that any way to answer a phone?" he asked, a smile on his face as he heard the voice of his old Delta Force buddy, Command Sergeant Major Burt "Big Dog" Dawson.

"Dylan?"

"You got me. How are you, BD?"

"A little busy right now, I've got about two minutes."

"That's all I need. Listen, I understand you're in Colombia."

"How the hell do you know that?"

"I know everything."

And he began to relay the details as he knew them to the one person he knew was close enough to possibly help his old archeology professor, he on the other side of the world and about to begin a mission of his own that couldn't be interrupted for anything.

"You have the number?" he asked when done.

"Got it. I'll get in touch as soon as I have a chance. I'm in the thick of something right now so we might not be able to do anything right away."

"Whatever you can do is probably better than what they've got now."

"True. Listen, gotta go."

"Okay, good luck, BD. See you when you least expect it."

52

He laughed and ended the call, heading for the showers to cool himself off, Trinh having done one hell of a number on his libido, but as he showered in the cool water, his thoughts turned to his old mentor and his new wife, wishing there was more he could do to help them.

Somewhere North-East of Rio Negro, Northern Amazon, Brazil

Laura tried to control the adrenaline rushing through her system, it only making the situation worse, panic having set in almost from the moment she had awoken. Her captor had an iron grip on her arm, not to mention a menacing looking spear and set of sharpened teeth. There was no hope of escape at this point, it still nearly pitch black, the only light from the stars and a half moon overhead, little of which made it through the thick canopy of tree branches above them. Should she manage to break away, she knew he'd simply recapture her within moments.

But for some reason he hadn't seemed too perturbed by her shouting out, three times now. Each time she had called for help, her captor had glared at her, hissing slightly, frightening her back into silence. And the last time, when she had heard James' voice so close, she had a flood of hope, but then there was a flurry of shouting in the distance and a smile from her captor.

Then silence.

And she knew something had happened to her beloved husband.

But for now she had to survive, and to that end she did the only thing she could think of to do.

Leave a trail.

With every step of her right foot, her captor on her left, she put as much weight as she could on her heel, digging it into the ground so it would leave a mark, rather than drag her foot which was more likely to be noticed by her captor. If someone could just pick up her trail, they might be able to follow it to wherever they were going.

The fact she was alive for now had her hopeful that he intended to keep her that way. Then again, cattle were walked to the slaughter house, not carried. Her cooperating might simply be making things easier for her later demise. Cannibalism had been reported in the Amazon, but it was rare, and not in this particular area. Usually it was a war ritual—eat the enemy, gain his strength, not to mention scare the shit out of his friends the next time you might encounter them.

She had a funny feeling this was more of a counting coup situation, where the young man performed an act of bravery against the enemy to prove himself to his tribe. Perhaps by abducting her he was passing some sort of test. From what she could see of him he seemed rather slight, even for a native of the Amazon, typically known for being short and very fit.

The runt of the litter?

He had no obvious deformities which might have merited him a quick death at birth, instead he seemed to have simply been cursed with a short stature and slight features. She might have actually felt a touch sorry for him if he weren't in the process of abducting her.

Suddenly they stopped and he pointed at her feet several times, then slapped his chest, then pointed at the tree branches above them, all the while speaking a language she had absolutely no possibility of understanding.

"You want me to stay here while you climb the tree?"

He repeated the gestures, then shook his spear, which she took to imply he'd kill her if she didn't stay put.

She nodded.

This seemed to satisfy him and he sprang up the tree so fast, he could have been mistaken for a primate. Suddenly a hand dangled in front of her face, motioning at her.

I guess he wants me to climb.

She reached up to grab the lowest branch but instead he grabbed her arm by the wrist and hauled her up to the large branch he was on. She yelped in surprise at his strength and grabbed onto the massive branch, his hand steadying her until she found her balance. The branch was large, easily the width of a twin bed with a large concave in the trunk of the tree at the branch's root. Her captor quickly cleared out this area of accumulated debris then lined it with large leaves, motioning for her to lie down inside the protected alcove.

She nodded then obeyed the order, lying with her back to the tree trunk, her spine curving with the trunk, it oddly comfortable, and, more importantly, signaling he had no intention of killing her before morning, and should they stay put overnight, it might give James and the others time to find her trail.

James!

What were those shouts? It wasn't his voice she had heard but those of at least several others speaking a language that might be the same as her captor's. All she knew was it wasn't English, Spanish or Portuguese. But she also hadn't heard him cry out, which she hoped meant they hadn't killed him.

But why would her captor not join his friends?

She knew enough about the Amazon Rainforest to know that there were hundreds of tribes that minimized contact with the outside world, and dozens that had had no contact whatsoever. She wondered who her captor was, whether he knew of white people, or whether he thought she was some sort of demon or otherworldly creature.

If he thinks that, then he is either extremely brave or incredibly stupid.

Counting coup with an otherworldly creature had to take the cake for bravery. Which might make sense. His slight stature and features would probably have him marginalized among the men of the tribe, and undesirable to the women.

Oh!

The thought had her heart leap into her throat. Was she to be his mate? Was she about to be raped? She pushed herself back a little deeper into the alcove. She calmed herself, all the while keeping an eye on her captor as he continued to prepare their shelter, expertly weaving what was shaping into a wall around them, the large leaves providing an effective cover. Within ten minutes they were enclosed enough so no one from the ground would be able to see them.

A small, shallow clay plate was produced from what she would characterize as a satchel that hung around his neck. The bag appeared to be pieced together from different animal skins, and had gone unnoticed up to this point in her panic. A hand drill for producing fire was removed from the bag and within minutes they had a small fire sitting on the clay plate. He placed it close to her and she held her hands out, warming them, as she suddenly realized how cool it was as her body chilled, no longer kept warm by their constant running.

She shivered.

Her captor's eyes narrowed slightly, as if concerned. He pushed the plate closer, then stood, removing more leaves from a higher branch. Placing them over her body, he layered her with the greenery. She almost immediately began to feel the thermal effect as her body heat began to be trapped.

"Thank you."

The words startled him and he jumped back slightly. She realized from her training that if she were to survive this, unscathed and unmolested, she needed to establish a rapport with her abductor. She sat up, repositioning the leaves to cover as much of her as possible, then pointed at her chest.

"Laura."

He looked at her, eyes narrowed, confused.

"My name, it's Lau-ra." She pointed again at herself. "Lau-ra." She pointed at him. "What's your name?"

He was still confused, pointing at his own chest. "La-wa."

She smiled, shaking her head, then pointing at herself. "Lau-ra." She then pointed at him, using her best "tell me your name" expression, trying to convey that she was asking him something.

His jaw dropped and his head bobbed rapidly as he seemed to get it.

What sounded almost like a popping sound followed by a hard 'k' emerged from his mouth as he pointed at his own chest. He repeated it several times.

"Tuk?" she repeated.

He grinned, revealing his barbarous teeth as he slapped his chest, repeating his name.

She smiled. "Your name is Tuk." She pointed at her chest. "Laura."

"Lawa."

"Lowr-raa."

"Lowr-raa," he mimicked almost perfectly.

"Laura."

"Lau-ra!"

She smiled, giving him the thumbs up. "Perfect. You're Tuk, I'm Laura."

He smacked his chest. "Tuk," he said, then pointed toward her. "Lau-ra."

This seemed to excite him greatly, and after a few more repetitions, he sat down and pulled some dried food out of his bag, offering her some. He said a word with it, then pointed at it then his mouth.

"Food," she said. She took some and tried it. It wasn't bad, though she could imagine what Reading would say.

Like dried bloody oats!

But it was food and she didn't know when she'd get fed again. Besides, she wanted to establish a bond, and he was already repeating "food" over and over, handing her more. After several minutes of him feeding her, she was indeed full, having eaten a good sized meal earlier in the evening, so she begged off any more. He seemed to understand and pointed at her bed, saying something along with her name.

She nodded. "Laura sleep."

She lay down and he jumped forward, startling her slightly but she kept her control. He repositioned the leaves to cover her again, then jumped back, turning his back on her in what appeared to be an attempt to give her privacy.

She closed her eyes, her mind slowly settling as she tried to figure out the best way to handle things in the morning. It appeared at this point he meant her no harm, but that could turn in an instant should she not cooperate with him. There didn't appear to be any sexual component to the abduction, at least not yet, and they still weren't that far from the campsite.

She would have to figure out some way to delay their travel and continue to lay her trail.

If she didn't, she might very well be lost to her world forever.

Professor James Acton knew he was in deep shit. He had stumbled upon what appeared to be a hunting party camping for the night. The spear pressed against his throat felt ready to pierce the skin. He slid his hand with the phone into his pocket, pressing the button to turn it off when inside so they wouldn't see the display flash. He slowly raised his hands, keeping his expression as neutral as possible, and not exposing his teeth. He knew very well that in some cultures, the baring of teeth was considered hostile, and the fact they seemed to be showing him their own teeth had him clamping his jaw shut.

He had no idea how primitive these half dozen men were, whether or not they had ever seen a white man before, technology like his phone or his gun, or even if they had heard a modern language.

Staying quiet and cooperating seemed the best option at the moment.

Four spears were held on him as two men stepped forward, patting him down as thoroughly as any cop, his gun, magazines, phone and other supplies all tossed in a pile on the ground.

And as he eyed the phone, he realized what an idiot he had been. It contained a GPS locator in it, which meant it could be tracked.

But only if it was turned on.

His hands were bound along with his ankles and he was pushed to the ground, his back against a tree. Two of his captors crouched nearby, their spears aimed in his direction as the others returned to sleep. And with nothing else he could possibly do, he soon found his own exhaustion overtaking him as the adrenaline that had fueled him for the past couple of hours wore off.

God, please take care of my wife.

Rio Negro River, Northern Amazon, Brazil
Two days before the attack

Dawn broke suddenly, at least for Reading, he having fallen asleep at some point through the night. He glanced over at Milton who was awake, the satellite phone still gripped in his hand, the iPad on his lap. The sound of the motor and the motion of the boat had Reading on his feet.

"Where are we going?"

"Just upriver a bit, apparently there's a tribe there that might be able to help," replied Milton. He held up the iPad. "Do you realize we're only a couple of miles from the Venezuelan border?"

Reading shook his head. "No." He frowned. "If she's taken across the border, we're going to have bigger problems getting her back. The local searchers probably won't cross and the Venezuelans won't exactly be cooperative."

"We can't be sure of that."

Reading nodded, sitting down again. "No, you're right. But look at that map. Almost their entire population is concentrated in the north along the coast. For them to mount a search and rescue operation, even if they were willing, would take days at least."

"I got an email from Terrence a few minutes ago."

Reading's eyebrows climbed a little at the mention of Laura's star grad student. "And?"

"And he's contacted the head of her security team, Lt. Colonel Leather. Leather says the security team at the Peru dig site where Jim's students are is too far away. It would take them a few days to get here—it's a day just to get to Lima from that dig. He's bringing in a half-dozen men who will arrive in-country tomorrow. They're apparently going to try and charter a small plane and parachute in. We could have boots on the ground as early as tomorrow night."

Reading frowned. "Two full days after. And that assumes they can make the jump. This is dense jungle."

Milton glanced over his shoulder at the thick forest to their right. It was tall, dense, and unforgiving. And he was sure any clearings large enough to be seen from the air and targeted by a paratrooper were manmade and potentially occupied. "Could they land in the water?" he asked.

Reading looked at the river, fairly swift but from what he could tell, free of rocks. "Perhaps. How they'd get to shore though would be the challenge. They could be swept quite a distance, and their equipment would be pretty damned heavy. I doubt they'd be able to swim."

"These guys are pros. I'm sure they know what they're doing."

Reading nodded. "Anything else happen while I was asleep? Any word from Jim?"

Milton shook his head, closing his eyes for a moment. "No. He's missed all his check-ins since that voice mail. I'm really worried."

"Me too." It was almost a murmur, Reading not wanting to acknowledge exactly how worried he was that two of his best friends were missing. He barely knew Milton, but knew Milton was extremely close to Acton so was certainly taking this even harder. And he also knew what helplessness could feel like. He had no doubt Milton wanted to dive into that jungle and find his friends, just like he did, but Milton was hampered by his handicap, and he by his age.

To be twenty-five again.

He sighed.

Hell, to be forty-five again!

"Penny for your thoughts."

"Huh?"

Milton chuckled. "It's an American—"

"I know what it means," interrupted Reading. He shook his head, looking at Milton. "Just cursing old age."

Milton slapped his stomach. It had grown significantly when he was first injured, but was much more respectable now, though not where he wanted it to be. "Tell me about it."

"You've got an excuse."

"Bah, don't let the wheelchair fool you. I had packed on an extra twenty before I got shot. Working behind a desk kills you slowly. First your fitness, then your spirit."

"Thinking of a change?"

Milton shook his head. "Even if I fully recover, I'll never truly be fully recovered. My days of running marathons and chasing after Jim are over. Besides, I love the kids. Don't get me wrong, the job is great for the most part, but pushing paper isn't what I thought I'd end up doing."

Reading grunted. "You shouldn't have taken the promotion," he said, knowing exactly what Milton was talking about. "Leaving Scotland Yard is one of my big regrets. This INTERPOL job has me staring at computer screens more than anything else. At least in my old job I was visiting crime scenes, looking for clues, interrogating people, catching bad guys."

"You loved it."

"I bloody well did!" He chuckled. "You know, if it weren't for Jim and Laura, my life would be pretty dull. But between having to either bail them out or being dragged along for the ride, I've seen more action in the past few years than in my entire military career."

"You were in the military?"

"Early eighties. Falklands War. I was—"

"We are here!" called Fabricio, pointing to the shore.

Reading and Milton rose, both staring at the shore. A small village of what Reading couldn't help but think of as savages could just be seen through the trees. If you didn't know to look for them, you could just as easily miss them. As the Captain guided the boat around the bend, he sailed them into an inlet that bent out of sight from the Rio Negro. The calm, isolated waters were filled with several dozen natives swimming, washing, and performing various other tasks. Several small boats, perhaps better described as canoes, were pulled up onto the shore. Farther inland were several large communal buildings, a large central fire pit and various other smaller structures where it looked like they were stretching animal skins, curing meat and fish, and fashioning tools and weapons.

"Aren't they all supposed to be naked?" asked Reading, a small part of him a little disappointed as he spotted some gorgeous women nearby, waving at them.

Then he noticed their breasts were only covered by long hair.

He smiled.

"Not if they've had contact with the outside world. The tribes that haven't usually go completely naked, some with merely a loincloth to cover their most private of bits."

"I see."

"You sound disappointed."

Reading looked at Milton. "And you aren't?"

Milton grinned. "Devastated, I'm sure."

The Captain positioned the boat beside a perfectly serviceable dock, these natives clearly set up to trade with the outside world. Captain Fabricio waved at an approaching elder, shouting something in Portuguese, a response offered in the same. Fabricio turned to Reading and Milton.

"You wait here. I will see if they are willing to help." He lowered his voice. "And whatever you do, don't show your teeth!"

Reading's smile at the bouncing bounty quickly filling the shoreline was instantly wiped away. "Why not?"

"Teeth mean you challenge them."

"Good to know," said Milton, his own face slackening.

Reading found himself scanning the shore for tooth-filled smiles, but only found what to him appeared to be nice, non-threatening smiles of the closed-mouth variety.

Fabricio then looked to Milton. "And don't let them see wheelchair."

"Now wait a minute!" exclaimed Reading, jumping to Milton's defense.

Fabricio shook his head rapidly, raising his hands. "It is a sign of weakness. They must see only strength. It best you stay here."

Reading was about to open his mouth when Milton held out his hand. "No, it's perfectly fine. These cultures respect strength and vitality. Seeing a man my age restricted to a wheelchair, or weak, would make them think we're all weak, unwilling to put me out of the tribe."

"Huh?"

"In their society I'd be considered a burden. Only elders are permitted that privilege. Someone like me, who couldn't walk on his own, would leave the tribe of his own accord, never to be seen again."

"You're kidding."

Milton sat down, clearly fatigued. "Not at all. It's really quite common. When a member of the tribe feels he's a burden and can no longer contribute in some meaningful way, it is his duty to do the right thing and leave. That way the tribe, usually few in number, don't have to provide for the non-contributing member."

Fabricio's head bobbed in emphatic agreement. "This is right. What he say is right."

"Sounds bloody barbaric to me." Reading looked down at Milton. "Are you going to be okay?"

He nodded. "It's for the best anyway. Someone needs to mind the phone."

Reading had to agree with that one. Who knew how a ringing phone might appear to these people? Though they clearly weren't afraid of the new arrivals, how much technology they had been exposed to was questionable.

"We should go, they will think it rude to keep them waiting," said Fabricio, motioning for Reading to join him on the ramp. Reading put a smile on his face, careful to not show any teeth, and walked down the ramp after Fabricio. Bows and awkward handshakes were exchanged with the elders, there now almost one hundred people gathered, many with their hands extended to try and touch the strangers, especially Reading, his English skin probably some of the most pale they would have ever seen.

Reading kept the pleasant expression on his face despite his not being a fan of being touched, especially pet as if an animal. A few squeezes had him feeling like he was being sized up for dinner.

Someone squeezed his balls.

His head dropped quickly to see who did it, the culprit apparently a giggling beauty he had seen earlier on the shore. She let go, saying something, the response laughter, leaving his manhood to feel like it would shrink from embarrassment. Then one of the men grabbed it and squeezed. He swatted away the hand.

The man jumped back, shaking his spear then laughed when the woman who had begun squeezing the fruit in his grocery aisle said something.

He had to know. Talking under his breath while trying to not move his mouth, he asked Fabricio, "Any idea why they're laughing?"

Fabricio began to laugh himself, looking up at the imposing Reading. "They want to know if all of you was as big as you look."

I had to ask.

He didn't know if his ego could take the answer so he didn't bother asking.

"Apparently the woman and the man disagree."

Interesting.

He looked at the woman who was nearby, keeping pace with the procession as it moved into the building. She seemed to be eyeing him like a piece of meat. Visions of the chief gifting this gorgeous creature to him as some sort of custom that could not be refused breathed a little life down below, making Hugh, Jr. wish for another squeeze.

"Apparently she think you are no bigger than anyone else, but the man disagree. I think he like you."

"Huh?"

"He gay, you know, he like boys."

Reading looked over the man, he too sizing him up like the main course at dinner. "I got that." Reading's fantasy suddenly turned into a nightmare vision of being offered the man, refusing an insult that would get them all killed.

Suddenly everything stopped, a hush spreading across the entire village as everyone turned to Reading's right. Several men emerged from the forest, spears raised over their heads, shouting in triumph, their face paint a little more menacing looking than the simple reddish-purple and white most of the villagers were covered with.

But that wasn't what caused Reading to gasp in shock.

It was the two men behind the lead group carrying a long branch between them on their shoulders, their prey tied to it by the hands and feet. Human prey. Reading's heart slammed against his chest as the realization of what he was seeing was finally comprehended.

His friend, in agony, strung like a piece of meat between the two hunters.

"Jim!"

One day from the Rio Negro, Northern Amazon, Brazil

Tuk held Lau-ra by the wrist, gently now, there no longer any need to worry she might run away. From the shouts of the hunters last night it seemed clear the Spirit People looking for her had been captured, which confirmed what he suspected.

They lost their power the farther from the mighty river they went.

Which must mean that Lau-ra had no powers anymore. He had to admit he was slightly disappointed, but then he had always wanted a human for a mate, not a spirit, so the fact she had become fully human thrilled him.

Almost fully human.

She was still a ghastly pale, as unhealthy looking as anyone he had ever seen. In the morning light he had thought it might be paint, like the red clay much of his own body was covered in, the white markings on his cheeks and forehead identifying his clan and tribe. Several rubs of her arm, even licks, failed to remove it though, leaving him to fear his intended mate might not be long for this world.

Could that be the curse?

Doomed to live on the river, never to set foot on land again lest they die all over again?

It would seem to make sense. The Mother was infinite in Her wisdom, and if the Spirit People were free to roam the land at will, life would be intolerable for Her children that dwelled there. It would be a terrifying existence for his people to see their ancestors roaming freely about. Though the medicine man sometimes claimed, with the help of certain plants, to communicate with the Spirit World, Tuk had always had his doubts. He had tried some of the herbs with Pol once and they both heard voices and saw a lot of strange things, but it had been gibberish.

But fun.

His heart again sank at the thought of his friend, dead, and wondered if he were on the mysterious craft that plied the mighty river. Was he on that very boat, or another one? Would Tuk even recognize him if he saw him? Tuk looked over at Lau-ra and wondered what she had looked like in her previous life, when she was alive? Would she have been beautiful like TikTik, or plain? It was hard to tell, her features so completely different from anything he had ever seen before, she was almost a creature unto herself.

But he found her attractive.

Maybe it was the way she had laughed last night as they learned each other's names. Maybe it was just the way she seemed so exotic in the morning sun. He looked up at the patches of sky he could see through the canopy above then at the shadows cast. It was approaching midday and they had a long day's journey ahead of him before he could begin the Cleansing Ritual.

Then present her to his tribe as his intended mate.

Laura had decided escape was pointless and that cooperation would be the order of the day. So far her captor, Tuk, had given no indication that he was aware she was marking their trail, and seemed perfectly content to lead her toward wherever they were going, frequently exchanging smiles with her, animatedly talking about their surroundings from time to time. If she didn't know better, it was as if he were out for a brisk walk with a friend.

The more time they spent together the less she thought this was a counting coup situation. He didn't seem to be full of bravado at what he had done, and her impression of him suggested bravado wasn't even in his nature. She was convinced he had self-esteem and self-confidence issues, his sometimes shy glances at her when he thought she wasn't looking and his habit of trying to make himself appear bigger when she was, suggesting he felt diminutive in her eyes.

She was not a tall woman, but not short either. However at five foot eight, she was definitely a few inches taller than Tuk, and her posture, always considered excellent, had her taking full advantage of all sixty-eight inches—none lost to a slouch. Tack on some heels and she began to approach James' six foot two.

James!

She wondered what had happened to him, wondered if he was okay. With hours of daylight having passed, she had to assume that if there was some sort of rescue operation being undertaken, it had begun already. But then again, the nearest sign of civilization was five days by boat from where they were. They would obviously go faster, but you could only go so fast without risking hitting something in these mostly uncharted and ever changing waters, and nighttime travel at high speed would be foolish.

It would take at least three days.

And by then Tuk might have her so far buried in the jungle, she'd never be found.

She dug her heel in a little harder, determined to try and make it as easy as possible to be found, despite how little faith she now had that she would ever see her beloved James again.

A tear rolled down her cheek and she turned her head away from Tuk so he wouldn't see it. The last thing she needed was him thinking she was missing her husband.

Jealousy could be a cruel master.

James Acton's wrists and ankles screamed for mercy, the bindings biting into his skin, tearing it in places, and the elasticity the branch had that made the journey a little more comfortable for those carrying him, made each step an agony of yanking and shredding with each bounce.

At first he was certain he was dinner, or a late night snack seeing as it was the middle of the night when he had been captured, but when everyone had gone to sleep except his guards, he had made it a point to get some rest himself. In the morning he had been tied to the long branch he now hung from, and his agonizing journey had begun.

He knew quickly he had to create a mental wall between him and the pain, so he instead focused on the details. His lead captor had a bag over his shoulder made from animal skins that contained everything they had taken off of him when he was captured. He knew he had to keep track of that bag, the phone it contained possibly his only hope of survival. If he could just get a moment with his hands in the bag, he might be able to turn the phone on so it could be tracked.

But how to get a moment?

Hanging from the branch, carried like a piece of meat, didn't seem to give much hope of a moment alone with his phone.

One thing that hadn't occurred to him, at least initially, was that these men were all wearing at least some clothing. Amazon tribes were known to wear usually nothing unless they had been "shamed" into wearing pants by contact with the outside world. Some wore loincloths not for modesty sake, but for convenience. Sometimes you just didn't want certain things hanging out when running through the jungle or sitting on insect ridden ground. Shirts or tops of any type were unheard of.

Yet one of these men clearly was wearing shorts. Tommy Hilfiger's by the looks of it. Well worn, threadbare in fact, most likely acquired in a trade not so long ago.

And if that were the case, then the tribe these men belonged to had been exposed to Western culture, so would most likely not be cannibals—though that was incredibly rare now in South America, and many believed it simply didn't happen anymore, at least amongst the exposed tribes. The untouched tribes, those that had no contact whatsoever with the outside world, may still practice the eating of human flesh, but for the moment, he was quite confident he was free from that fate.

Would they cook but not eat?

He felt like he was on a spit, and he certainly wasn't being treated like a guest. What their intentions were he had no idea. Perhaps they intended to trade him for something of value with other Westerners, or to another tribe. All he knew was their intentions couldn't be good, and the deeper they went into the forest, the harder it would be for his friends to find *him*, let alone Laura.

But with his constant view of the sun over their heads, caught through occasional breaks in the canopy, it appeared to him like they were moving almost north-west, which would take them toward the river if they kept going. This gave him hope. The closer to the river, the better chance of Western contact, the better chance of rescue or trade.

And less chance of being dinner or tonight's entertainment at the Thunderdome.

Two men enter, one man leaves.

If that were his fate, he'd do whatever it took to be that one man.

Because if he died, Laura had almost no hope.

Something smacked the back of his head, a rock or incredibly hard tree root. Whatever it was had his eyes watering, wincing in pain as he felt a warm, trickling sensation as blood began to flow. His heart started to slam into his chest, his ears filling with the roar as his head began to throb. He calmed himself, his thoughts of a concussion or worse beginning to wane when he heard what sounded like a loud crowd of people then suddenly silence.

He must have been mistaken, the rush of blood through his ears in his moment of panic playing tricks on him.

"Jim!"

Heathrow Airport, London, England

Retired Lt. Colonel Cameron Leather, formerly of the British Special Air Services, the country's most elite of military soldiers, sat at his gate, his flight for Brazil boarding in fifteen minutes. He was fortunate to have been in Norwich visiting his mother when he had received the call from a panicked Terrence Mitchell about his client's latest fiasco.

There never seemed to be a dull moment with Professor Laura Palmer or her new husband, Professor James Acton. Though he himself had only been involved in one of their skirmishes in Egypt, it had been bloody and good men were lost. He had learned a lesson that day.

Never underestimate the value put on some ancient discovery, especially when religion is involved.

He had doubled their detail at the Egyptian site immediately, along with the Peruvian site that his company was now providing security for as well. After retiring from the SAS he had quickly found it necessary to keep in the game. Private security gigs kept coming up, men with his background in high demand. He quickly realized that the middlemen were making the money off of his and the other men's backs, so he created his own firm, employing a bunch of his ex-SAS buddies, many who had served under his command, and paid them a far bigger cut than the other outfits were offering.

He was the "go to" guy for post British Special Forces employment and now had a couple of hundred men scattered around the world. He had staff he could trust in London handling the business end—mostly wives of his men—leaving him free to gallivant and do what he loved.

But Professor Palmer was a special case.

She paid a premium for *him* and a handpicked team. She wanted the best, and she paid for it. A ridiculous sum every month, but it was what she wanted. And one of those codicils to the standard contract was that whenever possible, *he* would be personally involved in any crisis situation.

And this was definitely a crisis, though not one he had ever expected to have to deal with.

A mega-millionaire being taken hostage? Absolutely. He trained for that. Negotiation techniques, forced retrievals, all standard stuff in his business.

But rescue from a primitive native in the middle of the Amazon rainforest?

No, he hadn't expected that.

He could honestly say *this* was something new. They would be entering a possibly hostile jungle environment, up against possibly one or more tribes that according to his preliminary research could number anywhere from twenty to twenty-thousand in number, and who knew the jungle like the back of their hand.

Not to mention the massive territory.

About the only good news would be that the only form of "rapid" transit would be by water. There were no cars, roads or horses to contend with here, the primitive, limited or noncontacted tribes never having been introduced to the beasts. This meant, hopefully, a limited search radius.

Leather and his small team were going in armed and well equipped, a "special" courier already arranged to deliver their weapons at the rally point in Manaus. His hope was that they could enlist the help of another tribe which from his understanding was a possibility. With local support, *true* local support, not government support that didn't know the jungle, they might stand a chance at finding the now *two* missing professors.

He didn't blame Professor Acton for going after his wife. He would have done the same, but it did make his job more difficult. For one thing, they had no idea if he was dead, injured or captured, and if captured, whether or not it was the same people who had captured Laura.

His work had doubled.

"Are we too late?"

The voice was familiar.

And unexpected.

And unwelcome.

Just what I don't need.

He stood up and turned as Terrence Mitchell, his wife Jenny directly behind him, rushed up, oversized carryon luggage flailing behind them. Leather forced a smile on his face as the rest of his men sitting nearby hid their delight in his discomfort, several of them having met the young and ridiculously awkward Mitchell while rotating through the Egyptian dig.

"What are you two doing here?" he asked as pleasantly as he could.

"We're going with you." Mitchell was breathless. Leather knew it wasn't from being out of shape, the boy did the workouts and training with the rest of the students, so they must have run through the entire airport.

And just my bloody luck, arriving just in time.

"Out of the question."

Mitchell and Jenny seemed taken aback by his rather abrupt response. "Why not?" demanded Mitchell's new wife, still shiny and happy in the post-wedding glow, years of bitter reality yet to destroy her hope in the future.

Bitter much?

His own wedding had ended in disaster, Annie a big city girl marrying the dashing soldier, getting posted to small towns in Britain and equally small towns in foreign countries, not matching the cosmopolitan lifestyle she had planned for herself. And when he had made the Special Air

Services and began to deploy on a moment's notice without being able to tell her anything, she had snapped.

Apparently it was quite the scene on their lawn after he had left.

It was his umpteenth deployment on a special op to Iraq that had finally done her in. When he came home she was gone. She had left a note telling him to sod off and never contact her, then cleaned him out of everything she had some sort of attachment to. Everything from the furniture to the pictures on the walls. Christ, she had even taken the wood toilet seats from the toilets, leaving the original plastic ones behind.

That was when he realized that there had never been any hope.

What kind of sick bitch takes the toilet seats!?

He looked at the two young, energetic and still filled with hope youngsters in front of him, wondering if his past was their future, and hoped not.

The wife of a military man isn't for everyone.

He had since spoken to his wife, many times in fact, the breakup years ago. She had remarried—some doctor in London—and was the fashionable woman she had always wanted to be. How she had ever thought she'd have that lifestyle shacking up with a soldier he'd never know.

Must have been love.

And he saw that same love in the two faces now staring at him, waiting for an answer.

"Why not?" repeated Jenny.

"It's too dangerous."

"I'm—we're willing to take the risk." It was Mitchell who offered up their lives, Jenny's head snapping in agreement.

"We will be jumping out of an aircraft at several thousand feet, precision diving into the Amazon River, then grabbing a line to take us to shore, that if missed, means we will end up either dead or so far down the river as to need rescue ourselves. Then we will be entering a rainforest filled with poisonous and deadly animals and insects, along with natives known to practice cannibalism, in the remote hopes to find Professors Palmer and Acton, who may not even be alive." He stared at Mitchell with no trace of a smile, knowing he was the weaker willed of the two. "Are you sure you're capable of that?"

Mitchell's bottom lip trembled slightly at the realization of what he had got himself into began to set in. Leather could tell however that the boy was looking for a way to save face with his wife so gave him an out.

"I would suggest that rather than come with us all the way as you had intended, you come with us to the staging area downriver. You can help us coordinate the evac once we've found them, and coordinate with the authorities. I had planned to leave one of my men behind to do it"—a lie, the job was a make-work project—"but with you two here, it gives me the opportunity to take an extra experienced man along." He looked from Mitchell to Jenny then back. "What do you think?"

Mitchell exchanged a quick glance with Jenny who also seemed slightly relieved for a way out, both their heads quickly bobbing in agreement. "I-I-I mean *we*, think that's probably a better use of resources."

"Agreed," said Jenny, gripping Mitchell by the arm.

"Good." Leather pointed at two seats at the far end of the row. "Now sit down and I'll brief you later."

The two nodded then dragged their unchecked bags to the two empty seats outside of earshot. One of his men, Michael Trent, leaned over.

"Dodged a bullet on that one, huh, boss?"

Grant hadn't met Mitchell, or seen his two left feet in action.

"You have no bloody idea."

Barasana Village on the Rio Negro, Northern Amazon, Brazil

"Bloody hell!"

Reading rushed forward, shoving his way through the crowd, not giving a damn about baring his teeth, and in fact he did several times as his anger grew, the sight of his friend trussed up like an animal being brought back from the hunt for dinner enraging him.

Fabricio cried out from behind him, urging him to stop, but Reading ignored him, continuing to barge through the natives barely half his size then came to a skidding halt when half a dozen spears blocked his progress, their owners' teeth bared, animalistic growls erupting from their throats. Reading's eyes flared, his teeth on full display as he returned their growl, adrenaline fueling him with rage and idiocy, there no way he could win here.

He reached behind his back for the gun tucked in his belt when someone grabbed his hand.

"No, senhor! You will get us all killed!" hissed Fabricio from behind him.

"Tell them to let him go!" shouted Reading, pointing at Acton who seemed in a confused daze.

Fabricio looked at the newly arrived hunters then, as if realizing for the first time who their captive was, he slapped his hands against his face, gasping, "Senhor Professor!" A rapid exchange in Portuguese ensued, the elder exchanging few words with Fabricio, mostly listening. Then there was an exchange between the hunters and the elder, then the elder held his spear up in the air, shaking it and shouting something.

Cheers erupted from all around, the spears threatening Reading were lowered, the mouths closed, the normal smiles returning, and Acton was gently lowered to the ground, his bindings quickly cut. Reading began to move toward his friend when he stopped. The men blocking him bowed slightly and parted, allowing him to pass unimpeded and he was soon on his knees, at his friend's side. He helped him up to a sitting position against a large tree, quickly checking for wounds, finding one on the back of his head that was bleeding but didn't look too severe.

"Water!" he yelled, Fabricio repeating the order and soon small clay bowls filled with water were brought, Reading holding the first one to his friend's lips, Acton drinking it slowly. A group of women sat down around them and Reading was about to object when they took Acton's arms, smiling at him reassuringly. The women quickly began to clean the wounds around the wrists and ankles, one tending to the head wound.

He gave his friend some more water and he slowly began to come around, his eyes finally focusing on Reading.

Acton smiled. "Thank God!" he murmured. "I thought I was dinner."

"You're lucky you weren't," replied Reading with a smile. He turned to Fabricio. "Get the med kit."

Fabricio nodded and shouted to someone on the boat. Moments later the med kit was at his side, opened, leaving Reading to stare at the mess of supplies.

If only Martin were here!

His old Scotland Yard partner, Detective Inspector Martin Chaney, had trained to be a doctor and would be perfect in this situation, but alas he was not. In fact it had been months since he had heard from the man whom he had considered one of his best friends.

No one had heard from him.

And it had him very worried.

He had seen him that night in Venice along with Acton and Laura, but he had then vanished without a trace, having filed an indefinite leave of absence before he had even arrived in Venice.

He knew he wouldn't be returning.

He had been shot and in a coma for months before waking just prior to their final mission for the Triarii, a two-thousand year old organization descendent from the Roman Empire's Thirteenth Legion. They had assumed it would be over for them, but with Chaney a member of the Triarii, he knew his involvement would continue, their mission to protect humanity from the perceived power of the crystal skulls never ending.

Reading prayed his friend was merely on some top secret mission for the organization, and would resurface one day as if nothing had happened.

I miss you, old friend.

Fabricio knelt down on the other side and began to expertly wrap the now cleaned wounds, first spreading a disinfectant powder causing Acton to wince.

"Laura?"

Reading slowly shook his head. "Nothing yet. We're here to try and get these people to help us." He patted his friend on the shoulder. "At least now we're only looking for one."

Fabricio began to wrap Acton's ankles when he spoke. "The Chief has agreed to help us look for your wife, Senhor Acton."

Acton grabbed Reading by the arm, relief on his face. "Did you get my last message?"

"The one with the coordinates? Yes."

"We'll start there." He struggled to get up when Reading pushed him back down.

"You're in no condition to go anywhere."

"I'll be fine."

"No, you'll just end up slowing us down."

Fabricio tied off the final bandage. "It no matter. They won't leave until tomorrow morning."

"Why?" cried both Reading and Acton.

"Today is a festival day. They no help today. But tomorrow, they all help."

Reading and Acton exchanged frowns. "I'm not sure what else we can do," said Reading, knowing Acton wouldn't be happy.

Acton struggled to his feet, failing, then glared at Reading. "Either help me or get out of my way."

Reading grabbed his friend by the arm and pulled him to his feet. Acton grabbed his head then immediately collapsed in Reading's arms. He was quickly surrounded by a group of natives who helped carry him into one of the communal lodges and lay him on a bed. They propped him up on piles of furs and brought him water and soup as Reading sat by his side.

Acton looked over at Reading. "Sorry for snapping at you."

Reading batted the words away with a flick of the wrist. "Nothing doing. I would have decked you if I was in your position."

"No doubt." He peered out the door. "What time is it?"

Reading looked at his watch. "Coming up on two in the afternoon. We've already lost half the day. Rest up, heal up, eat and drink lots, and you'll probably be able to come with us."

Acton nodded, then winced. "Can you check if we've got any Tylenol on the boat?"

Reading rose. "Be right back."

As he left a group of giggling girls rushed into the lodge and began to tend to Acton. "Have fun, Jim, just remember you're a married man now."

"Not a word of this to Laura!"

Reading roared with laughter as he quickly covered his mouth in case his teeth were overexposed. Suddenly he felt someone grab his arm. He looked down and it was the girl from earlier. She was smiling up at him, her expression suggesting to him she wanted a good shagging. Someone else gripped his other arm and the suddenly intimidating thought of a threesome flashed across his mind. He tore his smile away to look at what other beauty was also expressing an interest and nearly shite when he saw the gay man from earlier, smiling at him, his expression suggesting to him he too wanted a good shagging.

God help me.

One Day's Travel from Rio Negro, Northern Amazon, Brazil

Tuk was pleased. They had made very good time, Lau-ra cooperating with him and keeping a good pace. He had chatted with her the entire time, hoping that she would learn to understand his language. Perhaps it would come back to her, since in her previous life she must have been able to speak. He had even tried several of the other dialects from neighboring tribes, but had garnered no reaction other than smiles and motions.

Communication was progressing, however. Several hand motions had been established between them for such things as water, food, relieving oneself, and for having a rest. It was working quite well, and when they would rest, she would ask him for the names of various things around them such as the sky, trees, ground and the river. She already knew more words than he could count, and he was pleased that he was learning her way of saying things too. Surprisingly he found it much easier to learn her words than she did his, but then again he was always very smart, and this one may not be as gifted as he. By no means was she stupid, he could tell, there no dull look behind those eyes he had seen on some people, but perhaps languages were not her thing.

He had tried to teach her his full name, something she would need to know for the bonding ceremony, but she had failed. He had learned hers however. Lau-ra-pal-mer.

It was a three day journey to his village, but they had covered some ground last night, and were up at the crack of dawn this morning with few delays and a rushed pace to put distance between them and the Spirit People, so he was optimistic that by tomorrow morning they would be at her final destination, at least until the Cleansing Ritual was complete.

Then she'd be free to join him in the village.

It would be arduous, torturous even, but she was strong, and he was certain she'd survive it. Many didn't, but they were willing to accept their fate in order to be accepted back in the tribe, the Cleansing Ritual a way to purge the body of the evil that it had been exposed to, to allow the individual time to reflect on their misdeeds, and to prove their worthiness in the Mother's eyes. If at the end of the isolation they were still alive, then all was forgiven and forgotten, the Mother having found them worthy to remain amongst the living.

But should they die during their isolation with no food or water other than what the Mother provided them, they would be mourned for having tried, and buried with dignity. And should they have escaped somehow?

No second chances were given.

He wasn't sure how he'd convey what was expected of her to Lau-ra, but if she was of the Spirit People, surely she remembered the ways of the living? But then she didn't remember the languages of the living.

Unless she's from very far away, and it is a language I haven't heard before!

The thought excited him. He knew the river was long, so long no one had ever reached the mouth of it, or if they had, they had not been able to return.

But the Spirit People seemed to travel the river with ease, which might mean she was from many days journey away, where her language might be the norm.

It gave him hope that she might know what was expected of her.

Unless they have different ways of cleansing the shamed.

He was certain that when they arrived, much of what was expected would become self-evident, but she also needed hope. If she had no way of knowing how long she needed to survive, she might try to escape and be forever damned.

He looked up at the sky. There was less than an hour of sunlight left so they would have to find a place to spend the night. He bent over and picked up a bunch of small rocks, determined to teach the Woman of Light how to count before they went to sleep.

It's essential she understands how long she needs to survive.

Laura Palmer watched curiously as Tuk bent over and began to pick up small rocks. After he had found half a dozen on his own, she decided to help him, yet a further gesture of her being cooperative, and another opportunity for them to bond so he might have second thoughts about killing her at the end of their journey, no matter how certain she was that this was no longer his motivation.

But what if someone else decided to?

She knew some of the tribes in the Amazon demanded that the males find a mate from outside of the tribe and bring them back. This helped diversify the bloodlines and genome, and also proved the man capable of winning a mate. With his slight features, Tuk would probably have had an extremely hard time finding a mate which had her more convinced than ever that he was bringing her home to Mom.

And what if Mom rejected her?

Would she then face death? The stronger the bond she created with Tuk now, the less likely he might follow out any order to kill her should she be rejected by his family group.

She handed him several stones and he smiled, taking them and putting them in his bag. They then pressed on for several minutes before finding another perch off the ground and in a large tree quite similar to last night's accommodations. A bed for her was quickly made, along with a screen woven once again from the materials available to him. His mastery of surviving the forest was clear, skills she thought she had, but realized how without her modern tools to assist, she would be almost helpless.

Tuk disappeared for a few minutes, leaving her to debate making a break for it, but she knew she wouldn't get far and it would destroy any trust and bond she might have been able to forge to this point. Instead, she smoothed out her bed, again in an alcove in the massive tree, and took a moment to run her fingers through her knotted hair.

Something hissed above her and her head jerked back as she made eye contact with her visitor.

And screamed.

Tuk's head spun toward the tree, his eyes focusing on the branch where he had left Lau-ra. They bulged. A massive green yakumama snake uncoiled from her resting place on the branch above. It had apparently found a place exposed to the warm sun earlier in the day and was now either making its way back down, or had been disturbed by Lau-ra.

Either way it appeared to be at least ten arms lengths long, easily big enough to crush his future mate then devour her, most likely still alive.

He sprang forward, pulling his pipe with several poison, sharpened darts from his bag, blowing them in quick succession, each embedding themselves in the body of the massive snake. It hissed in anger, turning toward him, mouth opened wide as it spat its response, then turned back to its prey, the tiny darts not affecting it. Lau-ra continued to scream, the jungle around them now alive with every creature within earshot joining in. As the creature's enormous head continued to stare at Lau-ra, its body slowly lowered to the branch she was on, trapping her in the alcove he had left her in.

He readied his spear and threw it as hard as he could, which he knew wouldn't be enough. His aim was true, as he had expected, and the tip pierced the thick skin of the snake, as he hadn't expected. It continued through the body and the tip came through the other side, his hardest throw ever.

If only Father were here to see this!

The snake hissed in pain, its body writhing on the branch, its massive head thrashing back and forth, Lau-ra curled into a ball, her hands covering her head from the occasional impact with the head, easily the size of her torso. He raced toward the trunk of the tree, launching himself at it, his right foot expertly finding a hold then pushing off, hurling himself toward the body of the huge reptile.

"Tuk!" cried Lau-ra as he whipped a stone blade at her, its tip embedding itself in the wood just above her right shoulder. His right hand caught the spear and he swung himself up on the back of the writhing creature as Lau-ra yanked the knife free and began to jab it forward at the head of the creature, every second or third thrust making contact, angering the beast even further. He knew it was barely weakened, and their only hope was to get it out of the tree. He gripped the other end of his spear, then rocked his entire body to the right, pulling with all his might, his legs gripping the creature tightly.

He fell to the side, a few arm lengths on either side of the spear coming with him, but not enough. He saw the tail begin to coil around the branch and knew he had only moments before the mighty creature secured itself. Jerking his body back and forth, he let go of the snake with his left leg and pushed against the tree, bouncing as hard as he could and felt several more lengths begin to lose the grip on the branch. Out of the corner of his eye he saw Lau-ra sink the blade into the creature's eye, it hissing in pain, jerking back and sending even more of its body over the edge, gravity taking over.

The huge beast fell from the tree, falling almost the height of two men, with Tuk under it. He twisted, trying to move himself out of the way, but failed, smacking hard against the ground, crying out in pain. He tried to scramble away but couldn't, his legs stuck under the stunned beast. He grabbed the end of the spear and pulled with all his might, the long shaft slowly freed of the thick skin and body, easily the thickness of the great warrior Bruk.

The spear free, he jabbed at the body, hoping the yakumama would spasm and free his legs, but instead he felt it begin to wrap itself around him and he knew he wouldn't be long for this world once it began to squeeze. He continued jabbing as hard and as fast as he could, blood from the snake spurting out with each blow, but not enough it seemed to slow it down.

Suddenly he heard a cry. It was Lau-ra jumping through the air, the blade gripped tightly in both hands. She landed on the body, then plunged the knife deep, pulling it toward her as she scrambled backward, slicing the creature wide open. It hissed in agony, forgetting him, flipping over on its back, freeing his legs. As Lau-ra continued to slice, the creature's head swung around swiftly, knocking her to the ground, but it had given Tuk the moment of distraction he needed.

He shoved up with the spear, puncturing the beast's head, the spear going completely through. He shoved forward, twisting the head upside down and impaling it on the ground. Lau-ra jumped to his side, plunging the blade into its neck, slicing across as deep as she could. Tuk, satisfied the spear was holding the head in place, took the knife and hacked at the neck, slowly severing it until the beast finally stopped hissing and thrashing.

He dropped to the ground, flat on his back, exhausted. Lau-ra collapsed beside him, both of them gasping for air. He rolled over and looked at her, a smile on his face realizing he and his future mate had together taken down one of the mightiest beasts of the jungle, alone.

And that together they would be a match for certain to be blessed by the great Mother.

Barasana Village on the Rio Negro, Northern Amazon, Brazil
One day before the attack

Acton rubbed his eyes to find sunlight just beginning to pour into the clearing containing the communal lodges of the villagers. At least a couple of dozen were still asleep in his particular lodge, including one Hugh Reading who was at the far end, under a blanket with a particularly gorgeous native girl who seemed to have a ravenous sexual appetite, their love making having gone on half the night.

Way to go old man!

He sat up and found his headache to be gone. Gingerly testing his arms and legs, he winced as he rotated his still raw wrists and ankles. He stood, stretched carefully, then fully, and stepped outside. It had been one hell of a party from his vantage point. He hadn't been alone a single second, attended to by native women who had a hard time understanding the concept of a monogamous marriage, he finally having to roll over and feign sleep before he was left alone.

He had quickly told Reading to enjoy himself, the poor man so confused as to what to do, it was almost cute. It was just too bad he wouldn't be able to take her back with him, this truly a one night stand with no further risk of commitment.

Acton hoped his friend had used some sort of protection. The last thing the poor girl needed was a half-white baby, or he catching some STD Western-medicine had no cure for.

Some sort of brew had made the rounds, the entire crew of the Juliana passed out around the camp, some spooning women, other alone, and one with the gay man who had had his eyes on Reading for most of the night.

That could prove awkward if he's straight.

Acton chuckled, thankful he hadn't partaken in the drinking. He boarded the boat and found Milton asleep in his cabin, the satellite phone still gripped in his hand. He gently pried it loose, his friend grumbling in protest, then rolling over, falling back to sleep.

There were no messages, but there had been an incoming call that had been answered. He looked at his watch and realized he had to begin waking people up, daylight already burning away.

He gently shook Milton's shoulder. "Greg, wake up," he said, quietly at first.

A moan of protest.

A slightly harder shake, and a slightly louder demand had his friend turning toward him, pushing himself up on his elbows. "Wh-what did I miss?" he asked, still trying to get his bearings.

"Just a big drunken party from what I can tell." He stepped back as Milton swung his legs out from the bed, wincing as he suddenly grabbed his back. "Are you okay?" asked Acton, immediately concerned.

"My back is acting up." Milton extended a hand and Acton pulled him to his feet. "I think this trip was a mistake."

Acton felt a pit in his stomach form as guilt racked him. "I'm sorry, I shouldn't have pushed you—"

"Oh piss off, you know it's not your fault. I wanted to come as much as anyone, and there was no telling me it wasn't a good idea."

"Let me guess, your wife said you shouldn't."

"Wrong."

"Really? And here I thought she was a smart woman."

"Ha ha. Pain in my ass sometimes her always being right, but she was wrong this time. Both of us were. Seeing the World Cup wasn't a problem—she and Niskha had a fantastic time though I think soccer will never be her thing—it was this boat trip. They were wise to not come. The bed is just too uncomfortable. My back muscles never get a chance to rest properly."

"Is there anything I can do?"

Milton shook his head, plopping himself into his wheelchair, slight relief written on his face.

Acton motioned toward the chair with his chin. "Maybe you should try sleeping in that tonight."

Milton's head bobbed in agreement as he guided himself out the door and down the hall toward the deck. "Not a bad idea, but it might compress my spine being upright so long."

Acton sighed, two worries now on his mind. He had to get Laura, but he also didn't want his friend to relapse, perhaps losing the mobility he had gained through such hard work. "Maybe we should send the boat back with you on it. This might take a few more days."

Milton shook his head. "No can do. Got a call late last night. Leather and his team are here." Acton's heart leapt with hope. "They'll be parachuting in late this afternoon, early evening. And they're going to need the boat."

"Why?"

When Milton explained the plan, Acton shook his head in disbelief. "Those Special Ops guys are effin' nuts."

"Tell me about it. Thank God we have them."

"Amen to that." Acton looked at his watch. "But we can't wait for them. We'll lose another day, especially if they don't get here until evening."

"Agreed," said Milton, positioning his chair at the aft of the boat, Acton perching on the edge of a chair beside him, looking out at the village. People were starting to move, most like zombies, their joints still impaired from the overindulgences the night before. "Where's Hugh?"

94

Acton grinned. "Our friend got a little somethin' somethin' last night."

"No kidding!"

"All damned night from the sounds of it."

"Hugh Reading, breaking hearts the world over."

Acton laughed knowing full well Reading would cuss Milton out if he heard that one, last night's actions not in the man's character from what Acton knew.

But sometimes you just have to let go.

The poor man had been alone for so long, blowing off some steam with a willing partner in the middle of the jungle was well deserved. Acton was happy for him and couldn't wait for the ribbing to begin.

"You're never going to let him forget this, are you?"

Acton winked at Milton. "You know me so well."

Reading woke to find himself under a blanket, his head still thick from whatever godforsaken homemade alcohol had been handed about through the night around the communal fire. As he tried to remember all the details, one thing became abundantly clear as it wiggled beside him.

He had had sex.

Oh god! Please don't let it be—

A face popped out from beneath the blanket and he sighed in relief as the young woman from yesterday smiled at him, kissing him gently. She said something to him, words that had no meaning, but she seemed content.

"Honey, I have no idea what you're saying, but you have no idea how relieved I am to find you here."

She kissed him again and he returned the kiss, which was when he discovered he was naked, a hand suddenly gripping his growing manhood. He looked about and realized he was in a communal cabin, but most people seemed to still be asleep.

Oh, what the hell!

His hands began to roam her incredible body, she far prettier than he was handsome. As his mind began to wonder what kind of protection they had used last night, he not in the habit of carrying condoms at his age, he remembered being tossed a strip by one of the crew.

Thank God!

But where were they now? As things began to grow more heated, and hard, he pushed himself up on an elbow and smiled when he found one more unopened sitting on the floor. He grabbed it then the girl yanked it from his hand, putting it on for him, obviously well versed in how they worked.

I hope she learned that last night, otherwise she's the camp tramp.

But at this moment he didn't care.

She pushed him on his back and mounted him, both sighing in ecstasy as he got one last memory of his time with this woman whose name he had no clue of. And this time alcohol wasn't going to interfere with the memory.

He pulled her down and kissed her hard, hoping he wasn't going to regret this, and as their love making progressed, slow and steady at first, then quickening in intensity as he heard her begin to climax, he did his best impression of a twenty year old in a fifty something body, leaving them both gasping and satisfied, he quite pleased with himself in the end. It was the best sex he could remember, and he was happy they had one more go at it, one that he could remember and savor for years to come.

Somebody yelled, nothing panicky, more like an announcement, and the entire lodge stirred. He suddenly blushed, his British sensibilities returning, but his lover refused to move. Instead she continued to lay on top of him, quietly cooing in his ear, whispering words he wished he understood.

I hope she's not falling in love.

He'd hate to break this young girl's heart, but then again, it was more likely she'd break his. He was a novelty she was trying out for one night, a story she could tell her friends about, about the night she spent with the tall white man. She was a memory he could tell no one about, he the dirty old man who had "taken advantage" of a young naïve girl.

Though that wasn't how he felt.

If anyone was taken advantage of here, it was him—that much was pretty clear. She knew what she wanted from the start, and she pursued him.

He was just a little surprised and pleased that he had let her.

The desire to just continue lying with her, to continue feeling her warm, soft body against his, to continue to make love to her throughout the day was overwhelming, but he knew he had to get up. The search for Laura would be getting underway soon, and she was far more important than another roll in the hay.

"We have to get up, beautiful." The words meant nothing to her, but a quick double-tap on her bum and him pushing himself up on his elbows was enough of a hint. She grinned, pushing him back down as she climbed out of bed, revealing her entire spectacular body for the first time.

He gasped, shaking his head at how damned lucky he was.

Nobody would believe me if I told them.

He wondered if a cellphone picture would be appropriate, just to remind himself.

What are you, sixteen?

At the moment he felt it, but he thought better of capturing the moment. She quickly donned her short skirt from yesterday, then motioned for him to stay put. Returning several minutes later, she had water and some sort of plant roots that she crushed in a small bowl then mixed with the water. She then took an incredibly soft animal skin, soaked it in the mixture, and began to give him the best sponge bath he had ever had, a happy ending had by all.

By the time they were done they were alone, sounds of activity outside making him feel guilty. He kissed her one last time, rising from bed and dressing, his clothes in a pile beside the bed. He shook out his boots, some massive insect dropping out causing him to start.

He shook harder, smacking them together.

Nothing.

He tentatively put his feet in the boots, hoping to not feel anything squish or worse, bite, and was relieved to reach the steel toes without any surprises. Dressed, the young girl grabbed his arm and led him out. As they emerged into the sunlight, the entire camp turned and cheered, turning him a shade of red he hadn't seen since he fell asleep on the French Riviera during his honeymoon so many years ago.

The crew of the boat were particularly boisterous, jabs in Portuguese flying fast and furious, he for once happy he didn't understand the language.

And to his embarrassment, everyone seemed ready to go. He looked for Acton and saw him waving from the boat as he walked down the ramp, backpack strapped across his back.

"Have a good night?" asked Acton with a grin, his teeth covered tightly behind his lips.

"Umm, ahh, yeah, I guess you could say that."

Acton slapped him on the shoulder, returning the smile from the beaming young girl. "Well, I've got some good news and some bad news. What do you want first?"

Reading hated that question. *Just give me the damned news!*

"Bad news."

"Bad news is Greg's back is pretty bad, and we've got Leather's team parachuting in late this afternoon or early evening, and they need our help. I don't trust the crew to follow the instructions correctly, and I'm afraid Greg will overexert himself if he has to get involved."

"And the good news?"

"I need you to stay here with him."

"How's that good news?"

Acton looked at the woman on Reading's arm. "You've got nothing to do until late this afternoon, and a cabin on the boat that isn't being used that perhaps you'd like to give Kinti a tour of."

Reading felt himself flush as he glanced down at the woman's smiling face. *Kinti?* The memory of learning her name rushed back and he felt ashamed for having forgotten it. "Kinti," he said, smiling.

"Hugh," she replied, placing her hand on his chest.

Reading cleared his throat. "Umm, well, that sounds like a good idea. I mean, me staying behind to take care of Leather's arrival."

"Thought you'd agree," winked Acton. "Keep the satphone charged and on either you or Greg at all times. And try to make sure that Greg gets some rest."

"Will do."

"Fabricio is remaining behind, Sandro will be coming with the search party, so you guys should be safe."

Reading nodded. "I've been around a few years, lad. I can take care of myself."

Acton laughed. "Sorry, I'm acting like a mother hen, I know. I'm just worried about Greg. I know I'm leaving things in good hands." He slapped Reading on the shoulder then bowed slightly to Kinti who giggled, gripping Reading's arm even tighter. "We'll see you soon."

"With Laura."

"From your lips to God's ears." Acton walked toward the group, Sandro, the second mate on the boat, and the only other one who could speak English, beginning to bring him up to date on what was happening.

Apparently even Fabricio doesn't trust his men.

Reading pointed to the boat and Kinti nodded, smiling. They climbed the ramp and he introduced her to Milton, then made some excuse to go below. Milton grinned.

So I'm transparent.

He opened the door to his cabin and found it in shipshape condition, just like he had left it.

With an entire large box of condoms sitting on the pillow.

Kinti grinned, pulling him inside and closing the door.

She's going to be the death of me.

She quickly stripped him down, pushed him on the bed then jumped on top of him.

But what a way to go!

One Day's Travel from Rio Negro, Northern Amazon, Brazil

It was a feast Laura Palmer thought she could never partake in, but Tuk had insisted, in a pleasant way, and she was curious. She had eaten snake meat on several occasions, but never one as large as a female Green Anaconda. This thing must have been approaching ten meters in length, with the girth of a small man.

And they had killed it, together.

After lying on the ground for several minutes, Tuk had jumped up and immediately gutted and skinned the creature, taking large chunks of the meat and cooking it over a fire made from the fat reserves of the female. Tuk clearly was visibly upset about so much of the creature going to waste, it obviously not his people's way, but there was little choice. She was certain the jungle would lay claim to the rest of the carcass and none would go to waste.

The taste was as expected, it similar to other snakes she had eaten, but just with bigger chunks—chicken with a hint of fish, but not as chewy as chicken. The flavor really came from the roasting over the fire, and some type of herb mixture Tuk sprinkled over it, a tiny animal skin pouch for just such an occasion tucked away in his larger bag.

Once she got over what she was eating, and positioned herself so there was no risk of seeing their kill below, she had stuffed herself on the white meat, sleeping heavily, Tuk only feet away, both exhausted.

And this morning they were pushing forward, and had already been doing so for hours. Tuk had cooked a lot of extra meat and was liberally handing it out to her, to the point where she was too full, having to refuse him otherwise she might find herself throwing up with the pace they were keeping.

Why so fast today?

She had the impression that today he wasn't just heading in a direction, but heading to a specific location, he stopping occasionally it seemed to get his bearings. They were going at such a speed she was having a hard time marking their trail, and had to admit on occasion she just plumb forgot. This never lasted more than a few minutes, but she had to remember she was a hostage. Stockholm Syndrome was real, and if she weren't careful, she'd fall into its trap. She was creating a bond with him for her survival so that James and the others would have time to follow her trail and rescue her.

She couldn't risk thinking that Tuk was a real friend with no maleficent intentions. He had kidnapped her, he had some obvious plan, which she still thought involved eventual marriage or their tribal equivalent. And that meant sex.

Which meant rape, no matter how nice he planned to be about it.

I need some way to delay whatever ceremony he has planned!

She again thought of faking an injury, perhaps a twisted ankle, and again thought better of it. It was essential to mark their path if she were to survive.

And if she were to be ultimately raped while awaiting rescue?

She'd deal with it when the time came.

She felt her chest tighten slightly at the thought of it, at the thought of what her beloved James might think. She knew he was a good man, a fair man, and wouldn't blame her, but she would have been with another man, voluntarily or not.

And if she wasn't careful, Stockholm Syndrome might just have her forgiving the poor, simple, weak man who had kidnapped her, allowing him to do with her as he pleased to make things easier until rescue.

Are you kidding me?

A flash of anger overcame her defeatist attitude. Rape was rape. Sex without consent was rape. And she'd fight any bastard who intended to rape her tooth and nail, no matter how nice they were, or how good a friend they became. She was the master of her own body, and no one was going to take it without a fight.

Tuk seemed to sense a change in her demeanor and he gave her a thumbs up with a questioning, "Okay?", something she had taught him last night after their ordeal.

She nodded and forced a smile on her face. "Okay."

They crossed a small creek and he suddenly seemed excited, pointing slightly to the left of the meandering water source and urging her forward. As they pushed through the underbrush, suddenly they came upon a clearing and what she saw in the center had her heart leap into her throat.

"James, help me!"

Tuk was quite pleased at the time they had made, and as they entered the clearing, he was also pleased to see no one else was making use of the Cleansing Pit. He wasn't surprised, it was a rare ritual, but the pit was always kept prepared just in case there was a need.

And today there was a need.

Suddenly Lau-ra screamed something and turned to run. He grabbed her by the arm, pulling her toward the pit.

"Don't worry, the Mother will protect you!"

She struggled against him, the first time she had really done so in the two days they had been together, and it almost shocked him at first. *Didn't she come willingly?* She was a Spirit Person, the Woman of Light. If she hadn't wanted to come, there was no way he could have taken her, but she had let him.

"Please, calm down, you won't be hurt. It's just the Cleansing Pit. You need to be cleansed before we can be mated. I thought that was what you wanted?"

They were at the edge now, a rope, tied to a nearby tree, hung in the pit just in case someone happened to fall in accidentally. He had heard of the occasional animal being found at the bottom, but that was rare, the pit not hidden like a trap. Most animals gave it a wide berth. He grabbed the rope with his free hand and placed it in Lau-ra's hand. She threw it away, shaking her head, shouting something.

It sounded negative.

And it angered him, slightly.

If she weren't going to climb into the pit voluntarily like most did, then he had no choice but to put her in himself. But it was the depth of almost two men, so tossing her inside might kill her. He quickly wrapped the rope around her arm, yanking on it, causing her to yelp in pain, then he pushed her over the edge.

Instinct took over.

She reached up with her free hand and grabbed the rope as she fell, smacking into the earthen wall with a grunt, tears pouring down her cheeks as she screamed at him. He pointed at the floor, jabbing his spear for emphasis, and she lowered herself, finally letting go of the rope. He yanked it out, tossing it away from the pit.

He motioned for her to be quiet and she acquiesced, apparently realizing it was too late for her now. It was essential she remain calm. She would need her strength for the upcoming ordeal. But how to explain it to her?

She certainly recognized the pit from her previous life before the Spirit World.

Perhaps she had died in one?

If that were so, then the Mother hadn't found her worthy.

Would that mean now, in this second chance at life, the Mother would once again find her not worthy? Would he return here at the end of the ritual to find her dead, once again departed to the Spirit World?

Was that even possible?

He wondered. He had heard of spirits taking human form, but had always been told it was usually forbidden unless there was some specific purpose to be served for the Mother. In this case he had simply assumed the purpose was for him to find a mate so he could procreate and help his tribe expand and continue to honor the Mother.

But if she had died before in the pit?

Or was that a false assumption?

Perhaps she had no idea what the pit was, and was simply reacting to it like anyone might. No one wanted to be put into a pit. Outside of the Cleansing Ritual, there could be no good reason for a person to be put into a pit.

That must be it!

That would be why she had let herself get taken. If she had known about the Cleansing Pit, she would have known that it would be necessary for her to endure it if she were to transition back to the world of the humans. So if she knew, and she still went voluntarily, then she wouldn't be reacting the way she were now.

He sighed in relief.

She just didn't know!

Which meant that she hadn't died in the ritual in her previous life, which meant the Mother may very well still find her worthy.

He pointed at her. "Lau-ra."

She stopped pacing the pit and looked up at him, saying nothing, but her eyes glaring at him in hatred and fear.

He pointed up at the sky. "You must survive the challenge. If you are worthy, the Mother will provide." His words were lost on her. He frowned, then pointed at the sky again, then made a circle with his fingers to represent the sun. He pointed to where it rose each morning, then traced the route across the sky toward where it would eventually set.

"Day," he said, making the arc again. "Day. You understand?"

She nodded, saying something.

He removed some of the small rocks from his pouch and dropped the correct number into the pit. He pointed at the rocks, then at the sky, moving his arm in an arc several times before pointing again at the rocks.

"You must survive that many days, you understand?"

She picked up the rocks, and when she counted them her jaw dropped as she cried out again, throwing all seven stones at him.

She understands.

"Seven days? Are you kidding me!" she screamed. How the hell was she supposed to survive in the bottom of a pit for seven days? She looked around and saw nothing, not even a stick to help her. "Why are you doing this?" she cried, slamming her fists against the earth, small round impressions left behind.

Tuk said something, motioning with his hands something that suggested she calm down. He seemed perfectly okay with this situation, there no malevolence whatsoever. If anything he seemed puzzled, disappointed even—as if her reaction were completely unexpected. Perhaps it was the fact she had barely resisted since her capture that had him thinking everything would go smooth.

But if his intention all along had been to put her in here to die, then why be so friendly.

But he had said seven days, at least that's what she assumed his hand motions and the seven pebbles had meant.

And seven days meant there was an end to this. If his intent was to leave her to die, then there would be no seven day limit.

This is a ritual!

It suddenly made sense. He *was* intending for her to be his mate, but as in many primitive cultures, there was a ritual before marriage, especially if the person was unknown. This must be his tribe's ritual. If she were expected to stay here seven days on her own, with no supplies, it must be some sort of test of worthiness.

A test that must result in most dying.

Seven days without water?

She made a drinking motion. "What about water?"

Tuk's arm waved at their surroundings, as if encompassing more than just the immediate vicinity. He said something, then, "Okay?"

If she didn't know better, she took his meaning to be, "the jungle will provide." And maybe it would. This was a rainforest, so it could rain, providing her with water. That was the most important aspect to her survival. If she dug at the soil she might find grubs or other sources of protein to keep her going.

"Okay?" he asked again, giving the thumbs up she now regretted teaching him.

She returned the thumbs up. "Go to hell you bastard," she said with a smile.

Tuk smiled, oblivious to her words, then disappeared.

She listened but could hear nothing but the sounds of the forest.

"Tuk?" she called, but there was no answer. "Tuk!" She yelled this time, and still nothing.

She sat in the one corner that still had light and assessed her situation.

Horrendous.

She knew she only had a few hours of sunlight left so went to work preparing herself as best she could. In the opposite corner, where the morning sun would first hit, she stamped down a sleeping area, making it as hard and smooth as she could to try and prevent insects from coming up through it. She then used the heel of her boot to create several holes in the dirt, tamping them down, hoping they might hold water long enough for her to scoop some of it out should it rain.

Lastly, in the dark corner away from her sleeping area, she used her heel to dig out as deep a hole as she could for a latrine. It would get nasty quite quickly, but tomorrow morning she would begin looking at means of escape rather than survival.

And with luck, perhaps James would be here with a rescue party, having found her trail.

She double checked that her pants were tucked tightly into her boots, then removed her bra. She buttoned up her shirt tight and tucked it into her pants, then folded the cups of her padded bra together, laying her head down gently, lying on her side with her back toward the wall.

Her lip began to tremble as a wave of self-pity rolled over her.

Seven days. Just survive seven days.

Acton followed the natives, careful to scan the area for any evidence of Laura or anyone having been there before, but his skillset did not include tracking techniques, something he would be addressing with Leather when they got themselves out of this current situation.

And we will get ourselves out!

He knew deep down in his soul that Laura was alive. He was certain he would know if she wasn't. He knew it sounded foolish, magical, spiritual, but something inside him told him she was still alive and that she would hang on until he found her.

But so far they had found nothing, and the daylight was fading. They had been searching for almost eight hours, a group of at least thirty tribesmen having split off into groups of three, fanning out in every direction from the village. It had warmed his heart that these people would not only welcome them into their village, but would help search for someone they had never met, who they knew nothing about, out of the goodness of their own hearts.

For it was just that. They had asked for nothing in return. Fabricio had offered food, blankets, trinkets, chocolate, but was refused. They only wanted to help. Something wrong had been done, and they felt it was their responsibility to correct it.

It gave him hope for Laura. She had been kidnapped, but he didn't know why. Perhaps the motive was not one of malevolence, but merely a misunderstanding. Perhaps she was perfectly okay, merely being held against her will, but her life not in danger.

He sighed.

He was grasping at straws of hope, he knew, but he had to otherwise he'd be going mad. He knew the search was about to end for the day, which would frustrate him, but he could ask no more of his hosts. And they were the experts. They could keep moving forward in the night, but if they did, they might miss something.

One of the natives whose name sounded like Skip to Acton said something, the others gathering around.

"What is it?" asked Acton. Skip spoke Portuguese, and said something to Sandro who then pointed at a mark in the ground.

"He say that made by person. It not a track from animal."

Acton took out his flashlight, the shadows already long, and knelt down by the indentation, shining the beam over the area.

And almost cried out in joy.

The mark was a distinct heel mark with an obvious tread.

A modern boot had made this.

Which meant they were finally on the right track.

"This is a heel mark, from a boot," he said, pointing at the same spot on his boot.

Skip nodded then waved his hand, as if disagreeing. He walked forward a step then as he stepped forward on his right foot, he put more pressure on the back, leaving a deeper indentation. He explained to Sandro.

"He said that if it is her, she is leaving the mark deliberately, or she is injured and can't walk properly."

Skip shouted, pointing at the ground about ten feet away. They all rushed over to see what he had found.

"Another footprint!" exclaimed Sandro. "We have found her trail, senhor!"

"We have to tell the others. We have to follow this now!"

Sandro translated but Skip shook his head, pointing at the rapidly darkening sky. And Acton knew he was right. They would have to wait until the morning, but at least now there was real hope, and rapid progress should be made.

He dialed the satphone to give Milton and Reading an update, but was surprised to find it not answered. He left a message then tucked it back in his pocket and began to set up his sleeping area, wondering what might be happening that they would miss his call.

Barasana Village on the Rio Negro, Northern Amazon, Brazil

"The rope is too low!" yelled Reading from the shore. "They'll never see it!"

"If it's too high, they'll never be able to grab it!" came the reply from Milton, still on the boat that was now about thirty feet from shore, a rope dangling between it and a nearby tree. Leather's men were arriving any minute, and they were arriving late. The sun had almost set, and by the time they got here, it will have.

And they had no way of making the rope visible.

Several of the tribesmen had set up a large fire on the bank of the river and the boat had all its lights on, so Reading hoped that the team would be able to at least see the two ends of the rope, but that would be little comfort to them if they missed the grab and continued down the fairly swift Rio Negro. Reading had little doubt these men would survive, but they could be many miles downriver by the time they made it ashore and could face hours or days of travel on foot along the dense shoreline before they reached the village.

Reading and Kinti had spent an unbelievable day together, one that would go down in his own record books as being the most intense and most pleasurable he had ever had. They had barely left his cabin, she bringing him all three meals, he only leaving to use the bathroom and to check on Milton who said little, merely grinning at him like he knew exactly what was going on.

Reading had blushed the first couple of times, then accepted it, resisting the urge to bump Milton's raised fist. But when Fabricio had knocked on the door, the pleasure was over and the recovery operation begun. Leather's plan was crazy in civilian terms, probably fairly routine in the Special Ops world. And there was very little choice, there not exactly a landing strip nearby, and the clearing for the village not so large when you went up to tree top level where the branches still extended over much of the clearing.

The only clear area easily targeted was the river.

"We need to make this rope visible somehow!" Reading looked around. "Do we have any lanterns or something that we could hang on it?"

"Nothing electric according to Fabricio," replied Milton. "They're all gas. They'd just be doused."

Shit!

Reading looked about and noticed Kinti had left his side, instead conferring with one of the natives who spoke Portuguese. He pointed at the rope, saying something, then Kinti disappeared into the forest. Reading had no time to wonder where she was going as he heard the roar of a plane engine overhead. He looked up and saw the lights above, the pilot having turned on his landing lights to make himself visible, and to highlight the river below.

He's way too low!

As if in answer to his question he heard the engine power up and the plane begin to climb. He felt a tap on his shoulder. Kinti was there, looking up at him, smiling. She pointed at a bowl she had, some sort of paste inside, the firelight seeming to give it a dull glow.

"I'm not hungry right now," said Reading, smiling at the poor girl who had no concept of what was going on. He felt a twinge of regret once again as he felt he had taken advantage of her.

She shook her head. "No eat." She stuck her finger in the paste then wiped a streak across her face, turning away from the firelight. It glowed. Brightly.

Reading's eyebrows narrowed as he attempted to piece together what the young girl was trying to communicate to him when she simply took action herself. And when she started, he immediately began to question who was the primitive. She took a handful of the paste and grabbed the rope, rubbing the paste over the surface. As she continued out into the water, hanging onto the rope with one armpit, the bowl in that hand, the other free hand rubbing the paste on the rope, everything began to glow.

Reading stood, mouth agape, as he realized the genius of it, then suddenly noticed the danger. "Kinti!" he shouted, waving for her to come back, but she waved him off, continuing to cross the rope, coating it with the paste. Reading simply grabbed the rope, trying to hold it steady, knowing if he tried to follow her he'd just rock the rope and possibly knock her loose.

"Keep it steady!" he shouted to Fabricio, who was watching what was happening too, the entire boat in shock.

It only took minutes, but it seemed an eternity, Reading's heart pounding in his chest the entire time, and it wasn't until she scrambled aboard the boat at the other side that he dropped to the ground, grabbing his head, suddenly realizing just how much he cared for this woman he had just met.

You've got it bad.

He sighed.

And that's not good.

She waved at him and he waved back, the glowing rope now obvious to him even with the firelight. To the men above, he hoped it was a crystal clear beacon they could home in on.

He saw Milton raise the phone to his ear then cup his hand around his mouth. "They're coming!"

Reading looked up and saw the plane, far higher than before, just north of their position. He had no idea how high they were, he had never been

Air Force, instead enlisting as a grunt. But right now he didn't think it mattered too much.

What goes up, must come down.

You just usually don't want that to happen in a raging river in the middle of the jungle at night.

Retired Lt. Colonel Cameron Leather stood at the open door of their plane, all seven men, including him, crammed in the back, the pilot and copilot up front. He could just make out the river below and the fire on shore with the boat lights marking their target. To his surprise, they had watched the rope slowly begin to glow, from one end to the other, and it now was clearly visible. However they had done it, it could prove to be a tremendous help.

He just had no idea how long it would last.

"Remember, you're the most important thing, then your gear. If you have to cut it loose, cut it loose. Use your hooks to grab the rope, then slide to shore. If you miss, try to get to the left bank, that's the East bank, then walk north along the shore until you reach the village. Understood?"

A chorus of "Yes, sirs" responded.

"After me on three's!" He tossed the waterproof duffle bag containing his gear through the door then stepped out of the plane, arching his back, his arms and legs to his sides. He tossed the pilot chute he was gripping to his side, the small chute yanking his larger one out, he preferring to have two backup options in this case rather than one. He felt the tug of the chute opening above him then the pull of his gear dangling below him as he quickly gained his bearings, grabbing the toggles overhead, guiding himself toward the river and the lights below.

He looked behind him and could see the chutes of his men opening, all six with good canopies overhead. Now they just needed to hit their target upriver of the recovery point. The water was coming up fast, their jump at well under a thousand feet, their chutes specially packed so they opened very quickly. He pulled his telescoping "wand" as he like to call it from a long side pouch on his leg. He hooked one end around his wrist, tightening it so he wouldn't lose it upon impact with the water, then extended it to its full six foot length.

The water was close now and he was in the pipe near the left bank. He just hoped the current would carry him straight toward the recovery point rather than take some twist and send him on the wrong side of the boat.

No time like the present!

He yanked the cord, cutting him free of his parachute and he dropped. His equipment hit the water first as he yanked another cord, inflating a life vest instantly. He took a deep breath as he smacked hard against the water, momentarily disorienting him. Kicking his legs and pushing with his arms, he bounced back above the surface, his goggles keeping his vision clear. He quickly took a breath and stabilized himself, his head now comfortably above water as the river carried him along the shore, more swiftly than he had anticipated, the water appearing so calm from above.

Fortunately that meant there was less chance of rocks being near the surface that they might slam into. He grasped for his wand, and found it, gripping it tightly in his right hand. He could see the fire ahead, the boat to his right, the rope glowing in the dark as he raced forward. There was no time to look behind him to see how his men were, this was do or die time.

He shoved the wand out of the water, high above him, the other end containing a special hook that would allow the rope to pass through it, but not back out.

But it only worked if you were able to get the rope to slide up the wand. If you hit the wand against the rope too hard, you were liable to simply bounce off the rope, the wand hitting the water behind you and missing the rope entirely.

I love my job!

The rope was less than fifty feet away. Forty. He gripped the wand high with both hands. Thirty. He began to gauge how high the rope was from the surface. Twenty. He angled the wand back slightly, lowering the hook to about four feet above the water, his head tilting back to get a bead on it, then forward to see the rope. Ten. Time to commit, no further calculated adjustments were possible.

It was seat of the pants time.

He saw the glowing rope whip over his head. His eyes followed, tracking it like a target on a Heads Up Display, then at the last minute shoved the wand higher as he realized he had just dipped too low. His heart leapt into his throat then he felt the rope hit as he pushed forward on the wand as hard as he could. His head dipped under the water as he felt the rope slide up the pole, then suddenly there was a jerk, the rope hooked by the wand, and he felt himself tugged hard against the current, slowly sliding toward the shore, the boat placed as he had instructed slightly farther upstream so nature would bring them to shore.

Hands grabbed him and he let them do their work, he having taken a lungful of water. Suddenly he felt ground beneath him, someone hauling him to his feet.

"You okay?"

He recognized the deep voice immediately. Special Agent Hugh Reading.

He nodded. "Good. Forget about me."

He unclipped his harnesses, shrugging himself out of his gear, his equipment bag already hauled out by Reading and a group of natives. Within a minute he was ready to assist, but the situation seemed well in hand. Two of his men were already hooked, one at the shoreline being pulled from the water, the other still sliding toward them. He looked downriver and could see the other four, barely. But one was too far to the right.

He's going to either go right of the boat, or hit the bloody thing.

There was no point in yelling, no point in waving. He could see from here that the man knew he was out of position. He was trying to swim to the left, but the current was simply too swift. The smack was horrible, heard even from the shore as he slammed into the opposite side of the hull then dragged along it. He had no idea who it was, and wouldn't until the last man was out of the water.

He began to ID his men when he heard Reading shout, "Kinti, no!"

Leather followed Reading's horrified expression and saw a young native girl plunge into the water, disappearing below the surface then reemerging farther downriver, swimming expertly toward his wayward man. Reading began to run downstream along the shore, it clear that this girl meant something to him, which Leather found a bit odd.

As the last man who had successfully hooked the line was hauled ashore, he pointed at his second-in-command, Warren Reese. "Equipment check then set up camp, I'm going after Trent."

Reese nodded, directing the men to follow some of the natives who were ushering them along the shoreline. The rope had been tossed free of the boat and it was turning around, apparently in an effort to recover his man and the native woman.

This wasn't the plan, but with the civilians screwing with it, he had to pursue. Trent should simply make his way to shore, but with the impact he took, he might not be in any shape to swim. And now with the native girl involved, he had a duty to save her.

And it was too late to pursue his primary target regardless, their departure for the drop zone delayed by mechanical failure.

Things never go smooth.

Kinti wasn't sure why she had jumped in the water after this stranger, but as she swam the swift river, closing the distance with the man, she realized it was for Hugh. He was supposed to have just been a fling, an experiment, a story to tell her children in the future of the great pale man she had met.

She had no idea it would be about the great pale man she had met and fallen in love with.

Her thoughts were consumed with him, consumed with the desire to please him, to make him happy, to make him proud. Perhaps that was why she had jumped. She knew he would be pleased if she saved this man. She also knew it was the right thing to do. He was a stranger, but he was a stranger here to help, not harm. She had heard many tales of the pale man hurting people like her, but they had been lucky. The stories were from far away, passed down from one tribe to the next, and she knew how those stories could become distorted over time.

She couldn't imagine Hugh or his friends harming anyone.

The man was almost within reach. She called to him but there was no response, no movement. He appeared to be asleep, probably knocked out when he hit the boat. She had seen this before and wondered how he managed to stay above the water. Reaching forward, she grabbed his shoulder, getting a grip on his clothing, then began to kick toward the shore. He was heavy. Extremely heavy, easily the weight of two men. She knew these pale people were bigger than her people, but this heavy? It made no sense.

She struggled against the weight and the current, drifting farther and farther downstream. The shore was slowly getting closer, but she was getting tired. Her hand screamed for relief, her grip now beginning to cramp from the strain, but the man had still not woken. She thought of Hugh, of the night and day they had spent together, of how she had got

118

him drunk and seduced the poor man, and how he had embraced her and treated her so well today when he was sober, not angry at all with her actions.

He loves me too.

It saddened her. She knew there was no way for them to be together, and as soon as his friend was found they'd be gone. Part of her wanted to let go of this man, just for an instant, in the hopes it might extend Hugh's stay, but she knew that was wrong. She had morals, her people had morals, and it would be wrong to sacrifice this stranger for her own carnal pleasures, even if her heart risked being broken.

The shore was close now, almost within reach. She'd need to grab onto something strong enough to hold both her and this impossibly heavy man. She knew Hugh and some others were following them, she had seen them when she first jumped in the river, but they were far downriver now, and it could take almost half a day to reach them.

She grabbed at a root that jutted out into the water, getting a grip for a moment, but it slipped through her hand, scraping it slightly, causing her to wince and rethink her exit strategy. A low lying branch was ahead. She reached up, grabbing it, the leaves protecting her palm slightly, but also making it slippery. She knew she couldn't hold long, but she took the opportunity to try and use her legs to push the man toward the shore.

That was when she saw a large bag attached to the man by a long flat rope.

What is that?

She let go, sending them along the slightly slower edge of the river, the eddies and currents created by the shore disrupting the swift flow they had been in, but still moving them along too quickly. She reached forward with her free hand, gripping his shirt, then released her grip on his shoulder, her hand crying in thanks as she clenched and unclenched it, trying to work out the kinks. Reaching once more, she grabbed the rope that was attached to the bag and pulled. The bag was heavy, as heavy as a man, and she suddenly realized why she was having so much trouble. She tugged at her end but the rope wouldn't come loose, and it didn't appear to have any knot that she could untie, instead some sort of loop made of something shiny and smooth had it attached to a loop that encircled his waist.

She smiled. She had seen Hugh take this loop off several times, and she had even helped him the last time. She pulled one end of the loop with her free hand, it popping loose, exposing a small shiny stick. She yanked on the loop and the stick popped free. She let go then pulled at the side of the loop, it coming loose. She grabbed the other end and tugged, yanking at it, it slowly slipping bit by bit, the free end inching toward the shiny loop holding the rope.

Suddenly the force of the bag tugging whipped the loop free and the rope flew loose, immediately lost in the water, the weight she was trying to rescue dropping significantly. She again made for shore, much more easily this time, though she knew she was nearing exhaustion. She spotted a small dip into the forest just ahead, the water digging into the shore line far enough for the current to be killed. As they rushed toward it she switched to his side, opposite the shoreline, gripping his clothing at the shoulder and waist, then kicked with all her might, shoving him into the small oasis of calm.

As his body slipped in she let go, continuing down the river then grabbing the first branch she could. She came to a halt quickly, and with both hands now free and no extra weight to support, she pulled herself ashore then collapsed on the ground, her chest heaving in protest. But she knew there was no time to rest. She forced herself to her feet, running back upriver, toward where she hoped the man would still be lying, and as she burst from the trees she found him just about to slip back into the current again.

"No!" she cried as she dove into the water and grabbed his body, pulling him back to safety just in time. She struggled to get him out of the water, and by the time she did, he was moaning slightly as he began to come to. Breathing a sigh of relief that he was still alive and her efforts hadn't been in vain, she looked about her to take stock of her situation.

That was when she heard a curious sound that took her a moment to recognize, then she smiled.

"Hugh!"

Hugh Reading stood at the prow of the boat, scanning the shoreline, calling Kinti's name repeatedly. The boat had several lights trained on the shore and scanning the water, and they were travelling faster than the current, the engine adding to their speed. Which meant even if Kinti and the rescue team member couldn't get to shore, they should eventually catch up to them.

As long as they didn't miss them.

And they haven't drowned.

He and Leather had been taken aboard as soon as the boat had turned around, precious time wasted. He was happy to be aboard however, as his own efforts were useless. If he had continued on foot, he'd still be miles back, the fires of the village probably still in sight.

"There!" yelled Leather, pointing to the shore. Reading looked and nearly collapsed in relief as he saw Kinti in the light, waving at them and calling his name. It sounded like the singing of angels.

You've got it really bad.

He couldn't hide his grin as Fabricio swung the boat around, pushing the engine hard to battle the current and bring them back upstream to where Kinti was. As they neared he could see she also had Leather's man with her, and his admiration for this young woman grew several fold. She had proven herself resourceful with the idea for making the rope glow, and selfless in risking her life to save this man.

If she were from anywhere else, she would make a perfect wife.

And the thought broke his heart.

She was intelligent, and probably would have excelled if she had been born elsewhere. She was friendly, beautiful, sexy. She was everything everyman looked for.

But she was untouchable.

Not in the carnal sense as had been shown the past twenty-four hours, but in the relationship sense. He could never stay here with her, and she could never come with him. She would be completely lost in modern society, and he would be completely miserable in hers.

If ever there were star-crossed lovers, they were them.

Leather jumped ashore, tending to his man as Reading leaned over and pulled Kinti aboard. She embraced him, hard, repeating his name several times as he held her tight. Several of the crew helped Leather and his man aboard, the rescued man now conscious and talking.

Leather emerged from below as the boat plowed through the waters, slowly returning them to the village inlet. He walked up to Kinti and Reading. "Does she speak English?"

"Only a few words."

He looked at her and held out his hand. "Thank you," he said, holding his free hand over his heart. "Thank you for saving my man."

She smiled, taking his hand and shaking it, saying something in her language. Leather looked at Reading.

"Sorry, mate, no idea. But rest assured she understands."

Leather smiled at her again, then returned below. Reading joined Milton at the rear of the boat, Kinti sitting on his lap, her head on his shoulder as she hummed a simple tune over and over.

Once again Reading didn't want this day to ever end.

He looked at Milton, who had a slight smile on his face, the grins having grown old. "I'm in trouble."

Milton chuckled. "No shit, brother. Let's just hope she understands the reality of the situation."

Kinti looked up at Reading and kissed underneath his chin.

"I think she's far smarter than what you think."

Milton nodded. "I have no doubt. People think these natives are primitive, savages, but that's only by way of technology. They are fully developed, emotional human beings, with a way of life and a belief system as intricate as any other. To think of them as anything less than us is an insult to them, and an arrogant assumption on our part. Take away our technology, and they'll be the ones that inherit the Earth, not us."

"But there's no way she can come with us," murmured Reading under his breath.

"No, there isn't," agreed Milton, Reading a little shocked he had heard him. "You would destroy her. Better to leave her here, heartbroken, with her own people who will comfort her, and eventually she will move on and take a mate, start a family, and be happy, telling the story of you for years to come—which is what I think she intended as well."

"I was just a challenge, a curiosity."

"As she was to you."

"Not much of a challenge, I'm afraid."

Milton grinned. "I didn't hear you protest too much."

"No I guess not." Reading sighed.

But who mends my broken heart?

Manaus, Brazil

"Is that a satellite phone?"

Terrence Mitchell looked up from his fish, Jenny doing the same. A white man, slightly disheveled, stood next to their table. He looked like he had been through hell, and by the way he was eyeing their food, hungry as well.

Mitchell glanced at the phone, wondering if it were about to be stolen. "Yes it is."

"Any chance I can use it to make a call. I promise, I won't be long, and when my friends get here, I'll pay you for it."

Mitchell shook his head. "I'm sorry, but we're waiting for an extremely important call."

Jenny jumped in, sensing the man's distress. "But as soon as we get that call, you're welcome to use it."

The tears of disappointment that were nearly about to pour from the man's eyes turned into tears of joy, and erupted down his cheeks. "Oh thank God, thank you so much."

Jenny pointed at a free chair. "Why don't you join us until then?"

His head bobbed in elation, dropping into the chair. That was when Mitchell noticed the stench coming off the man. It was as if he had been in the jungle for days with no access to any facilities.

In fact, his clothes were filthy, torn to shreds in places. His shoes were still in decent shape though filthy. He had at least a week's growth if not more and his hair was a knotted mess. His fingernails were filled with grime and his teeth were yellow, unbrushed for some time.

Which meant body odor, foul breath and smells better left to the latrine.

And others were beginning to notice.

"Are you okay?" asked Mitchell.

The man shook his head. "No. My team and I were doing some research near the tip of the Rio Negro, cataloguing species, when we were ambushed and taken prisoner."

Jenny gasped. "By natives?"

The man shook his head. "No, by what looked like soldiers. Special Ops types if you ask me. I managed to escape. They hunted me for a few hours but I was able to hide. They destroyed our boat so I was forced to walk along the shoreline for several days before I found a native canoe. I don't know if it was abandoned or not, but the owner wasn't there, so I took it. It took me almost a week to get here." He grabbed at his threadbare shirt. "And the authorities won't help me. They said we were there without a permit so they won't help."

"You're American?" asked Mitchell, noting that the restaurant owner was starting to take notice of the new arrival.

"Yes."

"What about your embassy?"

"I haven't been able to call anyone. I have no money, no passport, nothing. It was all on the boat they sank."

Jenny motioned toward the owner. "We better get out of here."

Mitchell nodded, standing and waving the man off. "We're just leaving." He threw some bills on the table, grabbed the satphone then motioned to their guest. "Come with us, we'll help you out."

They quickly made their way back to their hotel, rushing their guest, whose name they learned was Bob Turnbull, through the lobby and up the stairs to their room on the third floor, no elevator available here.

"We're still waiting for that call, Bob, so why don't you get out of those clothes, have a nice long shower and I'll see about getting you some extra toiletries."

Turnbull's shoulders slumped as the pressure began to lift. "Thank you, you two have been just—well, awesome!"

"Think nothing of it," replied Jenny. "Now go clean up and I'll find some of Terrence's clothes for you to wear."

Turnbull nodded then disappeared into the washroom. Mitchell called the front desk and had a toiletry bag brought up, adding it to their bill, then took the liberty of ordering dinner for all three of them, they barely having touched their meals earlier, and it clear Turnbull hadn't eaten in days.

And lots of bottled water.

"What do you make of his story?"

Mitchell shrugged, looking at his wife from the bed he was lying on. "It sounds pretty farfetched, but look at him."

"But Special Forces in the jungle? Taking researchers into custody?"

"That's the part that sounds fishy," agreed Mitchell.

There was a knock at the door and Jenny answered. A young boy handed over a toiletry bag and Jenny slipped him a few coins, eliciting a grin. She tossed it to her husband. "You put it in there."

Mitchell jumped from the bed, knocking on the door.

"Yes?"

"I've got your toiletries here!"

"Great, just put them on the counter, thanks!"

Mitchell complied as Jenny handed him some clothes. Mitchell put them beside the toiletry bag and closed the door. Returning to the bed, he lay back down. "He said tip of the Rio Negro, didn't he?"

Jenny nodded.

"That's exactly where the professors were going, at least from a Brazilian standpoint. Any farther up and you're in Colombia and Venezuela."

Jenny's eyes widened. "Do you think we should warn them?"

Mitchell nodded. "When they call we'll let them know what we know. I doubt it's anything but you never know." The shower turned off and he lowered his voice. "For now let's humor him and see what additional info we can get."

Jenny nodded, suddenly not looking as comfortable with their decision to help this stranger.

Two Day's Travel from Rio Negro, Northern Amazon
Day of the attack

Laura lay curled into a ball, shivering, the nights of the jungle cold, especially on hard earth ten feet down. And the sounds were terrifying. What was beautiful from the safety of the boat, or even the camp with James beside her, took on a sinister quality in which everything was closer, everything had an agenda.

She tried to block the sounds out mentally, then physically covered her exposed ear, but it was of no use. Instead she began doing math in her head, a trick James had said worked for him, just simple factors of two, easy at first, more difficult when you got into the five and six figures. And it worked.

Her mind occupied, she slowly gave in to sleep, awaking to find a cool, steady rain falling. She shivered in the cold, but immediately jumped to her feet to take advantage of this fresh source of water. She held her head back, catching as much as she could in her mouth while cupping her hands to act as a spout to deliver even more. She continued to drink as much as she could, even beyond what she needed, not knowing when she'd get another chance, and preferring a belly full of water than nothing. The rain suddenly stopped and she returned to her now muddy corner, deciding instead to leave it be and sit against what she was thinking was the western wall where the sun would hit first, and fortunately had been left almost untouched by the rain, it coming in slightly from the west.

She shook almost uncontrollably from the cold, her legs drawn up, her hands clasped around her shins as she tried to warm up. Still shaking, she closed her eyes and lowered her chin into her knees and began to count, deciding sleep was better than this, and within minutes she once again felt herself begin to pass out, exhaustion taking over from the cold.

Tuk woke at the crack of dawn and left TikTik's village, having said his goodbyes the night before. He hadn't mentioned the Woman of Light to anyone, though they had grilled him for answers, his demeanor so happy they knew something was up, he usually so shy and demure. He simply kept repeating that he was excited for TikTik's wedding, which was usually enough to change the conversation, TikTik a very popular girl within the village.

"Bruk is a lucky man!" they kept repeating, and Tuk would agree. *But so am I!* He wanted to scream it, but he wouldn't dare. Couldn't. If she didn't survive the Cleansing Ritual, there would be no mating ceremony, no future, no hope.

He sighed as he took one last look at the village of several hundred, a much more thriving and exciting place than his own. It was amazing how much damage could be done in a single day to a village. The boys who had died from the boar incident would have fathered at least a dozen children by now, and the more of those that were boys the more their village might grow. But they were gone, and one of the few left of mating age was him.

A great disappointment to the elders he was sure.

They never said anything to him, but he knew there was talk. His mother would be gloomy sometimes, cussing under her breath about one or more of the elders, and when he'd ask her why, she'd simply say they were going crazy and it was past their time to join the Spirit World.

But he knew. He knew she had been forced to defend him once again.

Too often he cried himself to sleep on those days, the long communal lodges they slept in difficult to hide emotions in. Sometimes when he would be crying in his sleep he would wake to find Pol shaking him by the shoulder and they would leave the village, out of earshot so they could talk. Usually so *he* could talk and Pol listen. Pol was great that way, offering advice when needed, and an ear when not.

I miss you!

His journey home was a mix of melancholy and joy. He would think of his lost friend and his difficult life, then of Lau-ra-pal-mer, the Woman of Light from the Spirit World who the Mother had given him, a gift of beauty and wonder that would change his life forever, and make him if not the envy of the other males, at least an equal to them when it came to having a suitable mate.

I wonder how many children we'll have?

He hoped they would all be boys. And one daughter. He always loved little girls, but he couldn't imagine the heartbreak their parents would endure when they took a mate and left.

Six boys and one girl. That's what he wanted. Six boys was a good number. And if half survived until mating age, they just might be able to help the village recover and survive another generation.

Entering the village he saw his mother just waking. She waved, a look of relief on her face as she held out her arms and rushed up to him, hugging him tight.

"Where were you?" she cried, holding him at arm's length. "You left without saying anything!"

"I just needed some time," he mumbled, feeling guilty now for having left so abruptly.

She took his hands, squeezing them knowingly. "Pol?"

He nodded.

"I still can't believe he's gone." She sighed then motioned toward the other side of the village. "TikTik was asking of you." She gave him a look that he knew meant she knew exactly how he felt about her.

Why are you torturing me?

"I'm sorry for not telling you I was leaving."

She hit him lightly on the arm. "Don't you dare do that again." She led him to the village center where several of the women were preparing breakfast. TikTik was brushing the hair of her future mate's grandmother. He stared at her, her beauty overwhelming, her smile intoxicating, her laughter like music from the most beautiful bird the Mother had created.

She was perfection.

He pictured the Woman of Light, and how different she was. Beautiful in her own way, impossibly unique, but not TikTik. He knew who he truly wanted, and the Woman of Light would be settling, but at least she was a close second.

They would be happy together.

And he knew his mother would be delighted he had found a mate. She was desperate for grandchildren, and her chances were few, he her only son, the other children all dead before their first cycle. And then his father had been killed, ending her hopes of further children.

He stared at TikTik, her beauty once again overpowering him. He knew if he was strong like Bruk there was a good chance she would be with him instead. But that wasn't to be.

TikTik caught him staring and smiled. He quickly moved his head, pretending to stare at a nonexistent bird, and wondered how he'd survive the next six days, waiting for the Cleansing Ritual to end.

Bruk grabbed TikTik from behind, Grandmother scolding them.

He couldn't take it any longer.

I've got to get out of here.

Retired Lt. Colonel Cameron Leather looked at the GPS and motioned in the direction they were to follow. Two villagers were accompanying them, one of whom spoke broken Portuguese, two of his men fluent, handpicked for that very reason. The two villagers could prove useful as guides and trackers, but more importantly they could smooth out any ruffled feathers should other natives be encountered.

He didn't want to be trussed up like Professor Acton had evidently been.

They had left Reading and Milton back on the boat along with his injured man who would survive, but his bruised thigh and mild concussion would simply slow them down on their journey, of which speed was the essence. They had Acton's coordinates from where he had apparently found a trail, and without having to actually look for the trail, they were making extremely good time, able to jog for most of the way. They anticipated reaching the Professor before nightfall, giving them a large search party with plenty of firepower should things turn ugly in trying to retrieve his client, Professor Palmer.

He hoped it didn't end with a firefight.

She had been kidnapped, of that there was no doubt. It was a hostile act, of that there could be some doubt. Who knew what these natives were thinking. He was one to never underestimate his enemy, and he made few assumptions about them either, except that they were probably smarter than most gave them credit for.

But smarts wasn't the issue this time.

Motivation was.

What was the motivation of her kidnapper? The fact that she was still leaving a trail behind said she was walking on her own two feet, which meant alive and conscious. The fact she seemed to be going voluntarily also seemed to suggest she didn't feel any immediate fear. He would have assumed she would have made much more of a struggle than she had if she thought death was the end game.

Then again she could just be playing for time, hoping she would be found before that moment.

And he was trained to assume the worst.

He had to assume that whenever she reached their destination, she was going to be killed.

He just prayed they could reach her before that.

"What the hell is that?"

Acton pointed to a large tree at the base of which was the largest dead snake he had ever seen. It was massive, at least ten yards long and the thickness of a man. His immediate instinct was to run, and he almost had before he noticed it was gutted. The natives quickly surrounded it, poking it with their spears, then Sandro and the Portuguese speaking guide Skip rapid fired a series of questions and answers back and forth.

Sandro turned to Acton. "They say it killed probably one day ago. They also say it probably one person, maybe two."

"How do they know that?"

"If it was organized hunt, nothing would have been wasted."

Acton nodded as he circled the beast, it already crawling with the smallest denizens of the forest. "Makes sense. And the trail leads here, doesn't it?"

Sandro pointed to a heel print. "Yes."

Skip pointed up in the tree, saying something to Sandro.

"He says someone slept up there." Skip jumped up the tree, climbing it with startling speed, then shouted down to Sandro. "He say two people eat there and sleep there."

"I can't believe he would hunt a snake that big!"

Sandro shook his head. "No one hunt Anaconda that big. It probably attack, they defend."

Acton felt his stomach tie itself into a knot at the thought of this creature attacking. He dropped to one knee, his eyes closed as he felt faint, images of this creature devouring his beloved Laura too much. Sandro's voice sounded distant and he felt his face breakout into a cold sweat as he began to sway.

"Senhor!"

He felt a hand on his shoulder, shaking him, and he opened his eyes, the massive head of the snake staring back at him. He turned his head, too quickly, a wave of dizziness almost overwhelming him as his mouth filled with bile. He shoved his thumb into the pressure point just above his wrist and began to massage the bundle of nerves, his nausea slowly going away as the world came back into focus.

"Senhor, are you okay?"

Acton nodded, holding his hand out. Sandro pulled him to his feet and Acton steadied himself, making a point not to look at the now dead predator. "We're wasting time," he finally said. "Let's get back to the trail."

Sandro shouted the order and they were soon moving forward, and with each step, Acton felt his strength return. He took a swig of water from his canteen and nodded his appreciation to Sandro, who seemed relieved the episode had passed.

Skip pointed out several heel prints and a flush of relief washed over Acton as it was now confirmed Laura was alive and not in the belly of the dead beast's partner.

Mentally shoving the visuals of what he had just seen aside, he focused all of his attention on the trail and his wife that had left it.

Reading lay in his hammock, Kinti splayed across him, her head snuggled on his shoulder as she gently slept. But sleep eluded Reading, his mind filled with horrible visions of what could have happened to Laura. Acton had just checked in with the news they had found where Laura and her captor had slept two nights ago, and that there had been a battle with an Anaconda.

He shivered.

Kinti moaned, waking slightly and kissing him on the neck as she snuggled closer, falling asleep again within moments. Milton was resting in his bed, Kinti having brought a large amount of very soft furs for him to lie on once she understood his back was sore. She had also delivered a massage that Reading was sure had helped Milton understand part of the attraction he felt for Kinti.

The more time he spent with her, the stronger the connection became, and he wasn't sure what to do. He knew he had to end it, but it had been so long since he had not only a physical connection with someone, but an emotional one, that he missed it dearly. It wasn't just the sex, which was unlike anything he could have imagined before, it was the companionship, the knowledge that someone cared for you, liked you and wanted to spend time with you. It made him realize how much of a void he had been living with all these years. He didn't regret leaving his wife, that was the right decision otherwise they would have killed each other, but he was now regretting the decision to swear off another relationship. He had his dalliances when he was younger, but it had been a long time since he'd "blown off some steam".

And he felt great.

He felt wonderful.

Sexual satisfaction was one thing, emotional satisfaction was an entirely different beast, a beast he hadn't realized had been preying on him for decades. His heart cried out at the time he had lost feeling this way, and it ached at the knowledge that what it had found would be gone in a matter of days, if not sooner.

There was no future for him and Kinti.

And it broke his inexperienced heart.

He looked down at her and kissed the top of her head. She wriggled happily, and returned to her slumber, content.

It made him wonder what she was thinking.

She must realize the same thing he did, that this would soon be over, but she didn't seem to be letting it bother her.

She's got the right attitude.

Enjoy the moment, don't think about the future.

And if that was what she was thinking, it was the right choice.

"Help!"

Reading bolted upright in his hammock, almost spilling the two of them to the deck, as he looked for the source of the desperate cry. Kinti immediately woke, grabbing onto him as he swung his legs to the floor, helping her out.

"Help me!"

The voice was desperate and coming from the entrance of the small inlet they were docked in. Kinti pointed to the shoreline near the mouth where the river was and Reading gasped.

A man, clothed, was wading through the water along the river's edge, waving at them with one arm.

The other limp at his side, covered in blood.

Three Day's Travel from Rio Negro, Northern Amazon
Day of the attack

TikTik hummed as she pulled the brush through the hair of her future mate's grandmother Trin, it a chore she was happy to do, the old woman so pleased with the result. She looked out of the corner of her eye and saw Tuk staring at her again. She liked Tuk. They had grown up together, her village and his always on friendly terms and so close that the children would often accompany their parents when visiting.

They had become friends, and when she was younger, had even declared to her mother that she wanted to be mated to Tuk when the time came. Her mother had dismissed the idea, even discouraged it, saying he was too weak to be a husband, too small to be a good provider. She had thrown something at her mother, what she couldn't remember, and stormed out of their village and hid in the forest, her father and several others having to come search for her.

She had cried in her father's arms as he carried her home, refusing to tell him why she was so upset, her mother apparently too ashamed to share her revelation. He hadn't been mad at her, it was clear to him she had been upset by something, and that night she had cried herself to sleep, her dreams of living in Tuk's village and having children with him destroyed.

She knew Tuk still longed after her, but he had no idea how much she longed after him. Bruk was wonderful, of that there was no doubt. He was a prize mate, strong, handsome, and a good provider, but he wasn't the intellectual that Tuk was. Tuk was so smart that she could listen to him for hours talk about the various creatures in the forest, the sounds they made, their habits, their tracks. If you needed something or someone found, Tuk was the man to go to.

He'll amount to nothing, he's too weak!

Her mother's words still cut her like a blade. Tuk's village seemed to accept him as an equal, and TikTik knew Tuk's mother was desperate for grandchildren, and TikTik would love to be the one to give them to her. But Tuk had never asked. No matter how many hints she had dropped, no matter how many bashful glances she had returned with a smile, he had never had the courage to ask.

Because he too was convinced he would amount to nothing.

Of that she was certain.

She had heard the jokes made about him at her village, even within earshot of her poor friend. She had cried herself to sleep on many of those nights, sometimes even shouting at those making the comments to shut up, to leave Tuk alone, and she had simply been teased and taunted.

It wasn't fair. Just because he was smaller and weaker than the others didn't mean he couldn't provide for her and a family. His tracking was legendary, and he often led his tribe on hunts, he quickly picking the signs of their prey from the uncooperative forest floor. He could organize groups to build things like none she had ever met, his leadership skills second to none that she had seen.

But only when he didn't realize he was leading.

He would jump in to help with any project his village undertook, even helping at her village, and his intelligence quickly resulted in him telling where to cut, where to tie, where to place. Whenever she saw him in action, she felt so proud of him, and it made her want him even more.

But it was not to be.

She smiled at Tuk, trying to send him a message of her love, but he quickly looked away, staring at the sky as if seeing something fascinating. She didn't bother looking up; she knew there would be nothing there.

Her chest ached.

Arms grabbed her from behind and she yelped as she was lifted into the air, the roar of her future mate filling her ears. She squealed and he flipped her around, giving her a big kiss, which she returned willingly. Bruk was a good man, and she did have feelings for him, and in time she knew she'd love him more than she loved Tuk. Part of her always felt guilty when there was some sort of public display of affection between her and Bruk in front of Tuk, but it couldn't be helped, and if she were to live here, he would have to get used to it.

Bruk put her down and she stole a glance over at Tuk but he was already heading into the forest, his shoulders slumped.

"Stop that or the Mother will curse you with ugly children!"

Bruk and TikTik laughed as he put her down, one last kiss snuck before he disappeared into the forest with several of the men, tonight's main course still undetermined.

She resumed brushing Grandmother Trin's hair, her humming resumed, her thoughts returning to poor Tuk. She hoped he would find a mate someday. It would be hard, he having to marry outside the village and there only being a few villages within easy travelling distance. But perhaps at one of those villages there would be some poor girl, in a predicament similar to his, that would take him as her mate and perhaps they could make each other whole, each other happy.

She just wanted Tuk to be happy.

Because she knew she would never truly be happy if he weren't.

She felt an odd vibration on the log she was sitting on and stopped her brushing, looking about to see what was happening. A scream erupted from the forest, a scream she recognized immediately as Bruk's.

And it was one of terror.

A beast roared from the forest, unlike anything she had ever heard, the sound so loud she could only imagine it must be as tall as the trees. Legends of giants filled her head as she grabbed Grandmother and they retreated toward the center of the village. Suddenly creatures, black from head to toe burst into the clearing, quickly surrounding them all, at least two dozen in number, then a massive creature surged through the trees, the mighty trunks chewed through by the creature's spinning teeth, a high pitched wail emerging from its mouth as the trees were felled easily.

The beast was unlike any creature she had seen, it clearly from another world, perhaps that of the Spirits. Or worse. She had heard of course of where those with evil in their hearts were sent, a world of horrors where there was no joy for eternity, a world where those who would abuse the Mother's gift of life were doomed to live out the afterlife.

And she had no doubt this creature was from there.

One of the black creatures shoved her toward the center of the village, the hunters that had just left suddenly emerging from the forest, their hands high over their heads, their spears not to be seen. She couldn't see Bruk, and she wondered if he had somehow escaped, when her heart sank.

Two of the black creatures dragged his body into the clearing, dumping him on the ground.

She screamed.

Rushing toward the body of her mate-to-be she felt something hit her back and she collapsed to the ground, jerking, unable to control any of her limbs or even shout out in fear.

Tuk's voice erupted from behind as he cried out in anger. Her only thought was a message her mouth couldn't deliver as she lay paralyzed on the ground.

Run, Tuk! Run!

Tuk ran. As hard as he could. At first he had no destination in mind, then he turned to head to TikTik's village, then he realized there was only one person who could help him.

The Woman of Light.

She was of the Spirit World and so were the Panther People. She might know some way to stop them, some way to defeat them. From the little he had seen his people were no match for these cursed creatures. If he hadn't have seen it for himself he wouldn't have believed it.

Panther People!

The very idea was insane, but there was no doubt at what he had witnessed.

He had witnessed TikTik's death.

He suddenly stopped and bent over, emptying his stomach on the forest floor, his retching continuing as he pictured TikTik's body twitching on the ground then unmoving. How she had been taken down, he had no idea. Her attacker had merely held up its hand and she had dropped.

It was magic.

And he needed a medicine man.

And he couldn't picture a medicine man more powerful than someone from the Spirit World.

Lau-ra-pal-mer would save them.

Lau-ra-pal-mer would save them all.

J. ROBERT KENNEDY

Laura Palmer stood in the middle of her prison. Overhead the sun shone brightly through the tree tops, large swaths of warmth making it down to her. She had removed most of her wet clothes, putting her bra back on, and had slung her shirt and pants up over the wall so they hung down the side, the sun shining on them. She used her makeshift latrine, burying her waste, then drank as much of the water she could from the small holes she had dug.

Now for food.

The idea of using her shirt as a lure, rubbing it over her body then tossing one arm over the edge like a fishing line occurred to her, but she didn't know what she might catch. If the creature were too big, it might simply tear her shirt away from her, leaving no cover for nightfall.

Or worse, it might fall in the hole with her, trapped and scared.

The chance of it being a small creature was good, but not worth the risk.

No, she would have to do with whatever Mother Nature would provide.

That meant grubs, worms and insects.

The thought wasn't appealing, but she had eaten most things at least once in her life, but never as a matter of survival. To understand cultures you needed to experience their way of life, and the anthropologist in her insisted she try everything, no matter how disgusting. Which had meant insects, spiders, worms and grubs.

Even many of them alive.

She had wretched a few times, even tossed her cookies once, but in time she had learned to stomach most anything.

And it would keep her alive.

The pit looked like it had been there some time, so she decided the ground she was standing on may have begun to develop its own ecosystem similar to that above. She began digging in the corners, along the edges, and

142

was soon rewarded with a few wrigglers, quickly swallowing them without thinking about it.

Ugh.

Well, almost without thinking about it. She couldn't help it, especially with the knowledge that this might be all she ate for the next seven days.

Six and a half!

She sighed, shaking her head, wondering again why the hell Tuk had done this to her.

And where the hell James was.

She admonished herself for getting mad at him, knowing that there would be almost no hope of him finding her unless he had picked up the trail, and there was little chance of that without help, help that was days away at best.

And they had travelled over two days, fairly swiftly, Tuk clearly knowing the forest.

A branch snapped, the sound echoing through the forest overhead. She froze. Was it wildlife or man? Friend or foe? Was it a predator that wouldn't hesitate to leap down here and eat her, or a herbivore she could lure down and possibly snap the neck of.

Or was it a search party.

Or worse, a group of cannibals.

She heard something, what she couldn't determine, but she moved to the center of the pit, slowly spinning, her head monitoring the edge surrounding her as panic began to set in, the image of a massive anaconda slithering into the pit and crushing her to the point of near suffocation, then swallowing her whole—and alive, to be digested over days, never to be found again.

More sounds, another crack, making her think either the creature approaching was huge, or careless.

And only humans were careless.

If it were members of a hostile tribe, she could find herself in a worse state than she was now, but if it was a search party, they might walk right by her.

Do I yell?

It was a debate it hadn't occurred to her she might have to have. Of course she had to yell, she had to call out to let them know where she was. Anything was better than here.

Hostile natives could kill you or eat you!

She knew she could survive here seven days as long as she had rain at least every couple of days. There was plenty of food to scavenge that would meet her minimum needs, and as long as nothing entered the pit that was able to kill her, she should be okay until Tuk arrived.

Who then might kill her anyway.

The sounds were getting farther away now, slowly fading.

What do I do?

Then a thought occurred to her.

Natives would never step on a stick and reveal their position.

And she committed.

"Help!"

Acton stared at the ground in frustration. They had lost the trail, the overnight rain washing away many of the heel prints his Laura had been leaving, their trackers only able to find every fourth or fifth imprint, sometimes less, and now they had found none for the past five minutes.

He stepped on a stick, it snapping loudly sending several birds from their perches, silencing the immediate vicinity of some of its non-stop racket for a few seconds. And it was a racket. What had been beautiful two days before was now annoying. He hated the jungle. He wanted out of the jungle. He never wanted to see a jungle again. He knew his hatred was irrational and linked entirely to the situation, but his level of frustration, impatience and fear was so high, he was ready to snap and tear someone's head off.

Another branch snapped, Sandro the guilty party this time, and Acton cringed. If they were close to Laura's captor then he would certainly hear their approach with all the noise they were making. The native guides were silent in their progress, their bare feet seeming to sense the ground under them, but the inexperienced Westerners with their large boots and thick soles were blazing a trail of noise.

"Help!"

Everyone froze, ears cocked to detect where the cry had come from.

But Acton already knew. He plunged through the trees to the right, running as fast as he could toward what was unmistakably Laura's voice. He knew he had to get to her before she was silenced by her captor, or worse, killed for giving away their position.

He crashed through the trees, the jungle protesting at the disruption, branches snapping and cracking loudly, and he didn't care. Speed was what was important. He could hear the others behind him, and he hoped it was because they agreed he was heading in the right direction, not simply following him.

"Help me, please!"

He adjusted slightly to the left then burst into a clearing, skidding to a halt on the wet grass that greeted him. In the center was a large pit, easily ten by ten feet. He stepped up to the edge and looked in, the sun shining in his eyes, the pit dark. He shielded his eyes and dropped to his knees in relief.

"James!"

"Laura!"

She was the most beautiful sight he had ever seen despite her disheveled appearance. Standing in the center of the pit, a pit which was at least ten feet deep, she rushed toward him as he dropped to his stomach, reaching out for her. Their fingers could barely touch, but it was enough for them both to know they weren't imagining things. Sandro and the others arrived and within moments a rope was lowered as she dressed. They hauled her to the surface where she quickly leapt into Acton's arms, the two of them simply holding each other, sobbing in relief.

Acton's chest hurt with the shock, the relief, the anger of the situation. What had been intended for his wife? He could only imagine the worst, and his imagination was running wild with images of leaving her there to die, to tossing in wild animals for entertainment as she fought for her life.

He sucked in a deep breath and let it out slowly, instead focusing on her.

"Are you okay?" he asked gently, without letting her go.

Her head nodded against his chest.

"No injuries?"

She shook her head.

"He didn't—you know…" He couldn't bring himself to say it, he didn't know how he'd handle it. He knew it wouldn't be her fault if he had raped her, and he would think of her no differently, it was just something so alien to his experience he didn't know how she would want to be treated should it have happened.

She vehemently shook her head, pushing back slightly and looking into his eyes. "No, he never touched me." She cupped his cheeks in her hands, wiping the tears away with her thumbs. "In fact, Tuk was quite the gentleman for the most part."

"Tuk?"

"That's his name. We learned to communicate a little."

"Did he say why he took you?"

146

"A little, darling, a little. Like yes, no, toilet, food." She wiped her own face dry. "If I had to guess, however, I'd say he was taking me back to be his mate."

Acton felt a flash of jealousy, his cheeks flushing.

Laura grinned at him, patting his cheek. "Now, now, dear, I only have eyes for you."

"Uh huh. Your Tuk boyfriend better hope I don't see him."

"I don't think we have to worry about that. He's not coming back for another six days."

"Six days!" Rage again surged through his body as he tried to fathom what possible reason this Tuk bastard could have for leaving Laura in the bottom of a pit for a week.

"I'm guessing some kind of purification ritual," replied Laura to Acton's unasked question. "Leave me there for all the evil and impurities to leave, and if I survive, I was found worthy by their gods."

Acton nodded, still refusing to let her go. "Sounds plausible."

Sandro approached, everyone having given them a few moments alone. "Senhor, we should be leaving now. If we hurry, we can maybe make the village before nightfall."

Acton looked at Laura. "Are you able to walk?"

"Try to stop me!"

"Good, then let's go." He motioned for their guides to lead the way and Skip soon had them racing back through the jungle. As they proceeded Laura drank some fresh water and ate plenty of the food they had brought. Acton fished out the satphone. "I better give Leather a call, he's supposed to rendezvous with us by nightfall."

Laura swallowed a bite of her granola bar. "He got here quick."

"Yeah, apparently they parachuted in at night, straight into the river!"

147

Laura tore off another chew from the bar. "Intentionally?" she mumbled, covering her mouth.

"Yup. And Hugh's girlfriend saved the life of one of the men who missed the hook line."

"Girlfriend!" Laura nearly choked, beginning to cough, some granola going down the wrong pipe due to her sudden inhalation. She drank some water, her cough subsiding. "What are you talking about?"

"Her name is Kinti. She pretty much seduced him the first night in the village they went to for help. They've been inseparable since, apparently."

Laura shook her head, a smile on her face as she resumed chewing. "Good for him. I hope he doesn't get his heart broken though."

"He's a grown man."

"Who hasn't had a serious relationship in almost twenty years."

Acton frowned. "True. You don't think he'd actually fall in love?"

"Is she cute?"

"Beautiful. Not as beautiful as you, of course!" he added quickly for the save.

"Good one. Sex?"

"Absolutely. Here?"

"Not you, you pervert! Hugh."

"All damned night from what I heard."

"You were there?"

He nodded, describing his incident with the tribe's hunters.

"Well, I think I should meet this Kinti, see if she's worthy of our friend." The smile disappeared from her face. "In all seriousness, I hope he doesn't fall for this girl. He has to know there's no future."

"He knows. Just let him enjoy the moment."

"If the moment goes on too long, the heartache afterward will just be that much harder to get over."

"But it's his heartache to get over, and none of our business. Let him have his fun, and when we leave here tomorrow—"

"Tonight!"

Acton laughed. "Okay, tonight, we'll help him forget her. Who knows, maybe it will open him up to the possibility of finding a woman back in civilization."

Laura seemed pleased with that idea. "That would be nice. I always feel sorry for him. He must be so lonely."

"Some men are confirmed bachelors."

"Some. But I think Hugh has so much to offer."

"So do I. If I were a chick, I'd be all over him."

Laura smacked him. "Be serious."

"I am. I *would* be all over him."

She shook her head and put her arm around his waist, laying her head on his chest for a moment as they slowed their pace. "I'm so happy to see you," she whispered.

Acton stopped and wrapped his arms around her, kissing her deeply. When the kiss finally broke, he held her tight, his chest giving a single heave as he fought his emotions. "I thought I'd never see you again."

"Come! Faster!" yelled Sandro, waving to them from about thirty feet ahead. Acton waved and they followed, holding each other's hand as they rushed toward safety, either the heavily armed former SAS team, or the village itself.

Barasana Village on the Rio Negro, Northern Amazon, Brazil

Reading pulled the new arrival ashore with help from several of the natives, Kinti at his side. The man flopped onto the ground, exhausted, and simply tried to catch his breath as Reading checked him for wounds, finding nothing beyond scrapes and bruises except for his shoulder which had been bleeding profusely at some point.

"Is that a bullet wound?"

The man nodded.

"Who shot you? Border patrol?"

The man shook his head. "Some sort of Special Ops team. We stumbled upon them about a week ago."

Reading's eyes narrowed, the man's statement not making any sense, and the fact he was speaking perfect American accented English raising all kinds of red flags. *Drug trafficker?* "What makes you think Special Ops?"

"Black uniforms, faces covered completely, no identifiable markings."

"Brazilian?"

The man shook his head as he was lifted onto a stretcher from the boat, wincing as they did so. "We were in Venezuela when it happened."

"What were you doing there?"

They were quickly on the boat, the stretcher set on top of a large table. The wounded member of the security team, Michael Trent, was at the ready with the med kit. He expertly cleaned the wound as the man continued to talk.

"We're part of an environmental group, Protect Amazonia Now. PAN, maybe you've heard of us?"

Reading shook his head. "Can't say I have."

"What's your name?" asked Trent, a question Reading hadn't thought to ask for some reason.

"Steve. Steve Parker."

"Okay, Steve, this is going to hurt."

Parker nodded then cried out in pain as Trent dug into his shoulder with tweezers. A few moments later the tweezers emerged, Trent triumphantly holding up the bullet. He examined and cleaned the wound some more then gave Parker the thumbs up.

"Looks like there was no fragmentation and nothing major hit. I'll patch you up, give you a shot of antibiotics and you should be good to go. When we get back to civilization though you'll need to get that looked at properly."

Parker nodded, relief evident on his face. Trent proceeded with the bandaging as Reading continued his interrogation.

"You said you were part of an environmental group. What were you doing in Venezuela."

"We heard reports of some illegal logging going on so we decided to check it out. By treaty this entire region—Brazil, Venezuela, Colombia and Peru, are supposed to be protected. There are estimated to be seventy-seven uncontacted tribes in this area and illegal logging forces them out of their natural habitat and into the traditional grounds of other tribes, and eventually us. Their entire way of life can be destroyed, or worse, if they catch something as simple as the common cold from us, an entire tribe could be wiped out."

"Did you find anything?"

Parker shook his head. "No, we never had a chance. We were only a day into our hike north when these guys came out of nowhere, guns raised. I managed to run away, but got shot for my efforts. I don't know what happened to the others."

Reading looked at Milton who had taken a seat nearby, the excitement having woken him. He gave a "sounds fishy to me" type expression, to which Reading agreed.

Special Ops protecting a logging operation?

It made no sense.

Scratch that. Not Special Ops. Assumed Special Ops.

That made more sense. "They might have just been paramilitary, Venezuelan police. These countries quite often hide the identity of their police to protect them and their families."

Parker winced as Trent plunged a needle into his arm then pushed the plunger. "That's possible. I only saw them for a few seconds."

"Did they say anything?"

Parker sat up, slowly rotating his shoulder, testing the bandage. "Thanks," he said to Trent, "that feels a lot better."

Trent pointed at the dressing. "Take it easy with that, it could open up if you're not careful and you've got an infection that might take a week or so to clear up."

Parker nodded and stood up from the table he had been lying on then took a seat in one of the chairs on the deck. As the area was cleaned up by the crew, Reading sat, Kinti in his lap once again, this time her attention focused on the new arrival rather than her lover, and Trent occupying the final chair.

One of the crewmen came on deck with water and food for their new arrival, and as Parker shoveled it into his mouth, he continued answering Reading's questions between bites. "It's funny," he said, swallowing a large bite. "I couldn't understand anything they were saying. That didn't really surprise me though since I don't speak Portuguese or Venezuelan." He paused. "What do they speak? Spanish?"

Reading shrugged. "I think so."

"Yes, Spanish," confirmed Trent, obviously better versed on the region than Reading was.

"Well, I couldn't understand them. I know enough Spanish though to know it wasn't that, but it didn't sound like anything European either."

Reading's eyebrows narrowed as he exchanged a glance with Milton. "What did it sound like?"

"Well," began Parker as he took a swig of water then a big bite of thickly sliced bread smeared generously in butter. He held up his finger as he chewed the oversized helping and finally swallowed. "If I didn't know better, and really I can't be certain, but if I didn't know better it sounded like—" Suddenly he sucked in a sudden gasp, his eyes bulging and Reading leaned forward concerned.

A belch erupted, relief expressed on Parker's face.

"Excuse me," he said, "ate a little too quickly. I haven't eaten in days and the water I've been drinking is probably questionable. Who knows what kind of diseases I might have picked up."

Reading nodded impatiently. "You were saying, what did their language sound like?"

"Oh yeah, well, if I didn't know better, I'd say Chinese!"

Terrence Mitchel woke suddenly, the satellite phone vibrating on the end table. It had been a late night, a very late night, and everyone, including their guest Bob Turnbull, who had happily slept on a cot brought by the staff, were still asleep. After waiting hours for a call that never came, Turnbull had called his people in the United States, he apparently part of some environmentalist group called Protect Amazonia Now, an organization he had never heard of. He had heard only parts of the conversation, Turnbull making the call on the balcony of their hotel room, almost as if he didn't want to be overheard.

And the scraps he had overheard had him troubled.

The way Turnbull had originally spoken it sounded like they were scientists cataloguing species, at least that's how Mitchell remembered the conversation, but the snippets overheard in the phone call had him questioning his memory and Turnbull's original story. References to 'mission' and 'failure', words he wouldn't have used to describe a scientific expedition being attacked, floated in from the balcony leaving he and his wife very nervous.

And what Mitchell had learned over the year he and Jenny had been together was that when she was nervous, she became confrontational, dealing with whatever was making her nervous.

"I thought you were a scientist?" she had asked when Turnbull reentered the room.

He handed the phone back to Mitchell and sat down, Mitchell's clothes fitting him almost perfectly. "I am. Most of us are. I have a PhD in environmental studies from Berkley. A lot of people don't like environmentalists, especially down here, so I thought it better to say we were on a scientific expedition cataloguing species."

"What were you really doing?" Again it was Jenny with the balls.

"Trying to prove that the Venezuelans were illegally logging. We heard some rumors over the Net so a team of six of us came down to check it out."

"Why not go through the government?"

"Washington? They're part of the problem, not the solution, man. Once you get them involved, you know there'll be a cover up for sure. We couldn't risk that. We wanted to get direct evidence and show the world by exposing these bastards on the Internet where they couldn't deny it."

"But you were caught."

"Yeah, but not by loggers. These guys were paramilitary or something. Special Forces. Head to toe gear, all black, like something out of Call of Duty, man!"

The rest of the conversation had seemed truthful and had put them at ease slightly, enough that they let him stay in their room overnight, he still clearly having been through an ordeal.

The phone vibrated again, demanding attention. Mitchell grabbed it as the rest of the room stirred. "Hello?"

"Terrence, is that you?"

He immediately recognized the voice and jumped out of bed, thrilled. "Professor Palmer! Is that really you?" He couldn't believe his ears. Jenny jumped up on her knees in the middle of the bed as Turnbull groggily awoke. "Are you okay?"

"Yes, I'm fine now. James and some local natives found me, I'll explain later. We're going to rendezvous with Leather's team shortly, then try to make the boat before nightfall. I just wanted you to know I'm okay."

"That's fantastic news, mum." Jenny waved at the phone, tears of relief flowing freely down her cheeks. "Jenny sends her best."

"Hugs and kisses to her. I'm going to let you go now. Let the university and anyone else you can think of know we're okay. I'll contact you when we reach the boat."

"Okay, mum."

"Is that your missing Doctor?" asked Turnbull, standing up.

Mitchell nodded.

"The one with the heavily armed security team coming to get her?"

Mitchell's eyes narrowed. "Yes. Why?"

"Ask her if she saw or heard anything about my friends."

Mitchell frowned, thinking the poor woman had enough on her mind, but decided to ask anyway. "Mum, did you happen to see or hear anything while you were out there, specifically about a team of environmentalists being captured by a team of Special Forces types?"

"Are you joking, Terrence? You know you have to work on that sense of humor a little more."

"No, mum, I'm not. It's just that we met someone here who claims he and his friends were attacked while they were trying to find some illegal logging operation. He managed to get away but his friends didn't."

He heard muffled talking then suddenly Professor Acton's voice came on the line. "As a matter of fact, I do know something about that," began the professor to Mitchell's amazement, amazement which was apparently written across his face as Turnbull jumped up, grabbing the phone from him and putting it on speaker.

"Please, Professor, tell me everything you know."

"Who's this?"

"This is Bob Turnbull," replied Mitchell. "He's the environmentalist we ran into here."

"Bob, I'm Professor Acton. Do you know a Steve Parker?"

Turnbull's jaw dropped as his head bobbed. "Yes! He's one of the team!"

"Well, I just got a call from our boat. We have him. He's okay. Have Terrence call the boat after this call so you can talk to him."

"That's fantastic, professor." Turnbull paused for a moment. "I understand you have a security team with you?"

"We will be rendezvousing with them shortly."

"Can you please help us? Your team can rescue the rest of my team. There's only four left!"

"I'm sorry, Mr. Turnbull, at the moment our priority is to get ourselves to safety. Once we're all safe we can discuss how to help you get your team out."

Turnbull said nothing, his face slowly turning red, his eyes filled with tears. Suddenly a burst of sobs, words almost incoherent, erupted from him. "You need to help them! You have to help them! They're going to die!"

He jumped at Mitchell, grabbing him around the neck, locking his elbow around Mitchell's throat. Mitchell could feel himself already struggling to breathe as he grabbed at Turnbull's arms, pulling at them to no avail. Jenny screamed, jumping out of the bed as Professor Acton demanded to know what was going on, his voice drowned out by the struggle. Mitchell could feel Jenny pulling at Turnbull as well, but his grip was unbreakable.

"I'll kill him if you don't send your team to find my friends!" he screamed. Mitchell could feel the blood flow being cut off to his brain as he slowly passed out, the world becoming a fog.

"Everyone calm down," came the professor's voice. "I want to know exactly what's happening."

"He's choking Terrence!" cried Jenny, still beating at Turnbull, the thuds vibrating through his attacker's body and into Mitchell's.

"If you don't let him go, there's no way we will help you." The professor's voice was calm but firm. "Do you understand me?"

"I understand that I have your man and I'll kill him if you don't give me what I want!"

"Your name is Bob Turnbull," replied Acton. "We have your man Steve Parker. If any harm comes to my people, I won't rest until you go to prison for the rest of your life. With one phone call I can have your name and photograph at every single airport in the country. There will be no escape. And if you're rotting in jail, how are you going to help your friends then?"

Mitchell felt Turnbull's grip loosen slightly as he sobbed, and just as he was about to try and wrench himself free he heard an incredible bang with a slight ringing sound directly behind him, then suddenly he was free,

Turnbull collapsing to the ground. Mitchell turned to see Jenny holding the large, old rotary phone from the nightstand.

Try that with a cellphone.

Acton's voice erupted from the phone on the bed. "What's going on?"

"I'm okay, Professor," replied Mitchell, coughing and collapsing to his knees as he tried to regain his breath. Jenny dropped the phone and threw her arms around him, crying into his chest. "Jenny knocked him out with the phone."

"Okay, tie him up and call the police. Then call the American Embassy for him, he's going to need some help."

"He was just starting to let me go, Professor. I think you got through to him."

"Are you sure?"

"Not a hundred percent, but pretty sure. He definitely loosened his grip and I heard him sort of start to cry." Mitchell couldn't believe he was defending his attacker, but he felt sorry for the man, and knew what desperation felt like, he having gone through it in the Egyptian desert just last year. "I think he was just desperate. If we tell him we'll help, I'm sure he'll cooperate."

"But we can't send Leather's team in," replied Acton. "That's Venezuela. We have no permission to be there." Mitchell heard a sigh through the phone. "Listen, you're there, on site. It's up to you on whether or not you want to trust him. Tell him we will do everything we can to help, but if he touches either of you again, all bets are off."

"Okay, Professor. I'll let you know what happens."

He ended the call and looked at Jenny. "What do you think?"

"I think we call the bloody police and have him locked up for trying to kill you, that's what I think!"

Mitchell laughed slightly, his feelings mixed. He was terrified. The man had attacked him and could have killed him if Jenny hadn't of coldcocked him with the phone. But would he have done any different if the roles were reversed? He couldn't say for sure. And it had him torn.

Turnbull groaned.

And Mitchell's decision was made.

"Help me get him into the chair," he said, standing.

Jenny stared at him, mouth agape. "Are you daft?"

Suddenly the door burst open, flying off the hinges. Jenny screamed and Mitchell jumped in front of her, nearly shitting his pants as half a dozen police officers stormed into the room, guns drawn, screaming in Portuguese.

It appeared Mitchel's decision to give Turnbull a second chance had been countermanded.

To say Acton was concerned was putting it mildly, and his concern was clearly shared by Laura. Their conversation with Mitchell and his wife Jenny had taken place nearly on the run, there no time to waste if they were to arrive at the river before nightfall. He was more and more convinced that they had to reach the safety of the boat in case this Tuk kidnapper came back with friends. He had faith that Leather's team could hold their own in a firefight, but poison arrows in the dark of the jungle were almost impossible to defend against.

"Hold your position!" ordered a voice, the accent unmistakably British, from what part of the Empire Acton had no idea, still trying to figure out the diverse country's many different facets.

Everyone froze, Sandro quickly translating for Skip who ordered their guides to hold.

Bushes rustled and almost immediately retired Lt. Colonel Cameron Leather appeared from the foliage, a smile on his face. "Good afternoon, Professors. We could hear you coming from a klick away."

"Thank God you're here!" cried Laura, giving the man a hug and smiling at the rest of his team as they emerged from their cover. She introduced Sandro and Skip and it was quickly conveyed to their guides that these men were friendly.

Skip said something, pointing in the direction they had been heading.

"He say we must go. No time to chit-chat." Sandro was already following their guides, leaving the rest to catch up.

"Are you okay, Professor?" asked Leather, keeping beside Laura, their guides setting the pace at a near jog.

"Other than being tired, sore and embarrassed, I'm fine."

"You've got nothing to be embarrassed about, honey." Acton looked from his wife to Leather. "She took on an anaconda!" It was said with pride and awe, Acton having only believed the story because he had seen the carcass himself.

Leather's eyes widened. "An anaconda?"

"Dove out of a tree with a knife, sunk the blade into its head, then sliced the damned thing right open. I saw the carcass myself."

"Holy Christ!"

"Then she ate the effin' thing!"

Leather shook his head, laughing as he deked around a tree. "You never cease to amaze me, ma'am."

"Nor I myself, apparently." She frowned. "There's been a development since we were last in contact."

"What's that?"

"Apparently some environmentalists have run into some trouble. They were captured by what two survivors are calling Special Ops types, possibly Chinese?" She looked at Leather. "Does that make any sense?"

"Where?"

"North of here, just across the Venezuelan border."

"That's where we figure you were found, just across the border, a couple of miles into Venezuelan territory," said Leather.

"Did you have permission to cross the border as part of the search?" asked Acton.

Leather shook his head. "Negative. And I wouldn't bother asking. In this part of the jungle, the chances of getting caught by the authorities crossing the border are slim to none. It's a protected ecological zone that's supposed to be left alone so the natives can go about their business. I figured if we needed to cross to get you, we just wouldn't mention that in the report," he said, winking at Acton with a smile that lasted only a moment. "What makes these environmentalists think it was Special Ops?"

"The way they were dressed," answered Acton. "Head to toe black, faces covered, no markings."

"Could be paramilitaries, Venezuelan police."

"That's what I was thinking as well."

"And Chinese?"

Acton shoved aside some branches, holding them back for Laura. "That's what the guy said. He said he heard them talking and it wasn't Spanish or Portuguese, but sounded Chinese."

"That could mean anything. There's dozens of languages that sound Chinese. Hell, most people can't tell the difference between Chinese, Japanese and Korean. Can't tell the people apart either. But Chinese is probably the correct guess."

Acton was surprised at Leather's conclusion. "Why?"

161

"Venezuela is one step away from being a full-on communist state, China *is* communist, Venezuela hates America, China loves pretty much anyone the West doesn't. There's lots of business ventures between China and Venezuela. If I remember my briefing notes on the region correctly, China is Venezuela's second largest trading partner, and Venezuela is China's go-to country for Latin American investment. They are *very* tight. Makes me wonder why you Yanks would rather buy your oil from them than Canada."

Acton shrugged as Laura shook her head. "But Chinese Special Ops? What could they possibly be doing in the middle of the Amazon Rainforest?"

"No idea, but they probably weren't Special Ops, just advisors. China has military all over the world but call them 'advisors'," said Leather adding air quotes. "We do the same, so do the Americans. It's pretty standard practice. They could be providing security for something in the region, picked up the environmentalists on a security sweep."

Acton didn't like the sounds of this, the PAN environmentalists' story sounding more and more plausible. "Would they shoot first, ask questions later?"

Leather nodded. "Absolutely. They don't operate under the same Rules of Engagement as Western troops typically do. If whatever they're protecting is important enough, they'd kill without hesitation."

"So the captured environmentalists?" asked Laura, her voice telling Acton she didn't want to have the answer she already knew confirmed.

"Are most likely dead."

It was said with the certainty of experience, and was the same conclusion Acton had come to as well. He just hated to hear his pessimistic side confirmed.

"And an excursion to confirm that?"

Leather looked him directly in the eye. "Strongly discouraged. We are a small team, already down one man, designed to rescue two missing persons, one the hostage of a primitive tribe, not take on possible Chinese Special Forces. I recommend we stick to the plan—get to the village, evac by boat, tell the authorities. Let them investigate."

Acton was in full agreement, but he could tell Laura wasn't. "But what if it's true about this illegal logging operation. It could destroy the entire ecosystem here, or worse, destroy a way of life for the indigenous people."

"Which is why I think we should leave it to the authorities. They're trained for this, they have the diplomatic ties."

Laura frowned, the reply evidently still not sitting well, but she said nothing. Acton instead responded. "Then that's what we'll do, leave it to the Brazilians to sort out with the Venezuelans. Let's just get our asses on that boat and out of here."

Tuk sprinted through the last of the trees before the clearing containing the Cleansing Pit. The screams and terrifyingly alien sounds of the Panther People and their mighty beasts were long gone. He had bypassed TikTik's village fearing they might delay him from reaching the one person who might be able to help.

Lau-ra-pal-mer.

The Woman of Light would know what to do. She would know how to fight the Panther People, to stop them in their wanton destruction. His fear was he'd be too late. They had already killed Bruk and TikTik. Would they kill the others, or take them captive, forcing them into slavery to serve their cause.

He had heard of other tribes taking people as slaves to work their fields, but it was rare and he had never met anyone firsthand who had seen it. He could understand the appeal of slavery—if someone else was forced to do

163

the work, it left you free to pursue other useful activities that might benefit the community, or simply be able to rest from time-to-time.

It was the entire idea of *forcing* someone against their will to do it. That he couldn't understand. Why anyone would think they had the right to force someone else to do work was beyond him. Which made the entire concept of slavery unpalatable to him, and he was determined that his family and friends would not suffer long in that role should that be the intention of the Panther People.

The past few harvests his village had been forced to get help from TikTik's village due to their shortage of manpower. In exchange those that helped got a share of what they harvested. *That* seemed to Tuk to be the right way of doing things. Fair compensation for work well done.

Everyone won.

But for the Panther People to come and raid villages to steal people to work as slaves? Completely unacceptable.

But he prayed that was exactly what was happening.

For if it weren't, the alternative meant death.

He burst into the clearing and fell to his knees as he reached the edge. Looking over his heart sank as he felt his ears pound and the world begin to lose focus.

The pit was empty.

The Woman of Light was gone.

And his village was doomed.

He double-checked, not believing his eyes, then realized how obvious the answer was.

How stupid can you be?

She was a Spirit Person, and though she had led him to believe she had lost her powers, she obviously hadn't. When he had left her she must have simply left the pit, perhaps floating out like a feather caught on the wind.

Which also meant she had either not understood the Cleansing Ritual she was partaking in, or worse, had decided not to partake.

Either way, she wasn't here and all hope was lost for his village.

He sat back on the cool grass of the clearing and began to sob as he thought of his mother, condemned her remaining life to serve the Panther People as their slave, left to wonder what had become of her son.

Her cowardly, weak son.

I'm not a coward!

He slammed his fists into the ground then pushed himself to his feet, wiping his tears of self-pity off his face.

I am not a coward!

He looked about the clearing then at the ground. He smiled. There were tracks everywhere, not just Lau-ra's but several others as well, including two with curious markings from the strange leathers they wore over their feet like Lau-ra did.

Which meant the Spirit People had rescued her.

They are indeed powerful!

He examined the relatively fresh tracks and noticed they led out of the clearing and back toward the river. He set out after her, determined to retrieve what was willfully given to him.

And to convince her to help his village.

For without her, he feared all were doomed.

J. ROBERT KENNEDY

Amazonas Detachment, Delegacias de Polícia Federal
40 Av. Domingos Jorge Velho, Manaus, Brazil

The phrase 'arrest everyone and sort it out at the station' may not have seemed like a bad idea to Terrence Mitchell yesterday when he was safely within the borders of the British Empire, but today he was not, and the practice was not sitting well with him. In fact he was terrified, his cramped cell filled to the brim with drunks and general malcontents, including Bob Turnbull, the man who had attacked him.

And worst of all he had no clue where Jenny was.

When the police had burst into their hotel room part of him had felt relieved. Turnbull would be arrested and the decision on whether or not to trust him taken away. But that's not what had happened. Instead, after a large amount of screaming and yelling, they were all handcuffed and taken away, not a word of English spoken by the police.

Jenny had been separated from them, kicking and screaming, when they arrived, and he had already vomited once, much to the annoyance of his cellmates, thinking of what might be happening to her. Having grown up on a steady feed of the bullshit 24-hour news cycle, he had heard horror stories of gang rapes by police officers in the third world, Mexico specifically coming to mind.

How different would it be down here in the middle of the jungle?

He clung to the bars of the cell, determined to not be dragged out of sight of the cop sitting at a desk just down the hall. He had lost track of Turnbull and at this point, frankly, didn't give a damn what happened to him. His only thoughts were of self-preservation so he could find Jenny. He had begged the guards for a phone call, for someone to call the British

166

Embassy. All it had earned him was a rap on the knuckles and several games of grab ass from some of the inmates interested in sampling "Carne Britânica"—what that meant he was terrified to know—until some shouts from the guard settled them down.

He now sat on the floor, his right arm hooked through the bars, his left hand loosely locking it in place, his head resting against the cool steel, his feet curled up under him in a pile of his own vomit. He couldn't believe how quickly he had degenerated to vermin. His clothes had been torn apart during the arrest, his valuables including watch, wallet, phone and wedding band stripped from him when he arrived, then his shoes and belt, along with his pants, were stolen within seconds of being shoved into the cell.

The welcome beating hadn't helped, and he was sure the ribs bruised by the police batons were now at least cracked, it hurting with every breath taken. His sobs had at least subsided, he realizing it only brought more misery in the form of taunts or the occasional kick.

Now he was silent, broken and ashamed.

He prayed for rescue, but deep down he just wanted to die, the prospect of anyone he knew seeing him like this too humiliating.

"Bob Turnbull?"

The voice was American, questioning, and directly in front of him. He looked up, the man looking down at him. "Help me."

"That's why I'm here," replied the man, smiling as he knelt down. "My name is Rick Henderson; I was sent by PAN from Rio. Sorry it took so long but arranging a flight out here isn't the easiest of things. First we have to get you out of here though. I've posted bail and they assure me it will only be a few minutes."

"Did you say 'Bob Turnbull'?"

Mitchell didn't bother looking over his shoulder to see who had asked the question, he recognized the voice.

"Yes. And you are?" Henderson rose.

"Bob Turnbull."

Henderson looked down at Mitchell. "I thought *you* were Bob Mitchell."

"No, I am."

Mitchell looked up. "Please, help me. My wife. At least help my wife."

A guard shouted something and everyone moved back, Henderson stepping aside. Keys were produced and the cell unlocked, the gate swinging aside. Turnbull walked out and the gate was slammed shut and locked. He and Henderson followed the guard.

"What kind of human being are you?" cried Mitchell. "I'm in here because of you! My wife is in here because of you!" He pulled himself to his feet, his hands still gripping the bars as he shoved his face through as far as he could, not making it quite to the ears. Looking sideway down the hall, he continued shouting. "*You* attacked *me*! *You* tried to kill *me*! Tell him that! You have to help us! You can't leave us here!"

Henderson looked back, pausing, saying something to Turnbull, a quick conversation in whispers occurring before they resumed.

Mitchell's chest tightened and he felt his world begin to close in around him as a panic attack began, the only glimmer of hope he had seen since arriving about to disappear through the door now held open for the two Americans. "We're the only ones who can help you!" he cried as he collapsed to the floor, sobbing uncontrollably, not caring what happened to him anymore as the taunting already began.

"You should have helped me last night when I begged you!"

Mitchell yanked himself to his knees, pushing his head through again. "So this is revenge? Revenge because we said we'd help you, but couldn't send our rescue team across the goddamned border? You call yourself an environmentalist but you're not. You hate humanity. You're probably one of those nutters who belongs to the Voluntary Human Extinction

Movement. What were you really doing in the forest? Were you spying on illegal loggers like you claim or were you actually there to sabotage their equipment and spike the trees so people would get hurt or killed? Are you one of those barmy bastards that think the life of a tree is worth more than the life of a human? If you leave us here, especially Jenny, then you're no better than the scum you say captured your team and tried to kill you!"

It took a few minutes for Mitchell to realize he was screaming at an empty hall, Turnbull and Henderson having left. He felt a hand on his shoulder. He shrugged it off, but it grabbed him again, this time hard, and yanked him away from the bars. Suddenly he found himself in the midst of a crowd of men, pawing at him, grabbing at him, and as he tried to protect himself, lowering his head and covering it with his hands, they continued to tug at him.

He was shoved to his knees and a man positioned himself in front of him, dropping his pants.

And Mitchell made a decision.

He would die with dignity.

His hand darted forward and grabbed the man's testicles. Squeezing as hard as he could, he yanked back quickly as the man screamed. He didn't have time to look at the end result as he tossed whatever was in his hand aside, turning his attention to the next nearest attacker. He drove his fist up hard into the man's groin, then grabbed the first wrist he could see, bending it forward rapidly while applying intense pressure to the top of the hand, causing the man to drop to his knees in agony. Mitchell's left thumb plunged into the man's eye, shoving hard until he felt the eyeball collapse.

Today everyone dies.

The horror he had caused had most of the men backing off. Mitchell jumped to his feet, grabbing the nearest one by the arm and yanking him toward him, spinning him so the man's back was facing him. He wrapped his elbow around the man's neck and locked it in place with his other arm, then squeezed, pushing his would-be rapist's knees out from under him. With one push on the back of the man's neck, it snapped. He tossed the body aside, his breathing heavy, his chest heaving as he gasped for air, his eyes surveying the circle of men around him, none within reach at the moment.

He lunged toward one man and the entire crowd scurried back several feet, nobody daring approach the crazed Brit. One was dead, another partially blinded, and still another writhing on the floor, gripping himself where his scrotum used to be.

He was now the alpha male.

He stood up straight, taller than most in the room, and pointed a finger, it slowly singling each out.

"Touch me again, say a word to me again, and I'll kill you. Is that understood?"

The entire room that a moment ago didn't speak English, nodded in terror. He pointed at the men in front of the bars and motioned for them to get out of the way. They scurried to the sides like cockroaches revealed by a light, and he returned to the bars, draping his hands through the metal and resting.

Someone came up from behind him.

He spun around in a defensive stance drilled into him by Leather and his men to find an old man carrying a stool.

"For you, senhor."

Mitchell nodded and allowed the man to place the stool near the bars for him, then sat down, relaxing for the first time since he had arrived. As his thoughts began to clear, he glanced over at his handiwork and couldn't believe what he had done. Leather's training had paid off, and the words of one of his men echoed through his head.

When it's life or death, there are no rules. You do whatever it takes to survive.

"Terrence!"

He spun, jumping to his feet and knocking the stool over as he saw Jenny running down the hall, the American lawyer Henderson behind her with a smiling Turnbull. As soon as she came within sight of the inmates a few whistles erupted. Mitchell spun around, glaring at the men who quickly dropped their heads, all suddenly quiet and looking for their missing contact lenses.

"Terrence, love, are you okay?"

He lunged through the bars, grabbing her, not sure if she was real, not sure if any of this were real. As his heart pounded in his chest, the rush of blood roaring through his ears, he barely heard the sound of the gate being unlocked and the bars swinging open. He collapsed into Jenny's arms, sobbing as a group of policemen advanced into the cell, batons at the ready as they removed the dead and injured.

"Is it over?" he finally asked, looking Jenny in the face, her cheeks smeared with dirt and grime, her own ordeal apparently not easy. "Did they hurt you?"

She shook her head. "No, I'm okay. They yelled at me a lot then threw me in a cell for a while. Bob got me out!"

"Bob?" He turned to the smiling Turnbull and decked him, dropping the asshole to the floor in a heap. He was about to pounce on him and finish him off when he was grabbed by several policemen. "Let me at him! He left me here to die!"

Henderson helped Turnbull up off the floor, the latter nursing a bleeding lip. He waved off the police. "Let him go. I deserved that." The grips on him eased and Mitchell resisted the urge to jump back into the fray. "I'm sorry, Terrence, but I was angry. As soon as I walked out that door I knew I was on the wrong side of this and that you were right. I had

Rick immediately go to work. Just a couple of phone calls and everything was cleared up. I'll still face charges unless you guys drop them, but I'm willing to face the music after what I've done."

Henderson stepped in front of Mitchell. "You and your wife are free to go, no charges. Mr. Turnbull has confessed to attacking you and causing the disturbance at the hotel. He will return at a later date for his trial unless those charges are dropped here and now."

Mitchell said nothing, continuing to glare at everyone around him, adrenalin fueled anger still his commander.

"Terrence." It was a whisper accompanied by a tug on his arm. He looked down at Jenny who was imploring him to respond.

A burst of air he hadn't known he was holding erupted from him and his shoulders slumped, his entire body releasing the taught, clenched muscles as he finally realized everything was over, and revenge a selfish treat he didn't need.

"I don't want to press charges," he mumbled. He looked up at Henderson then at Turnbull. "It's over. Let's go back to the hotel so I can clean up."

"It is not over, senhor," said an older police officer, stepping forward. "We have a dead man and two seriously injured prisoners here. They say you do this to them."

Mitchell's heart leapt into his throat for a moment, but after everything he had been through, there was no way this situation could scare him. Instead, he laughed. He pointed at the dead man then the dickless wonder. "He tore this guy's bollocks off, then the other guy jumped in to try and stop him. The dead guy shoved his thumb through the guy's eye but he hung on and killed him in self-defense." He pointed at the Cyclops. "He deserves a medal for stopping the guy."

The old cop smiled. "Then why do you have so much blood on you, senhor?"

Mitchell held up his hands. "I have first aid training. I tried to help but there was little I could do."

The smile spread as the man pointed to the wall behind him. Mitchell's heart sank as he saw a camera pointed directly at the cell. "Fortunately for you, senhor, the camera is broken. But I like your story, it cleans things up very nicely." He jerked his thumb toward the door at the far end of the hallway. "But I don't ever want to see your faces again."

Mitchell's head bobbed up and down rapidly as Jenny's grip tightened noticeably on his arm.

"Let's go," said Henderson, his tone revealing a needed sense of urgency. Jenny pulled the still stunned Mitchell toward the door, Turnbull and Henderson leading the way. Mitchell was given a set of clothes, his old ones stolen or covered in blood, a chance to clean up, then after a flurry of signatures on Henderson approved paperwork, everyone was soon on the street. The four of them climbed into a waiting car, Turnbull wisely in the front, Mitchell in the opposite rear seat, Henderson apparently not willing to trust their fight was over.

As the car put some distance between them and the police station, Mitchell finally began to relax, the adrenaline rush over, his body slumping in exhaustion. Turnbull looked at Mitchell as if he wanted to say something.

Mitchell frowned. "What?"

"I just have one question for you, then I'll leave you alone."

"What?"

"Did you really rip that dude's balls off?!"

All eyes were now on Mitchell. He paled.

"Oh my God! I guess I did!"

"Dude!" Turnbull offered him a fist bump which Mitchell automatically returned, not even registering the contact, shock beginning to set in.

"Did you kill that man?" asked Jenny gently, still holding his arm tightly.

He nodded. "I broke his neck, just like we were taught."

"Taught by who?" asked Henderson.

"Our boss' head of security. We've been trained in all sorts of self-defense techniques."

Henderson nodded, his hand reaching into his suit. Mitchell gasped and Jenny yelped as a gun was produced, pointed directly at them.

"Did he teach you how to dodge a bullet?"

Barasana Village on the Rio Negro, Northern Amazon, Brazil

Reading looked up to see where the hail had come from. A boat was pulling into the inlet they were moored at and several aboard were waving. Fabricio returned the wave, coming out onto the back deck.

"The rescue boat is here, senhors!"

"Just *after* the nick of time," muttered Reading as Kinti, who had been sitting at his feet humming as she weaved a basket, rose, helping pull him to his feet. He put his arm around her as ropes were thrown to lash the new arrival to the Juliana. A uniformed man stepped across a plank and onto the boat, Fabricio stepping forward to greet him in Portuguese. Words were exchanged rapidly, the new arrival pursing his lips as his head slowly bobbed. Finally he turned to Reading and Milton who was now at his side.

"I am Lieutenant Colombo. I understand your friends have been rescued."

Milton snorted then spun, apologizing as he did so. Reading glanced after him then turned back to Colombo. "They should be arriving any time now."

"This is good news. They are very lucky." He jerked a thumb over his shoulder. "We will wait until their arrival, then depending upon the time, leave either this evening or in the morning."

"There's a new problem," said Reading, stepping back and motioning toward Steve Parker, the Protect Amazonia Now environmentalist who until now had waited patiently behind them. "Mr. Parker here says he and his team were ambushed by Special Forces types several days ago."

The man's eyebrows shot up his forehead. "Special Forces?"

175

Parker nodded emphatically. "Yes. They were head to toe in black body armor, face masks, machine guns. Definitely not run-of-the-mill security guards."

Colombo frowned, apparently not convinced. "Where did this happen?"

"Upriver a bit, then inland about three days north-east."

Colombo's eyebrows rose. "That's Venezuelan territory."

Parker nodded nervously. "It might be. Does that mean you won't help us?"

"It means you need to deal with the Venezuelans."

"Can you help?" Parker sounded desperate. "We're just environmentalists looking into illegal logging. The rest of my team doesn't deserve to die."

Colombo looked at Reading then back at Parker. "How many?"

"There were six of us. I escaped, and apparently so did my friend Bob Turnbull. He's in Manaus with their people," replied Parker, nodding toward Reading.

"This is true," said Reading. "He apparently stole a canoe and paddled down to Manaus where he asked to borrow a satellite phone from two of our people coordinating things there."

"So your people may already be sending help."

Parker shook his head. "That's days away. They don't have days."

"What makes you say that?"

"They shot me!" Parker shoved his shoulder forward, wincing. "They're obviously going to kill them."

"Why would they do that? Did you see anything?"

Parker shook his head. "No, we didn't see anything. But I think we were close."

"Why?"

"There was a smell in the air. Something different. I can't really describe it because we were just catching wafts of it. Bob thought it was diesel, but I couldn't be sure. Whatever it was it wasn't natural and it was being carried on the winds."

"It could have been a boat."

Parker's jaw dropped. "Are you intentionally being difficult?"

Reading almost chuckled but caught himself, though there was no preventing the smile before it spread across his face. He caught the twinkle in Colombo's eye. He knew the man was simply doing his job, drawing out information from Parker by playing part stupid and part Devil's advocate. He'd done the same routine many times in his career, and it was remarkable how much you could pull out of someone, especially when they got frustrated. They began to try to convince you of their story by revealing items they wanted to hold back, tidbits that might incriminate them in something, but should their need for you to believe them overcome their mouth-brain barrier, a font of information could be revealed with one slip.

He had no doubt this Colombo honored his fictional namesake.

I wonder if he's even heard of him?

He was certain if he had he had been teased about it when joining the force.

"I am not being difficult, senhor, I am merely asking questions. You are asking me, a Brazilian police officer, to help a group of people who have crossed the border into Venezuela—" He paused, his eyes narrowing. "You had permits for this incursion, yes?"

Parker blanched. "Well, ah, no, you see when we left, we didn't know it was going to be in Venezuela, we just sort of ended up there."

"I see." Colombo rubbed his chin, pursing his lips as if deep in thought. "This could be a problem. So what you are saying is you *illegally* crossed the border, were caught, then were shot trying to escape, and now you need our help to free your friends from the Venezuelan authorities."

Parker's eyes were wide open in shock. Everything the Lieutenant had said was true, except for the assumption it was Venezuelan authorities that had captured the group. Reading still wasn't convinced. Why would they not have markings on their uniforms, and why would they be dressed the way they were if merely border security. He decided he needed to step in.

"Lieutenant, is it customary for the Venezuelans, or for that matter, your government, to patrol the border in that area? Isn't it environmentally protected?"

Colombo turned his attention to Reading. "No, it is not common. In fact, unless the Venezuelan government has decided to violate the treaty, they shouldn't be there at all. They have a border outpost at the Rio Negro and several facilities along the river, but this area of the Amazon is supposed to be protected from all activity more than one mile from the shoreline."

"So whoever is there is violating the treaty."

Colombo nodded then held up a finger. "Or is not party to the treaty."

Reading's left cheek broke out into a smile. "Like a private security force guarding an illegal logging operation?"

He sensed Parker about to say something when he reached back with his arm and squeezed Parker's arm tightly and out of sight of Colombo.

Shut up if you know what's good for you!

Colombo smiled from ear to ear. "You are a police officer, no?"

Reading laughed. "Scotland Yard, over twenty years. Now I'm INTERPOL."

"Ahh!" Colombo's eyes widened with respect and awe. "I have read many detective books. Sir Arthur Conan Doyle, Agatha Christie. I love Sherlock Holmes and Hercule Poirot. I try to think like them when I have a crime to solve. And what was it that Holmes once said? 'When you have eliminated the impossible, whatever remains, however improbable, must be the truth'? And if we assume the Venezuelans haven't broken the treaty—though that is an assumption, not a confirmed fact—then it must be some private organization." He sucked in a deep breath, his chest swelling. "Mr. Parker, is it?"

Parker nodded.

"Sir, I believe your story. It would take a madman to shoot himself, and as you have a second witness in Manaus, it has been my experience that madmen don't often travel together, but when they do, once separated, it is every man for himself. But both of your stories apparently corroborate. Since we are no longer needed here, you will come with us and we will head north to the border and enlist the help of the authorities there. I will radio Manaus to have your friend picked up for questioning so we can confirm the story and get corroboration on a possible location for the ambush."

Parker seemed relieved, his shoulders slumping and some color returning to his cheeks. "Thank you, Lieutenant, thank you so much!"

"Daylight is running out. We have an hour to the border station if we hurry so we must go now."

Parker shook Reading and Milton's hand along with Fabricio's. "Thank you all for helping me. It's appreciated. If you're ever in Washington look me up, I owe you."

He climbed across to the police boat as the lines were untied and the new arrival pushed back from the Juliana. Moments later its engine was guiding them out of the inlet and onto the river where it banked right and was soon out of sight, its engine a mere memory a minute later.

Reading sat down, Kinti resuming her weaving as Milton stretched his back. "I'm going back down below," he said, wincing. "Wake me if any more excitement occurs."

179

"Why bother?"

Milton's eyes narrowed questioningly then followed where Reading was pointing. At the far end of the village a group of natives appeared followed by Leather and his team who were surrounding two exhausted looking professors.

Milton grabbed Reading with one arm over his shoulders and squeezed him. "They're back!"

Reading nodded as he looked down at Kinti, whose face was plastered with the sadness his heart was encased in.

They would be leaving within minutes.

And their whirlwind romance would be over.

Forever.

Acton waved to Reading and Milton on the boat, his arm now tightly around Laura's waist. The entire village was gathering around, smiles everywhere as a chant of celebration broke out. Leather's team herded them toward the boat and Acton was content to let them for now, but proper, formal goodbyes would be necessary for those who had done so much to save a stranger, asking nothing in return.

"Is that Hugh's girlfriend?"

Acton grinned as he saw the young girl, easily eighteen inches shorter than Reading, clinging to him. He felt a twinge in his heart as he saw the tears rolling down her face, and the mixed emotions on his friend's.

"Yes it is. Her name's Kinti. She seems to be a very sweet girl with a voracious sexual appetite."

"James!" Laura swatted his arm.

"Hey, I had to listen to it all night!"

"That's terrible! Let the poor man have his privacy!"

"Then he shouldn't have shagged her rotten in a communal hut!"

"I'm sure it wasn't like that."

"You're right, it wasn't. She shagged him rotten. I think he mostly laid back and enjoyed the ride."

He was slapped again, but this time at least there was a giggle accompanying it. "Stop, he'll hear you!"

Reading strode down the ramp to shore, Kinti holding his left hand as he one arm hugged Laura, lifting her off the ground. "Thank God you're alive!"

"None the worse for wear, but eager to get home." Laura stepped back as a thumping exchange occurred between Reading and Acton. "And who's this?" Laura smiled at Kinti, putting out her hand. "Hello, I'm Laura," she said, patting her chest.

Kinti shook Laura's hand, smiling politely. "Kinti."

"Such a pretty name." Laura smiled at Reading. "Does she speak any English?"

Reading blushed crimson. "Just a few that I've taught her."

"Portuguese?"

Head shake.

"Spanish?"

Head shake.

"So, how do you communicate."

"Body language," coughed Milton as he descended the ramp, finally tired apparently of waiting for them. He gave them both hugs and Acton could immediately see his friend was in pain.

"I think we better say our goodbyes and get underway," suggested Acton. He pointed to Fabricio who had joined them. "Please tell the Chief that we are thankful for his people's help, and are in their debt."

Fabricio translated and the Chief bowed deeply. He translated for his people who seemed very pleased, many whooping in pleasure. The Chief spoke and motioned to them all. Fabricio looked to Acton. "He say that you are all friends and you are all welcome to return at any time."

Acton bowed along with Laura and the others. "We are honored."

The formalities over, hands were shaken, hugs were exchanged, and Reading and Kinti left the crowd as they walked toward the trees. Acton kept the smile forced on his face, but his chest tightened for his friend. It was obvious he was hurting. He knew from experience what love at first sight felt like. The intensity, the emotions, the overwhelming sense of desire and need, were almost too much to handle. It compressed a lifetime of love into a short flurry of red hot passion that was so pure, it felt as if the world would end when it came to its sometimes inevitable conclusion.

And this was one of those times.

It was an impossible situation.

And Acton knew the way Reading was.

He would keep his pain bottled up inside, making it worse.

Reading was sick to his stomach. The hollowed out feeling he had was beyond compare in his memory though he was certain he had experienced it before, but not since a young man. At that age you were supposed to feel this type of pain, it was all part of growing up, of becoming a man. But today he felt like that boy, desperately in love, who had just been told the love of his life was moving away forever, never to be seen again.

His chest was tight, his throat almost sore as he resisted the urge to join Kinti in her sobs. The poor girl's shoulders heaved against his chest as she curled into a ball, allowing herself to be enveloped in his arms. He gently patted her head, stroking his fingers through her hair, his face buried in it as he enjoyed her scent one last time.

He glanced toward the boat and saw everyone boarding and knew it was time.

"Kinti." His voice was soft, gentle, not its usual gruff self, this lovely young creature having smoothed out the rough edges decades of solitude had honed.

She looked up, blinking away the tears. "I must go now." Tears finally spilled over his eyelids as he forced a smile on his face. Her lips trembled into a smile of her own when he closed his eyes and kissed her one last time, both of them now clinging onto each other in a desperate attempt to hold onto the moment, to tell the hand of time to wait just one more second before ticking toward a future of loneliness and despair.

He finally let her go and they looked into each other's eyes, words unspoken, their faces saying the thousand words that needed to be said. With one more peck, he led her to the ramp, then with one final kiss and hug, he climbed back onto the boat, the ramp quickly pulled aboard as the motor kicked into gear, sending them toward the mouth of the inlet. The entire village ran along the shore, Kinti in the lead, her hand raised in the air, part waving goodbye, part reaching for him, not wanting to let go of the bond they had created in two short days.

Reading gripped the rail with one hand, at the far back of the boat so no one could see his face. He waved to Kinti, his lip stiff as he fought back the tears his tough, reserved British upbringing told him were unmanly, but his face told her everything she would need to know.

He loved her.

And would never forget her.

Tuk heard voices ahead and slowed. He had spotted a village upriver of where he had camped the night before he had spotted the Woman of Light, giving it a wide berth as he was unfamiliar with their people and more importantly, wanted to be alone in his grief over TikTik's impending nuptials and the death of his best friend Pol.

He had been dismayed when the trail he had been following had headed directly to the village rather than back to the Spirit Boat for it meant far more people to deal with who might just slow him down in his quest to reach the woman who was to be his mate and the savior of his village.

Lau-ra-pal-mer.

He secreted himself behind a large tree and watched as a boat, the very same boat that the Spirit People had been on left the village, the entire population on the shoreline waving and shouting. On the boat he could see several of the Spirit People and his heart leapt when he saw Lau-ra waving at the crowd.

Then he frowned.

She appeared happy.

If she had willingly left the Spirit People to be with him, then why would she be happy to have been taken back? Perhaps it was merely a façade designed to set the others who had "rescued" her at ease? Or perhaps she really had misunderstood the Cleansing Ritual and thought he had abandoned her and was relieved to be with her own kind?

It made sense. She didn't know his language and she had definitely appeared scared when she saw the pit. He had been forced to push her in after all, and now in retrospect it seemed pretty clear she didn't know what the Cleansing Pit was at all.

She must have thought I had left her there to die!

He desperately wished he could speak her language, not only so he could win her heart, but to communicate to her the very real need he had of her help. As the Spirit Boat left the small inlet it turned downriver, back toward where he had first seen her. He rushed through the forest, knowing they had no choice but to pass by the same spot. His route was more direct, theirs requiring them to travel in an arc around the Mother's Forest. As he rushed through the trees, silently as to not attract the attention of the nearby village, he winced as his shoulder suddenly throbbed in pain. He looked down and finally noticed he was bleeding from the back of his arm, near the shoulder.

And it hurt.

There was an odd hole, as if an arrowhead had pierced it then fallen out. He wondered if it could have been a shard from the exploding tree trunks when he had made his escape, the curious sounds coming from the Panther People's short spears perhaps causing some magical, invisible arrow to strike the trees as they missed him.

He shrugged off the pain, it not important. Saving his people was what was important now. Saving his mother. Avenging TikTik and Bruk.

He burst onto the shoreline just as the boat came into view to his right. As it rushed toward him, the current and whatever mode of propulsion it was using—he could see no oars—moving it swiftly along, he realized he would have only moments to get their attention.

Can the Spirit People even see me when they are on their boat?

He began waving and shouting at the boat, his arm now noticeably hampering his movements. "Lau-ra! Lau-ra-pal-mer!"

A sudden rush of activity on the boat as Spirit People with their own short spears lined up on the edge proved to him quite convincingly that they could see him. He recognized no one then suddenly she appeared at the rear of the boat, her mate from the Spirit World with his arm around her.

And again he felt a flash of jealousy.

"Lau-ra! Lau-ra-pal-mer!"

He motioned for her to come to him but she said nothing, merely standing at the rear of her boat. He could tell she was sad, her eyes glistening even from this distance. She was barely a spear's throw away but he could tell she wasn't going to tell the boat to stop.

185

Then he yelled the one word he had heard her say several times.

"Help!"

Rio Negro, Northern Amazon, Brazil

"Hostile to port!"

Laura jumped, adrenaline suddenly rushing through her exhausted frame once again as Leather's men rushed to the port side, taking knees as they aimed their weapons at the shore. She was about to get up to see what the problem was when she felt James grab her.

"Stay down!" he hissed. Turning to Leather, he asked, "What is it?"

"Single native, war paint by the looks of it, naked. Not from the tribe we just left, I don't think."

"What's he doing?"

"Waving his arms and yelling something. I can't make it out."

"Silence!" yelled James. "Fabricio, cut the engine!"

"Yes, senhor!"

"Lau-ra! Lau-ra-pal-mer!"

James' eyebrows jumped. "Did he just say what I think he said?"

Reading and Milton's heads both bobbed in agreement. "He's definitely calling for you, Laura."

"Tuk?" She felt a surge of fear and relief as a mix of conflicting emotions overcame her. She definitely was happy to be here—ecstatic in fact—but she also felt sorry for the poor, simple native. His apparently weakened state meant he was probably condemned to a life alone, and she was convinced he had thought he had found a mate in her.

And she had led him on.

In her efforts in self-preservation she had convinced him there was a bond between the two of them, and in the end, she had betrayed that bond—at least in his mind. But if the bond wasn't real, why did she feel guilt, why did she feel she must explain herself to this poor man.

But it was pointless. There was no way to communicate with him.

"He appears unarmed." Leather was standing now, binoculars to his eyes. "And he's injured."

Laura jumped to her feet, concern pushing aside all other emotions. "How so?"

"Looks like he's bleeding from his left shoulder."

She moved to the aft of the boat and stood near the edge, looking at the poor man as he desperately waved and called her name. She felt James put his arm around her protectively, and almost smiled as she thought of him being jealous over the little man on shore who had stolen her from him.

Then suddenly everything changed.

"Help!"

She looked at James. "Did he just say 'help'?"

James nodded. "I think so. Does he know what that means?"

"He heard me say it several times but I never actually taught him it."

"Could he have picked it up from the context? Actually understood it?"

Laura nodded. "He's very smart. These natives may be primitive by our standards, but they have their Einsteins and Hawkings just like we do. I think he knows exactly what he's saying."

"Einstein, eh?" Reading shook his head. "I don't see it."

"And two days ago you couldn't see yourself falling in love with one of them, could you?" Laura immediately regretted her statement as Reading's face clouded with pain. She reached out and gripped his arm gently. "I'm so sorry, Hugh. I didn't mean that the way it sounded."

"Don't worry about it, you're right. I saw them all as savages, and now I realize they aren't. They're people just like us who are perfectly happy living their lives the way they are and don't need our modern ways to be fulfilled.

They live, laugh, love and cry exactly like us, perhaps even in a more pure way." He sighed. "I've learned a lot on this trip." He pointed at Tuk. "And if he says he needs help, then I think we should at least see what he has to say."

"But how are we going to communicate with him?"

Reading shrugged. "Take him to the village? Maybe someone there speaks his language."

James smiled. "If I didn't know you better, I'd say you were just looking for excuses to spend more time with Kinti." Reading was about to open his mouth in protest when James cut him off. "Like I said, *if* I didn't know you better." He turned to Fabricio. "Bring us ashore so we can take him aboard."

Fabricio's eyes widened. "Are you crazy, senhor? He could be a killer!"

Laura motioned toward her security team. "I think we're well protected, Fabricio. Please, he's wounded and needs our help."

"Okay, senhora, it your charter."

He fired up the engine and turned the boat around, Tuk having kept pace with them as they had continued to drift, all the while calling for Laura and for help.

And the entire time her heart broke as she heard the desperation in his voice, his pleads for her to help him, "Lau-ra help Tuk!" echoing in her head as she watched him plunge into the water as he saw the boat turn. He swam toward them then suddenly dipped below the surface, not returning. An arm shoved above the water, his head following as he sputtered for air, then disappeared again.

"He's drowning!" shouted Reading as James yanked off his boots.

"Be careful!" she yelled as her beloved husband dove into the water after the man who had kidnapped her. James broke the surface, swimming hard toward the relative position Tuk had been in when they last saw him, he obviously assuming the current would still be carrying the young man along with it. It was almost dark now and Fabricio's men were aiming every light they had at the area, Leather's men scanning the surface with their own flashlights.

"There!" yelled one of Leather's men, pointing farther downriver. Fabricio's men immediately redirected their lights and she gasped in relief as James broke the surface, Tuk gripped in his left arm. Fabricio guided the boat toward them as several lifebuoys were tossed in. James grabbed one and Leather's team pulled him and the unmoving Tuk to the side. Strong hands grabbed them and pulled them aboard, James rolling onto his back, gasping, as Tuk lay beside him, still.

"Is he breathing?" Laura asked as she rushed to his side.

"Doesn't look like it," said Leather as he checked for a pulse. He immediately began chest compressions as Laura knelt between James and Tuk. She took James' hand in hers, then Tuk's in her other.

"How's he doing?" asked James as he sat up, shoving his fingers through his dripping hair. Reading tossed him a towel and he stood, letting go of Laura's hand as he began to towel himself off.

Leather checked for a pulse again. "Nothing so far."

Laura leaned over, close to Tuk's ear. "Tuk! It's Laura. You have to breathe!" It was frustrating not being able to communicate, and she realized what it must be like for a true refugee—not economic refugees shopping for the best handout—thrust into unfamiliar environments where no one spoke their language. Finally she squeezed his hand in both of hers, saying the only thing she could think of to say.

"Tuk help Tuk!"

Everything was black. A roaring sound in the distance was all he could sense except for strange lights that seemed like those he would see at night when he looked up.

The campfires of the spirits.

He had often wondered about that. If they were campfires, then why were they white? And why were they moving across the sky in an arc? All of them. Did the Spirit World move? And if the Spirit World were in the sky, then what were they doing on the great river?

He believed in the Mother, proof of Her existence was all around him. But many of the stories taught to him as a child, and clung to in adulthood by most, seemed outrageous to believe in without some sort of proof. He kept his opinions to himself of course, sharing them only with Pol, but now he wondered about everything.

For he was dead.

He could remember swimming toward the Spirit Boat and Lau-ra, but his injured arm had proven too weak and the current too swift. He had been sucked under and soon lost the battle to hold his breath.

Or had the Spirit World punished him?

He had taken one of their own and then had the gall to try and board one of their vessels as if he were an equal.

He deserved to die.

The roaring in the distance grew closer and he wondered if he were nearing the afterlife his people believed in so fervently. Would the great Mother of all things embrace him, allowing him to live for eternity in her bosom that was the Spirit World where he would be reunited with the loved ones he had lost over the years.

Pol!

The thought excited him. To see Pol again would be worth dying for. He smiled as the thought of reuniting with his friend began to consume him and he beseeched the Mother to take him, to take him from this life of pain and heartache, and deliver him into the easy life of the Spirits.

But what of his own mother? She was a prisoner or worse of the Panther People. Did she deserve to live out her remaining days in horror just so he could be reunited with his dead friend, a friend who would be waiting for him whenever he actually did die?

NO!

He knew he had to get back, to somehow survive, but he didn't know how. *Please great Mother, do not take me yet! I have to save my people! Without me they are all doomed! Let me save my people, your children, then you may take me!* He listened for some sort of reply, something that had never happened in the real world, but perhaps here, in this strange place between his world and the Spirit World, the great Mother would respond.

"Tuk help Tuk!"

The voice was unmistakable.

Lau-ra!

Was she the Mother? Could she be the embodiment of the creator of all things? Or was she merely a messenger? Sent by the Mother to save him? That made more sense. He laughed. The arrogance of thinking that the Mother Herself would allow him to take Her from the Spirit World and willingly go with him to be his mate.

"Tuk help Tuk!"

He knew what she meant. She meant he had to help himself. But how? How could he help himself? He could feel nothing, hear nothing but the roar in the distance. What could he possibly do to help himself?

He frowned, pondering the conundrum of how to save one's life in the ether that lay between life and death.

If he were to help himself, he knew he had to beat death. So how did one beat death? Overcome what had killed one in the first place. That much was obvious. *So what killed me?* The water. He had drowned. Why did drowning in water kill someone? He knew he had struggled to breathe and he had finally felt himself gasp in the water, filling his body.

The water had obviously taken the place of the air he was supposed to breathe. So how to get rid of the water blocking air from getting in? He knew from enough roughhousing in the smaller rivers near his village that when water went down the wrong way, you would cough it out.

Cough!

He coughed, hard, and suddenly felt air rush into his lungs, the roar in the distance suddenly overwhelmingly loud. Someone was holding his hand, someone else was pushing on his chest. He opened his eyes and found he was surrounded by shapes, strange white lights pointed at him nearly blinding him.

"Lau-ra!" he cried, looking for his messenger in the horror of the Spirit World. Voices surrounded him, voices he couldn't understand, but one voice he recognized, near his ear.

"Lau-ra help Tuk. Okay?"

He raised his thumb. "Okay." His voice was weak and he was suddenly shoved onto his side, someone slapping his back. He coughed some more and several mouthfuls of water spilled out. He didn't know how long it took but he was soon breathing normally, though he was weak and shivering.

He felt something wrap around him and he gripped the strange skin tightly as he shook in the chill of the evening. He was helped to his feet and he looked to see Lau-ra was to his left, her presumed mate to his right. They led him to the rear of the Spirit Boat and sat him down on a strange, incredibly soft log with rests for his arms.

The entire time he kept his eyes glued on Lau-ra and her gentle, smiling, incredibly pale face. He was too terrified to look anywhere else but when someone removed the skin covering his shoulder and began to poke around, he winced, then passed out from the overwhelming pain.

"He's out cold," observed Leather. "Probably for the best." His eyes narrowed as he inspected the wound then opened wide in surprise as he looked up at his client, Laura Palmer. "This is a bullet wound!"

She gasped, her jaw dropping. "How did he get that?"

"The guard fired a shot after you two. Perhaps he hit him?" suggested Acton.

Laura shook her head. "No, he wasn't wounded when I last saw him. He was perfectly healthy."

"Are you sure?"

"Look at him. He's buck naked. It's not like it was hiding under a shirt and I just missed it."

Acton frowned. "Then who shot him?"

Leather pulled out the bullet, holding it up for everyone to see. "7.62 millimeter I'd guess. That's a thirty caliber for you Yanks."

Reading frowned. "Powerful weapon."

Leather continued patching up Tuk's arm. "I doubt any of the locals are carrying something that packs that much punch."

Acton rubbed his chin, puzzled. "Most of the locals have nothing more than spears. Some might have been traded guns in the past, not knowing they needed ammunition, but I saw nothing at the village that would suggest they even knew what a gun was."

Reading grunted. "Agreed. Perhaps we can ask them when we arrive. We're almost there." He nodded toward the inlet, lit by the lights from the boat. "Hope they don't mind late visitors."

"I know one person who won't mind," grinned Acton.

Leather looked up at Reading, the man trying to keep a professional visage but even he had to smile as he battled to hide his delight. Leather returned his attention to Tuk. He finished the final stitch and cut the string then saved his fellow Brit. "But you know who does use that type of ammo."

Laura seemed almost afraid to ask. "Who?"

"Military. Special Forces. Including Chinese Special Forces. Their Type 79's are 7.62mm and are their preferred submachine gun."

"Which fits in nicely with our environmentalist's account."

"It does," agreed Leather as he wrapped the wound. "But that type of ammo is used by pretty much every military in the world, so I wouldn't read too much into it. Let's just say though that I doubt he was shot by one of the locals."

As they approached the dock, the village erupted in cheers as those around the large campfire jumped to their feet and rushed to the shore to greet their returning guests.

And in the front, standing right at the dock, was the sparkling young woman Leather had determined owned the crusty old cop's heart.

Lucky bastard.

Manaus, Brazil

"What in the bloody hell is going on here?"

Terrence Mitchell's question was one that would go unanswered for the rest of the drive. He had tried the doors, despite the gun being aimed at him, to no avail. They were locked and controlled from the front and the deeply tinted windows kept the activities inside private. All he had discovered during their ordeal was that Bob Turnbull seemed as equally bewildered, he too ordered to raise his hands and shut-up.

Their benefactor, Rick Henderson, simply told them to relax and enjoy the ride.

Jenny was pushed hard against Mitchell, her feet shoving against the center console the entire time, and it was beginning to make him claustrophobic, he unable to take a full breath the entire ride.

"We're here," announced the driver, obviously an accomplice. The man was Asian, beyond that he had no idea of his nationality except that the two words he had spoken sounded perfectly American.

"Where are we?" asked Jenny, her voice quivering with fear.

"We're going to take a little flight."

Mitchell didn't like the sound of that. "Where?"

"That, you don't need to know." Henderson's smile was uncomfortably genuine looking. "I will tell you this. Helping Mr. Turnbull here turned out to be a *very* bad mistake on your part."

Dylan Kane lay prone outside the Kunlun Mountain complex, China's equivalent to Area 51. And it too didn't exist. With information so tightly under control in China however, it was much easier to keep its existence

196

from the Chinese people. And without the local population asking about it, the world didn't ask about it.

But hiding it from spy satellites was a different matter. The United States had known about it pretty much from the moment construction began, and the Chinese simply acknowledged that fact by not bothering to try and hide what was happening. They let the mountain overhead do that for them. It was a massive undertaking, built on the backs of tens of thousands of peasants looking for work. A massive complex had been built inside the Kunlun Mountains, and once hollowed out, no amount of spy satellites would be able to determine what occurred inside.

It had a massive runway, capable of handling the largest of aircraft, and it was used to test their newest designs, including the latest rip-offs of American, Russian and European aircraft. This was the fundamental advantage China had over every other developed nation on earth—a complete lack of immigration. Western nations had immigration, and China was one of the preferred sources, the population usually better educated, spoke English, were known for working hard, and usually didn't bring any religious baggage.

But what the politically correct West couldn't admit publicly, was that there was no way to know how many of these immigrants were legitimate, and how many were actually working for the Chinese government. Time and time again Chinese immigrants were being arrested for selling or giving secrets to their former homeland, yet there were just too many to know who else was involved.

And Kane had spied on enough senior Chinese officials to know that there were elements within the Party that were already developing a Fifth Column throughout the world should the day arise when they needed an enemy crippled. This was why the US government was secretly scrambling to figure out a way to make their telecommunications and power infrastructures redundant without alarming the public.

When all your tech is made in China…

His satellite phone vibrated a priority flash pattern in a pocket in his ghillie suit, one designed by him to fit this particular terrain perfectly. He would be nearly invisible to anyone and with the scopes he was using, he was so far away, he doubted anyone would think to look this far.

He slowly, carefully, curled his body away from the complex and fished his phone out, the display in dark-mode meaning the backlight had been disabled and instead the e-ink display showed him what he needed to know.

Leroux?

Chris Leroux was a buddy of his from high school, and one of his few friends. He was also a top analyst at the CIA headquarters in Langley and Kane had tasked him—on the side—to monitor any communications from the Professors' area.

He must have found something.

Kane took the call, and cursed after he heard what Leroux had found.

Command Sergeant Major Burt "Big Dog" Dawson kicked the corpse, just to make sure it was a corpse. It was. The operation had gone smoothly with the hostages rescued and the hostage takers eliminated. His team had merely provided support, taking out the guards with several sniper teams, allowing the Colombian Anti-Narcotics Brigade to enter the drug lord's compound swiftly and undetected—that is, until it was too late.

The entire op had taken a week of planning and ten minutes of execution.

"He overreached this time, eh, senor?" The Colombian commander, Colonel Rodriguez, kicked the same body. "He never should have kidnapped the American Ambassador's son."

Dawson, his face behind a ski-mask, as were all of their faces, nodded. "They think they're untouchable sometimes." Which was when guys like him liked to reach out and touch. The more arrogant, the more satisfying the takedown. *How I wish I had been there to take down Osama!* He had spoken to some of the SEALs involved and though they like he didn't glorify killing, they privately admitted it was one of their more satisfying ops.

Today was merely saving one idiot kid who had snuck away from the secure compound he lived on to see his Colombian girlfriend. She was the other hostage they had saved today. Lucky for the kid he was connected, which meant Delta had been sent in and US resources used to track him. He had been quickly found, an op put together, and now a couple of dozen body bags were filled, that many fewer vermin breathing the same air as he was, and the American Ambassador's son having hopefully learned to think with the right head.

His phone vibrated. "Excuse me," he said to Colonel Rodriguez, stepping away as he answered the call. "Speak."

"Hey BD, I've got some more info for you before you move on."

Dawson smiled as he climbed into an armor plated SUV that had just pulled up, Sergeant Carl "Niner" Sung behind the wheel, his Korean-American features hidden behind his still in-place ski mask. He settled in the passenger seat then motioned for them to roll. "How do you know I haven't rescued the professor already?"

"Considering you just finished your op, I'd say that would be a neat trick."

"How the hell do you know that?"

"I know everything. Now listen, BD. This situation just got a whole lot more serious, and a whole lot more dangerous."

As Kane dropped the bombshell on him, his head began to shake back and forth.

Even in the middle of the goddamned jungle those professors manage to find trouble.

"I've arranged for transport for you and your team. The details have been sent to your phone. Try to get there ASAP. It might already be too late."

"Keep the intel coming. We'll get there." He paused. "Has this been sanctioned?"

He could almost hear Kane smile. "Well, I've got no objections if that helps."

"It doesn't."

Dawson killed the call and read the file that had been sent to his phone. He activated his comm. "No rest boys, we're heading into the heart of darkness."

Barasana Village on the Rio Negro, Northern Amazon, Brazil

Tuk had been carried off the boat and placed in one of the communal huts on the suggestion of Laura. "He might feel more comfortable on dry land when he wakes up." It had made sense to Reading and his reunion with Kinti was delayed again, it initially little more than a hug and peck before explanations were given to the elders as to why, once again, they were disturbing their village.

And once again they had proven more than accommodating, inviting everyone ashore, food and drink offered as the young Tuk was carried by Reading and Acton to the lodge. By the time he was in a bed, covered, he was moaning, about to come to. Laura sat beside him, holding his hand, something Reading wasn't sure was wise.

The tosser kidnapped you just three days ago.

He of course knew exactly what Stockholm Syndrome was, and he also knew Laura well enough to know she wasn't the type to succumb. In this case he knew she was simply being herself—a caring, kindhearted woman who wanted to help people, even if they had somehow wronged her. As long as it was a wrong she could forgive. He had no doubt should someone hurt her husband or one of her students there'd be no controlling her vengeance.

She's the strongest woman I know.

He felt Kinti's hand squeeze his and he smiled at her. Tuk moaned and those gathered all leaned in. "Let's give the poor lad some space, shall we?" Reading's voice boomed, startling those who didn't know him. Fabricio translated and the crowd backed off as Reading decided he wasn't needed. He began to walk toward the other end of the communal home when Tuk began to babble. Kinti spun around, nearly breaking her grip with Reading. Her jaw dropped and she looked up at Reading, her eyes wide with excitement. She pointed at her mouth then in the direction of Tuk.

Reading's eyes narrowed as he tried to figure out what she meant, but Kinti saved him.

"I speak!"

She pointed again then rushed back to the bedside of the ailing young man, Reading following as he realized his "girlfriend" might be the solution to their problem. Their hope had been they might find someone who spoke his language, many of the tribes speaking those of neighboring tribes, it apparently common to send the girls to other tribes to meet prospective mates.

How Kinti hadn't found a mate, I'll never know.

It suddenly occurred to him that perhaps she wasn't considered attractive among her people. He had to admit most of the women he had seen did nothing for him, but a few were quite beautiful, like Kinti. Perhaps what he as a Westerner found attractive, her people didn't.

Their loss, my gain.

A twinge of regret suddenly haunted him, though. He knew this relationship would be over the moment they left, and no matter how he felt about her, he wanted her to be happy. And he knew that meant her finding a husband, marrying—or whatever it is they do—and having children. But he estimated her to be easily in her early twenties, which he assumed was quite old to not have yet married.

Maybe she is the town tramp? Bad reputation, not worthy of a mate.

He chastised himself silently, anger seething through him at the thought of imaginary people saying anything negative about her. He knew nothing about her tribe, about her ways, about *her* for that matter. He simply knew she was a loving, caring, kind girl who had given herself fully to him,

202

knowing nothing of him as well. Perhaps like he, she too merely needed comfort. Perhaps she had lost her husband years before and spent the time since alone, like he had after leaving his wife.

But now this young woman, who he cared for so deeply, so quickly, was talking rapidly back and forth with Tuk, whose eyes were lit with an excitement he hadn't yet seen at being able to communicate with someone.

And once again Kinti amazed him.

These people aren't at all what I thought. They aren't savages, they're just like us without the technology.

Reading moved closer as Kinti turned to the elder and translated. The elder's eyes opened wide, then he spoke to Fabricio, who finally translated Tuk's words to English.

"He say the Panther People have attacked his village."

Reading and Acton looked at each other. "Panther People?" asked Acton. "Is that a tribe?"

Fabricio asked the elder, who shook his head as he responded. "The Barasana haven't heard of them," translated Fabricio as the elder asked Kinti something. The conversation was slow and almost painful at times, but it eventually came out that the Panther People were a legend about a tribe of natives who had betrayed the Mother—the deity these people seemed to worship—prizing the skins of panthers, leaving the rest of the carcass to waste. The Mother exacted her revenge by sending a pack of panthers into the village, wiping them out, then rewarding them with the power of man to punish any others who might defy the laws of the Mother.

"Sounds like a children's story," observed Reading. "Scare the kids straight, sort of thing."

"That's exactly what it is," agreed Acton. "But he saw something that has him terrified and stories don't shoot guns."

Reading grunted. "Panthers are black, right?" he said, not waiting for an answer to his rhetorical question. "Special Ops sometimes wear black, and that Parker guy said his attackers were dressed in black head to toe, so…" Reading left the suggestion dangling, incomplete, waiting to see if someone would pick up on his thread.

Acton was quick to. "That makes perfect sense. Somebody in full body armor, helmet, goggles—Tuk wouldn't know what to make of him. He'd fall back to the stories he had heard growing up and these Panther People would fit." He paused a moment as the conversation continued between Kinti and Tuk. "If they attacked his village then that means they're almost definitely in Venezuela."

"Which means the Brazilians can't really help beyond going to the UN."

"Which is useless. They'll just blame it on Israel." Acton gasped as he looked behind Reading. Reading spun, not sure what to expect, but when he saw Milton in his wheelchair, holding out the satellite phone, he was ambivalent. He knew Fabricio and Milton had expressed concerns about appearing weak by not having sacrificed Milton to the great unknown, but he was certain they were far beyond that in their relationship with these people.

And the fact a smiling native was pushing him seemed to confirm it.

"Phone, Jim. It's important."

"Who?" asked Acton as he and Reading quickly exited the communal lodge.

"Kraft Dinner."

Acton's eyes narrowed for a moment then he laughed. "Dylan?" Milton nodded. "I told him to call back in five, I didn't want the natives seeing the phone working."

"Good thinking, though the guides definitely saw us talking on them. I'll head back to the boat with you. Hugh, you stay with Laura. I'll brief you as soon as I'm done."

Reading nodded and returned to the long communal sleeping chambers, joining the group still talking to Tuk. Kinti gave him a quick glance as he approached, beaming a smile that could freeze time.

And he wondered how much more of this his poor heart could take.

Acton, with the help of a couple of their new native friends, managed to push Milton to the ramp and up onto the boat before Kane called back. The entire time they struggled across the uneven ground, much of it sand, his thoughts were of how bad his friend's back must be.

Two weeks ago he would have walked over with the phone.

His pocket vibrated just as Milton positioned himself on the deck, thanking the natives with a polite smile and slight seated bow. They rushed off the boat as if afraid of it, as Acton sat down, putting the call on speaker.

"Hello?"

"Kraft Dinner here."

Acton smiled. "Hey, are we secure?"

"Yup. I understand everyone is safe?"

"Yes, we managed to find Laura and arrived back here at the village about an hour or two ago."

"I understand you have another problem."

Acton looked at Milton who whispered, "I gave him a quick update."

Acton nodded. "Yes, like Greg said, the native who kidnapped Laura came asking for help. He had been shot and we just learned he thinks the 'Panther People' attacked his village. According to our translator, they are a tribe of Panthers with human powers. Panthers being all black, we think he may have seen a special ops team attack his village."

"Makes sense and jives with some bad news I have for you."

Acton felt his chest tighten. "What bad news?"

"Your wife has two students in Manaus, a Terrence and Jennifer Mitchell?"

"Yes. Why, has something happened to them?"

"I've had a friend monitoring comm traffic in the area since your wife disappeared. Looks like her students got arrested last night along with a Bob Turnbull—"

"That's the environmentalist! He and his friend Steve Parker claimed to have been attacked by Special Ops soldiers. Parker just left a few hours ago with the Brazilian rescue team to talk to the Venezuelans upriver."

"Well, the Mitchells and Turnbull were released earlier today with all charges dropped, but never arrived at their hotel. In fact, an intercept suggests they left on a private plane heading for Venezuela a couple of hours ago."

Acton and Milton stared at each other, dumbfounded. "I can't see them doing that voluntarily," said Milton. "It makes no sense."

"No it doesn't," agreed Kane. "My contacts gave me a set of coordinates just inside the Venezuelan border where the plane disappeared from radar, presumably landing on an unknown runway. I'm sending those to your phone now."

The phone vibrated with a message and Acton quickly looked to confirm receipt. "Okay, we've got them. But what the hell can we do? We've got seven security guys with us, one who's wounded, and a bunch of natives who we shouldn't get involved. This is really a thing governments need to get involved with."

"I don't think we've got that kind of time."

Kane's statement sounded ominous, and Acton gripped the arms of his chair tight. "What do you mean?"

"I mean you've got a Special Forces team, possibly from China, in the area, killing witnesses. They are tapped into communications well enough to have known about Turnbull in Manaus. Now he made a phone call with Mitchell's satellite phone, which was obviously monitored. That means all calls on that phone would have been checked."

"You mean the calls made to here." Acton's voice was almost a whisper as he realized the implications.

"Exactly. They know about Parker, and they know he told you about what they saw. If they're willing to kidnap Turnbull and your students in broad daylight, then they're coming for you. I guarantee it."

"Then we have to get out of here now!" exclaimed Milton, turning in his chair as he surveyed their surroundings.

Acton shared his friend's feelings, but also knew that panicking had never proven useful in the past. "What do you recommend?" he asked the expert.

"I've got help on the way, off the books. They should be there before morning. I suggest you brief Leather. He's ex-SAS, he'll know exactly what to do. Now, I've got to go. I'm in the middle of an op but when this intel flashed my way I had to pass it on. Good luck, Professor."

"Okay, Dylan. Thanks for this. I'll keep you posted."

"Good bye."

The call ended and Acton quickly input the coordinates into the Google Maps app on the iPad. "It's the middle of nowhere. Nothing but trees!"

Milton nodded. "But somewhere in there, somehow, a plane landed."

"And there's something there worth killing for."

Steve Parker sat anxiously awaiting news, any news, on whether or not the Venezuelans were going to help. It had only taken an hour to reach the border, guarded merely by signs indicating the fact it was a border, and that all vessels crossing should report to customs upriver at the next town. Fortunately they'd been able to avoid that, a random boat patrol having just arrived when they did. The two boats were lashed to a dock that had been set up he assumed by both countries at some point, the Venezuelans on the northern side of the old wood structure, the Brazilians on the south.

Several radio calls had been made and apparently word was working its way up the chain of command, which in a near-communist state like Venezuela meant it needed to go almost to the top, decision making power rarely delegated to the first several layers of bureaucracy.

Parker looked at his watch.

Two hours!

It was ridiculous how long things were taking, but he had to be patient. He had to not look annoyed otherwise he might piss off the Venezuelans who were his only hope of saving his friends.

If they're alive.

He pushed the thought aside. They had to be alive. He couldn't give up hope now, now that he was so close to finally getting them help. Surely the Venezuelans would help, especially now that they knew the Brazilians were involved. He was relieved that Lt. Colombo had agreed to talk to the Venezuelans despite the fact he hadn't been able to reach Turnbull. He wasn't too worried about not having reached him, he just thanked God Turnbull was safe and working from the outside to get help. The phone belonged to the Professors' people so there could be any number of reasons why they hadn't answered.

He stood up, unable to take the waiting any more, and stretched. Lt. Colombo sat on the dock with a couple of his men and two of the Venezuelans, chatting in Spanish and smoking exchanged cigars, a flask of something being passed around as they passed the time on friendly terms. He got the distinct impression they all knew each other, and it might very

208

well be possible—he couldn't see there being too many people available to patrol this area.

Heads turned north, into Venezuela, as a boat motor made its presence known. Everyone rose, watching as a boat raced around a bend, making directly for them. He knew enough Spanish to know the Venezuelans had no idea who the new arrivals were, and he also knew enough to know that if help were that close, there wouldn't have been as much doubt expressed earlier about what they could do.

Colombo took a pair of binoculars from one of his men and peered into them. His jaw dropped, the cigar he had been enjoying falling from his mouth, onto the dock. He tossed the binoculars back and started barking orders, the Venezuelans confused for a moment, then following suit. Ropes lashed a moment ago to the dock were untied, motors fired up, and the Brazilian boat was pushed away, already turning down river, its motor in full gear.

"What's going on?" he asked, terrified to hear the answer. The binoculars were tossed to him and he looked through them to see the Venezuelan boat pulling into the middle of the river, several men lying on the prow, machineguns laid out in front of them. He heard something being announced over a speaker from the Venezuelan boat but he couldn't make it out, their own engine too loud, the distance between them growing rapidly.

He changed his angle slightly and suddenly the new arrival appeared. And he nearly shit his pants. Aboard the all black vessel were at least a dozen heavily armed men, all dressed head to toe in black.

"That's who attacked us!" he cried, pointing. "That's them!"

"We know, senhor!" cried Colombo, screaming into his radio. He slammed it on the side of the boat several times and tried again. "It's not working!"

"They must be jamming communications!" Parker had watched enough spy movies to know it was a possibility if you had the right hardware. Which meant that these guys were not only well-armed, but well-equipped with state-of-the-art equipment.

Could they be American?

The ones that had attacked his team were speaking some Chinese sounding language, definitely not English. And from what he had seen through the binoculars, these new arrivals were wearing the same gear as the team that attacked—hardly something he'd expect if they were from different countries.

Gunfire erupted from the arriving boat, tearing huge holes in the Venezuelan craft. The men on the prow returned fire, their bullets seemingly ineffective.

"We've gotta go faster!" yelled Parker, Colombo apparently shouting the same thing, the officer at the controls already giving the boat all she had.

And it wouldn't be enough.

A streak of smoke raced over the water drawing a line of death from the attacking boat toward the Venezuelans. When the rocket impacted the entire front of the boat erupted in flames sending the men on the prow spiraling through the air, screaming. The remaining Venezuelans jumped overboard as the fuel line ignited, the boat erupting into a large fireball as the wood it was constructed of splintered and flew in every direction. The men flailed in the water, surrounded by burning fuel and oil, desperately waving toward the Brazilians for help, but Colombo appeared to have no intentions of providing it.

And Parker was okay with that.

They turned a bend, losing sight of the chaos, the only evidence of it the distant pleas from the survivors, and a ball of dark black smoke smeared across the sky, slowly rising and dissipating as all evidence of the event was slowly wiped out by Mother Nature. Small arms fire suddenly was heard over the engine and within moments the cries of the survivors in the water were silenced.

Then the engine of the attacker's boat roared back to life.

"We're dead if we stay here!"

"Where would you have us go, senhor?"

It was a reasonable question, and the choices were limited. All Parker knew was that the choice of staying with the boat was the wrong one. He rushed across the deck toward the port side and jumped into the water, swimming as hard and as fast as he could, his heavy boots dragging him down, but he knew he'd need those if he were to survive. As he struggled toward the river's edge he glanced over his shoulder, taking a deep breath, and saw Colombo gripping the railing, shouting after him as the boat continued swiftly down the river, the high-pitched whine of their pursuers growing closer.

He reached the shore and looked to his left. He could hear the engine of the attacking boat nearing and suddenly it burst around the corner, banking sharply toward the Brazilians, Colombo's men opening fire. Parker sucked in a deep breath then dropped below the waterline, praying he hadn't been noticed in the split second he had been in view. The boat raced by him. He could hear the muffled sounds of weapons fire and what he thought was a splashing sound. His mind raced as to what that could be, and terror suddenly seized him as he realized it could be a crocodile coming for him.

He waved his arms and kicked his feet, pushing himself closer to the shore then finally came up for air looking downriver to see the boat he had just been on in flames, the men fighting a losing battle as the superior firepower of their foes overwhelmed them.

Parker reached for some roots and pulled himself out of the river, his waterlogged clothes slowing him down, and just as he was about to collapse onto dry ground, he heard something erupt from the water behind him then felt an incredibly sharp pain in his back. He screamed out in agony as he felt something heavy land on him, pinning him in place. Turning his head to see what had attacked him, he saw a man in a wetsuit, goggles covering most of his face, as the knife buried in his back was withdrawn then used to slice his throat open.

And as he slowly bled out, his attacker pulled his body deeper from shore and out of sight of anyone who might pass by, leaving him to be reclaimed by the forest, and the creatures that inhabited it.

Barasana Village on the Rio Negro, Northern Amazon, Brazil

"Colonel!"

Leather turned toward Acton as he rushed down the dock to the shore. He said something quietly to the two members of his team that were with him, then approached Acton. "Yes, Professor?"

"We've got trouble." Acton quickly summarized Kane's phone call and could see the concern growing on Leather's face the more he spoke.

"And he didn't give an ETA on when this 'help' would arrive?"

Acton shook his head. "Just that they *should* arrive before morning."

"And I assume this help is your Bravo Team buddies?"

"I assume so, but I don't know for sure."

Leather's lips were drawn back into thin lines as he surveyed the village, the village of over two hundred innocents who wouldn't stand a chance against modern weaponry.

Laura walked up to them, a smile on her tired face. "Tuk has gone back to sleep. Kinti was wonderful, she apparently learned his language when she was a child on a work exchange with a village near his. She thinks she might have actually met him but she's not sure, it was so long ago." She stopped, eyeing Acton and Leather, her smile disappearing. "What's wrong?"

Acton brought her up to speed, she too surveying the natives around them as he spoke. "What are we going to do?" she asked no one in particular.

"It's almost dusk now," said Leather, looking at the sky. "Leaving on the boat isn't really an option. If they're indeed coming for us, then they'll come either by boat, or on foot. If I were them I'd say boat since their home base

213

we assume is a good three day's hike from here. They could travel that distance in a fast boat in a matter of hours."

"So they could be here at any time."

"Or never." Leather waved one of his men over, a former SAS captain named Chester. He briefed him quickly then pointed upriver. "Hike fifteen minutes upriver, set up position and watch for any activity. Radio us if you see anything. If you do, do *not* engage, hoof it back here as quickly as you can. *If* we have already been engaged and captured, retreat and await the arrival of the Delta team. If they've killed us all, get the bodies home. If they've captured some of us, give them these GPS coordinates"—he showed Acton's iPad to the soldier who quickly wrote them down—"and tell them this is where we presume their base of operations is. Understood?"

"Yes, sir!"

"Now go, and good hunting!"

"Yes, sir!" Chester rushed over to the small camp set up by Leather's men and moments later reemerged from his tent fully equipped. He disappeared into the woods as the rest of the team began to approach, their curiosity piqued.

Laura lowered her voice. "What are we going to do, Colonel?"

"We could retreat by boat. That would at least in theory protect the villagers. But we also know they've killed or captured an entire village so it might *not* protect them."

"It sounds like they captured them," said Laura, relating Tuk's story about how he had seen everyone gathered in the village center, all alive except for two. "And one of the dead, a woman, it sounded to me by the way it was described that she may have been tasered. Apparently one of the Panther People as he calls them held out his hand and she shook as she hit the ground."

214

"If they're tasing people then they want them for something." Acton scratched behind his ear. "Slaves?"

Leather nodded. "That's the only thing I can think of. Whatever the Venezuelans have going on they must need labor for it, and if it's so top secret that they'll kill to prevent anyone from knowing about it, they probably want to minimize their own people which means laborers from the cities are probably out of the question. Natives however wouldn't be missed by anybody and don't need to be paid."

Laura shook her head in disbelief. "What the bloody hell do they have going on up there that they would do such a thing? It can't be illegal logging. That's not worth killing for, wiping out villages for!"

"I'm guessing it's something far more valuable than trees," agreed Leather, ending the conversation. "But now we need to make a decision. Do we leave on the boat and possibly leave the villagers to be taken as slaves or worse, or do we stay and try to defend the village, against a most likely superior force?"

"How superior?" asked Acton.

"Their boat would have to be pretty big to bring more than a dozen men, so I'm guessing squad or platoon size, ten to twenty. And we're seven, with one wounded."

"Correction. We're ten. Laura, Reading and I are all trained and can fight."

Leather grunted. "If these are truly Special Forces, especially *Chinese* Special Forces, they will be *highly* trained, and brutal. They don't fight under the same code we do. You *will* have to kill them or they *will* kill you. They're not likely to follow the Geneva Convention. This will be a fight to the total death."

Acton felt himself pale slightly as Laura grabbed his arm. He decided to let her speak first. "I don't see that we have much choice. These people have done nothing wrong. We need to protect them if we can."

Acton looked at his wife with a proud smile as he placed his hand over hers gripping his arm. He squeezed it three times.

I love you!

"Agreed," said Acton. "Our priority is saving these people. Hopefully we'll have the element of surprise."

"Very well," said Leather, his emotions well hidden leaving Acton to wonder if he agreed with the decision. "I suggest you try and get the natives to leave the village at once and take refuge as far into the forest as possible."

Laura nodded, immediately heading back to the communal lodge where the elders were. Leather turned to Acton. "You see if you can get the boat crew to help. I'm guessing they'll sail within ten minutes."

Acton allowed himself a single, wry laugh. "I wouldn't take that bet."

He watched as Leather left to brief his men, then returned to the boat to fill Milton in on what had been decided.

Decided *for* him. A near cripple now in the middle of a war zone with no safe method of escape.

I never should have invited him on this trip!

Undocumented Landing Strip, Northern Amazon, Venezuela

Terrence Mitchell stumbled from the small plane, out onto the dirt runway carved into the forest. As the plane was pushed into a small sheet-metal hangar, he watched in awe as two vehicles drove toward them from the opposite end of the runway, pulling massive camouflage netting between them. Within minutes of their arrival there would be no evidence from the air of a runway existing.

What was even more stunning however was what lay to their left. A massive strip mine, carved deep into the jungle floor. And overtop, similar, thicker, netting, covering the entire area from prying eyes. Unless someone happened to fly directly overhead, at a low altitude, they would never know it was there.

And how many planes actually fly low over this area?

Mitchell guessed few if any. He exchanged stunned glances with Jenny and Turnbull before they were shoved forward by several armed guards, all dressed like the Special Ops soldiers Turnbull had described earlier. As they entered a camouflaged building built among the trees, the windows capped with large overhangs he assumed were designed to prevent any reflection from the sun being seen from above, he heard a cry from within the mine, and some shouting. As he peered below in the fading light, he gasped.

Hundreds of natives were in the pit, toiling under the supervision of uniformed guards.

"What's going on here?" he asked, unable to restrain himself, the sight simply too horrible. "What are you people doing?"

"Nothing that should have concerned you."

The voice, near perfect English with a hint of an accent, came from behind him. He turned to see an Asian man in an impeccably maintained black suit, despite the conditions. The temperature was quickly dropping with the sun, the humidity still high, Mitchell already dripping from spots he'd rather not mention in polite company. Yet this man seemed oblivious to it all.

"Who are you?" asked Jenny, fear mixed with defiance in her voice.

He pushed up against her slightly, drawing and giving comfort from the contact.

"I am Dr. Chen. You are now my prisoners."

"You can't do this!" exclaimed Jenny. "We're British citizens! People will be looking for us!"

"That's right!" Mitchell decided he better join in to deflect any anger that might be directed at Jenny for speaking out. "We're both British. And he's American"—he motioned toward Turnbull—"you can't just abduct us like this. People know where we are!"

Chen smiled. "I can assure you, Mr. Terrence Mitchell of University College London, that no one knows where you or your wife or your unfortunate new friend are. This location is completely secure, and only a handful of people on the planet know where it is actually located. Not many more know of its existence. You, Mr. Mitchell, are quite alone right now, and I would highly suggest you cooperate, lest you find yourself laboring in the mines for the rest of your life."

Mitchell bit his lip shut, grabbing Jenny's hand and squeezing it to try and urge her to keep quiet, the secret of their connection apparently not much of one.

The room was silent.

Chen smiled. "Very good. Put them with the others," he said motioning to the guards. He pointed at Henderson. "Please follow me."

Mitchell, Jenny and Turnbull were herded in silence deeper into the facility then through what seemed to be an enclosed breezeway into another building that contained several jail cells.

The misery on the faces of those already jailed pushed the last bit of hope he had been clinging to out of him.

Dr. Chen stepped outside, the sun nearly set now, the slaves being gathered together for the long drive up the spiraling road that rimmed the ever expanding mine. It had been barely a blight on the landscape when he had first arrived to take over three years ago, and now it was a going concern, pulling out of the rock some of the rarest substances known to man.

The technology sector was dependent upon these scarce substances, names like Lanthanum, Terbium and Thulium barely known to the average consumer, yet their hybrid cars, permanent magnets and medical x-rays wouldn't function without them. And what the public didn't know, was that the world was running out of economical access to these substances. Which meant that any find, no matter where, had to be exploited until alternatives could be found. And if they couldn't be found on the surface of the planet, then companies and countries would turn to space.

Most Americans thought the Chinese space program was a vanity play like the Apollo program had been. Apollo was a race to the moon not for scientific or human endeavor, but to beat the Soviets. The Chinese were happy to leave the world thinking that their manned space program was simply a matter of national pride.

But it wasn't.

They had already put men in orbit and they had plans to build a space station of their own, a moon base, and eventual Mars base. All ahead of the Americans and now inconsequential Russians. Not to be first, of that they were quite certain they would be since America had bankrupted their economy. No, it was for the rare earth elements contained in outer space. It was the Chinese plan to be the first to be situated for mining asteroids, the moon, Mars, for the rare earth elements they contained. Not for national pride, but for world dominance in the marketplace.

The nation that controlled the supply of the building blocks of today's technologies controlled everything, from consumer electronics to advanced military weapons systems. And already China controlled 95% of the supply, with the United States so distant it might as well not be on the scoreboard.

And mines like this would allow them to secretly stockpile even more without the world knowing, to use for their own domestic needs, leaving the world prices to continue to rise as the earthbound supplies dwindled, and as China's space program marched on, unchallenged.

It made him proud to be Chinese.

Imagine what America could accomplish if it didn't waste money on the silly trappings of democracy? Of exercising its morality on the world and fighting wars for the national interest, then wasting billions upon billions in the vain attempt at nation building.

It was a sad joke.

"You were wise to bring them here," he finally said to Henderson as he stood at the edge of the pit, staring down as the lights shut off, the only remaining those of the headlights of several buses bringing the natives to the surface. They had cut a road from the Rio Negro to the mine several years ago, being careful to make certain it couldn't be seen from the air, the beginning hidden in an inlet that was invisible to anyone passing by on the river. With it they had sailed in all the heavy equipment and continued to get supplies along it, not the least of which was fuel and explosives, something any mine such as this needed in abundance.

And of course it was used to export their precious product.

"We were lucky. I had no idea who the other two were until that Mitchell guy started yelling at Turnbull. Once I heard that I realized the story had spread and they'd need to be taken in."

"Very wise thinking on your part." Chen rarely paid out compliments, especially to non-Chinese, but Henderson had proven capable, and useful. He didn't seem bound by the usual morals that he encountered in Westerners. That wasn't to say his people didn't have morals, it was merely that they thought of life differently. In the West, it was a moral dilemma on whether or not to sacrifice one life to save others, or to raze an old neighborhood to make way for the new.

In China, you sacrificed for the greater good. If someone should need to die to save others, it was done. It was insanity to leave someone with Ebola for example alive to infect others, when their immediate execution and disposal could save potentially hundreds of lives. It was also insanity to hold up progress for the sake of preserving the old. The ancient? Yes, he agreed the past should be preserved whenever possible, but China hadn't hesitated to flood entire ancient cities when building dams, because it was for the greater good.

And in the United States? Where progress was held up because some group didn't want a century old building destroyed to build a new skyscraper? It was laughable. On nearly every street in China you could find something older than the entire United States.

It was one of the many ways China prospered while the West buried itself in paperwork. The Keystone pipeline? It would have already been built. To fail to see the benefit to the United States was to be blind. China had its environmentalists, but fortunately they had no platform to speak from, so their impact was negligible. And their funding, usually from the West, quite often had them vilified by the public.

"What are you planning on doing with them?" asked Henderson.

"We'll treat the environmentalists as the useful idiots they are. Ransom them as if they were captured by some rebels, then kill them, dumping their bodies somewhere they can be found. No one will think they have any connection to us."

Environmentalists! If only Americans knew where their funding came from, they might not be so willing to listen so trustingly.

With countries like Saudi Arabia pouring tens of millions of dollars into the campaigns against Keystone and other projects that might give the United States its energy independence from the oil Sheiks of Saudi Arabia and the other eleven OPEC countries—none of which are considered true democracies—it was no wonder the debate had been muddied. Pipelines were the safest method of transport for oil—that had been proven over the past century without a doubt. Rail was far more dangerous, and truck even more so. To try and use trains and trucks to transport oil would waste an incredible amount of fuel, contributing to the very greenhouse gases that the environmentalists claimed to be against, and it would kill thousands over time if all pipelines were to be replaced.

So the alternative proposed by the truly nutty? Just don't use oil. Chen and his friends always had a good chuckle while watching CNN or the other Western broadcasters when they interviewed the truly delusional. It was even more entertaining to see that the press and the public were actually being swayed by these insane messages. Chen had no problem with America shutting off the taps from the Canadian Oil Sands. It meant more oil for China. China would continue to grow, and as it did, it would need more and more of the world's oil.

And if America preferred to buy its oil from Islamic states like Saudi Arabia and Iran, along with near-communist states like Venezuela, then so be it. It showed the hypocrisy of the entire environmentalist movement in his opinion. Clearly women were of no importance to them since these countries for the most part treated their women as second class citizens, and some like Saudi Arabia, like mere chattel. He found it quite humorous to see women's groups protesting the "tar sands" as they intentionally mislabeled it, while remaining silent on the atrocities committed against the women of the countries they seemed to prefer to buy oil from.

When was the last time a Canadian woman was stoned to death for kissing the man she loved? Or beheaded for witchcraft?

He shook his head.

Thank the ancestors I'm Chinese!

China would never be handicapped by the idea that everyone's opinion mattered. In China it was recognized that some people truly were stupid, and that their opinions weren't valuable. In the United States they could get elected. Like the Congressman who wasted everyone's time grilling an Admiral because the Congressman, elected to help lead his country, was concerned that stationing eight-thousand extra Marines on Guam might cause the island to tip over and capsize. In China he would have been 'disappeared', in the United States he was allowed to try and suggest later it was humor rather than idiocy.

The same man opposed Keystone.

Scary.

Chen resumed walking along the perimeter, his heart, beating a little quicker than it should, thoughts of the stupidity of others and the ability of his country to capitalize on it like no other, usually causing it to do so.

"And the other two? The husband and wife?"

"We'll hold them until we clean up the rest of this mess, then dispose of them with the bodies of their compatriots. Again make it look like rebels." Chen smiled. "The Amazon is a dangerous place, people die all the time."

"It might not be so easy this time, though."

Chen's eyes narrowed. "What do you mean?"

"I just found out before we arrived who this Professor Palmer is."

Chen stopped, turning to face Henderson. "She is a university professor, from London, England, is she not? That is what your report said."

"Yes, but I now have additional information."

Chen frowned. "You mean you sent me an incomplete report?"

Henderson gulped. "Well, no, I mean, yes, but I thought you would want at least the preliminaries so you could make a decision on what to do. The financial information hadn't come in yet, and I assumed you wouldn't want to delay my report for information on a university professor's credit report."

"Yet you bring it up now."

Henderson reached into his satchel, pulling out a folder. Chen waved it off. "Tell me what you missed in your initial report."

Henderson edged himself away from the precipice only feet away. "It turns out she is worth millions. Hundreds of millions."

Chen felt his chest tighten. "This changes everything."

"Yes. Perhaps we shouldn't be so quick to eliminate them?"

He prided himself on controlling his anger, and he did so even now as his arm darted out, his knuckles drilling into Henderson's esophagus, collapsing his windpipe. As Henderson doubled over, gasping for breath, Chen circled behind him, then pushed him over the edge of the pit with a single shove of his foot.

The collapsed windpipe failed to produce any sound as another idiot fell to his death, unable to fail him again.

Chen turned as footfalls quickly approached. It was one of his Venezuelan men, one who he was assured could be trusted.

"Sir, I'm sorry to interrupt," he said, keeping a noticeable distance from the edge.

"What is it?"

"It's the Lil' Jag, sir, she broken again."

Chen shook his head. One of their trucks, an old workhorse that was used to pull the runway camouflage into place was constantly breaking down. He had requested a replacement from Beijing but one had yet to arrive. It had proven so unreliable, the men had taken to calling it 'The Lil' Jag', the TOYOTA emblazoned on the tailgate painted over with 'JAGUAR'. He sighed. "Do it by hand."

"Yes, sir, we already are, I just thought you would want to know why we were delayed."

Chen smiled slightly. "A wise decision. Now go see if you can get that piece of Japanese garbage working for tomorrow's departure."

"Yes, sir!"

He watched the young man sprint away from him, casting a terrified look down the pit. Chen was pleased the execution had been witnessed by at least someone. It meant the entire camp would know before the morning, and discipline would be all the more the order of the new day.

TikTik sat huddled on some sort of seat. It felt quite soft to the touch, but the physical comfort it provided did little to make up for the mental torture she was under. She and Tuk's mother sat side-by-side, holding each other as they sat inside the belly of this beast that would carry them to the surface. She had never seen anything like it, and couldn't comprehend what it might be. When they had arrived earlier in the day at whatever hell this was, it had been the most terrifying experience of her life. No one spoke their language, no one could explain what was happening, and when they were forced inside the beast, several of the men fought back, but were beaten until they bled, then tossed aboard.

No one had fought them getting on for the journey back to the top.

They had survived being transported in the beast, its angry growl and stench almost overwhelming, but it proved to be nothing to the pain and torture that awaited them at the bottom.

Never had she worked so hard in her life.

They had moved, carried, pushed, pulled, more stone and other odd contraptions than she had thought possible, and she now ached and bled all over.

And poor Mother!

Tuk's mother slowly sobbed beside her, her body nearly broken, she far too old for the demands being placed on it.

And her heart was broken. No one had seen Tuk since the attack. In fact, TikTik was certain he hadn't returned since she had caught him staring at her, but others said after she had awoken that they had heard him scream and someone had thrown a spear at one of the Panther People.

It had bounced off.

Many assumed Tuk was weak, but she didn't. She had seen him lift things that any man would find challenging, and the fact that he had thrown the spear and it had hit its target proved to her that he might very well be an able hunter but lacked the confidence due to his failure at the skill when he was a boy.

She had been surprised how all day, while toiling, her thoughts had been dominated not by the death of her future mate Bruk, but by the missing Tuk. She couldn't stop worrying about him, wondering if he had survived, the Panther People sent after him returning empty handed according to Mother.

From what she had learned after waking during their forced march to this monstrous scar on the Mother's land, only Bruk had died. Other than Tuk, everyone was alive and uninjured, for which she thanked the Mother. As they had travelled they had all agreed that these strange creatures, wearing curious furs of black from head to toe, must be the fabled Panther People. She had heard the stories of course as a child, but never really paid them much mind when she got older, realizing that the bedtime stories were meant to scare children into obeying the laws laid out by their parents, the elders, and the Mother.

But now that they had proven true, it made her wonder about some of the other terrifying stories from her youth. *Could they be true? Could they all be true?* She simply couldn't believe it.

Yet here she sat, in the belly of a beast of transport, having seen massive beasts deep in the pit the height of several men, pushing stone and dirt around with ease, a man at the controls, a man who looked similar to her— not like these Panther People.

But these men who worked the mine with them weren't beaten, weren't yelled at. They were treated with respect, and often were the ones doing the beating and the yelling. She wondered what made them different from her except for their appearance and the odd skins they wore.

What makes them better than us?

The beast shuddered to a stop at the top of the hole, it gently growling as everyone was herded off and led into the darkness.

What more can they possibly do to us?

She trembled at what her imagination produced and instead focused on Tuk and her prayers that he was alive and safe, somewhere far from the horror they all now found themselves in.

Barasana Village on the Rio Negro, Northern Amazon, Brazil

Tuk looked to the girl named Kinti, his eyes questioning, hers filled with fear as she clung to the large spirit. She was clearly not afraid of him, and in fact he had seen many Spirit People in their village. It made him wonder if this village was blessed somehow by the Mother, or if they were merely friends.

Or maybe they are here because of you?

He had noticed when taken out of the communal lodge, much like those of his village, that the Spirit People here seemed to be either staying on their strange boat, or in their own strange buildings made of some type of super-thin skin, each shaped oddly like half a head lying on the ground. They had an appearance of being temporary, which made him think his theory of them being here because of him might actually be valid.

"What is going on?" he finally asked Kinti, she not having explained the frenetic activity around him. If he didn't know better, it looked to him like everyone was preparing to leave. Why anyone would want to do that in the middle of the night, when the jungle was at its most dangerous, was beyond him.

Then he felt himself pale, a wave of nausea sweeping over him as he realized what must be going on.

"Is it the Panther People? Are they coming?"

Kinti's head bobbed quickly and Tuk dropped to a knee, almost passing out. He felt a massive hand on his shoulder, the Spirit Man he had heard Kinti call Read-ing, and who also appeared to be her mate, was kneeling beside him, saying something in his strange tongue that seemed to be expressing concern.

"I'm okay, sorry," he replied, Kinti translating. The man smiled and helped him up, then gave Kinti a kiss as he left them, rushing over to help another Spirit Man who was on some sort of bed being carried by two other Spirit People who had darker skin than the pale faces like Lau-ra-pal-mer.

Kinti grabbed him by the arm and led him into the forest with the others, and before he knew it, the village and its large central fire were lost in the trees, even the glow disappearing within minutes. As he looked about, he couldn't believe the turn events had taken.

And it terrified him.

For not only were the villagers like him fleeing, but so were the Spirit People.

Which meant the Panther People must be far more powerful than he had feared.

And there was no hope for his family and friends.

Acton lay prone behind a large log with a clear view of the inlet, the village evacuated only minutes before. The assumption was that any attack would come from the water, and as he laid here, Laura at his side, both armed with Glocks and a healthy supply of magazines, he began to wonder if the assumption was correct. While he agreed that they most likely would travel here by boat, if he were attacking the village, he'd disembark and come through the woods.

The very woods he and his wife were hiding in.

He looked into the darkness but could see nothing. The large fire was still burning, it intentionally fed a little extra just before the natives left to hopefully give the illusion that all was well and the residents had simply retired for the night.

Leather's men were stationed at the other line of trees with a clear line of fire not only on the inlet, but the trees in which Acton was hiding. If they stood a chance, the element of surprise would be necessary. The boat was still docked, the lights dimmed as if for the night. The tents were zipped shut, a couple with lights on and fake bodies in their sleeping bags to give the illusion the visitors were all asleep or soon falling asleep.

The reality was the small encampment on the shore was a kill zone. Leather was to fire first, then all hell would break loose. If they were lucky, they just might be able to pull off their ambush.

But from Acton's experience, nothing ever went to plan.

The radio crackled. "This is Recon One. I've got a boat, dark, on the river, at least twelve, repeat twelve, hostiles onboard. At current speed, ETA five, repeat five, minutes, over."

"Roger that. Return to base when safe to do so, approach from east. Command, out."

Acton looked at Laura who was staring at the water, her weapon at the ready. He wanted to hold her, to protect her, to grab her and race into the forest with the others, but he knew they were needed. Leather's men were outnumbered, and they were only here because of them. Anyone trained was needed. Which was why Reading had put up a good fuss when Acton told him he wanted him to go with Milton.

Initially Acton wanted Milton evacuated on the boat, but when Leather explained that the boat provided no method of retreat or escape except for jumping in the water, at which point you would most likely be gunned down, Fabricio had bravely suggested that he and his men would go with the villagers to protect them.

That left Milton without a ride.

Reading had reluctantly agreed to go with the villagers. Acton knew it went against the man's natural instincts as a former soldier and current law enforcement officer to leave the fight, but he also realized there was a need to coordinate the evacuation and protect Milton and those like Kinti should they fail here at the frontline.

Acton looked at his watch, the hands glowing slightly in the firelight.

Surely it's been five minutes?

He stared out at the inlet, looking for anything, even a ripple, but there was nothing. He began to wonder if his previous fears of them coming through the forest behind them might be a more likely scenario. He listened carefully, hoping to catch any sound, even just the snapping of a twig, but heard nothing.

His heart was pounding hard now, his chest getting tight as the uncertainty of the situation began to control *him*, rather than *he* controlling the situation. He took a deep, slow breath and held it for a five count, then slowly exhaled, repeating the process several times, his heart slowly returning to a closer to normal state.

"Are you okay?" whispered Laura as she looked at him.

He nodded. "Just getting it together."

"Oh shit!" she murmured and Acton looked back at the water.

And gasped.

Laura froze up, fear taking over as a scene from a horror movie played out in front of her. Ripples approached the shoreline, too many to count, too many intersecting with others, confusing the numbers.

All she knew was it was too many.

The first broke the water, a glint off a face mask the first thing she noticed as they noiselessly walked out of the water. A second appeared, then a third and fourth. Before she knew it the count was up to twelve, exactly as Leather had predicted, and within seconds they were out of the water, a semi-circle created around the tents by half the men as the others spread out to establish a perimeter.

The first group opened fire, shredding apart the tents, the others taking knees, their weapons watching for activity from the surrounding area. She ducked as one stopped not five feet from their position and lowered a pair of night vision goggles.

Oh no!

She heard a round fire from James' gun.

Leather opened fire, someone else having beaten him to the punch from the Professors' position. He didn't blame them, he would have too if he had someone five feet from the muzzle of his gun with night vision goggles about to reveal his position.

They opened fire with their MP5's on full-auto, cutting down the unsuspecting team firing on the tents before they had a chance to respond. He wasn't worried about them, they were simply the easy targets, it was the other half dozen—scratch that five since one of the professors had dropped one—that were more his concern. Which was why two of his team of six were already picking the others off.

If it took twenty seconds he'd be surprised, but he called out the ceasefire before his second clip was empty. The two professors jumped up and waved, smiles on their faces as he activated his comm. "Stay down for Christ's sake!"

They dropped just as the second shoe did.

Chester raced as fast as he could toward the gunfire, tripping several times over roots and other obstacles. The forest was nearly completely dark, starlight and moonlight blocked by the thick canopy of leaves and branches overhead. As he neared, the gunfire dwindled and he smiled, breathing a sigh of relief as his trained ear detected the final shots were fired from an MP5, the return fire from a distinctly different weapon, a Type 79 would be his guess if they were indeed dealing with Chinese Special Forces.

He slowed up and activated his comm when he heard something behind him. He spun but it was too late, a knife plunged into his belly, the blade twisting. "Second…group…" he gasped, as the blade was withdrawn and slid across his throat.

Reading huddled with the rest of them, his Glock at the ready. As the gunfire dwindled, he prayed for his friends, frustrated at being left to wonder what was happening. The comm provided to him by Leather squawked in his ear.

"Second…group…" then a burst of static.

"Oh shit!" he muttered as a second burst of gunfire erupted from the village. "It's a bloody trap!" He turned to Kinti then looked at Fabricio. "I have to go help, they're being ambushed." He gave Kinti a peck on the forehead as she translated for Tuk. Reading sprinted back toward the village, veering to the right, making the assumption the new attack would be coming from the north. It didn't take long before he could see the glow of the village's fire pit to the left then muzzle flashes from both sides of the clearing.

Far too many muzzle flashes for him to take on alone.

He heard something behind him and felt his chest swell with pride as several dozen warriors, spears and blow darts at the ready, appeared from the forest, Tuk at their lead.

Maybe there was hope after all.

When Acton saw the first shot erupt from the forest they were hiding in he had immediately grabbed Laura and retreated east, out of the line of fire.

Several shots had chased them but the trees were thick and they had survived the initial counter attack. It made him wonder how Leather had known, his shouted warning the only thing that had saved them.

As he and Laura crawled deeper into the trees, trying to find a position to be able to fire from, the distinct sound of a Glock firing from behind the new arrival's position had him jumping to his feet, realizing there were only two possibilities. Either Chester was attacking alone from behind, or Reading was.

Either way they needed help. Shouts erupted, then cries, Reading's voice bellowing orders to what sounded like dozens of native warriors. He activated his comm to warn Leather of the new arrivals.

"Friendlies attacking from the rear of the new position, over!"

"Roger that, out."

He noticed the weapons fire from Leather's position immediately switched from full-auto to single shot.

But it didn't matter.

The enemy fire had stopped.

"Hugh, are you okay?" shouted Acton, praying to God for the umpteenth time on this trip.

"Yeah, over here!"

Acton followed the voice and the sounds of the excited natives, holding Laura's hand as he led her through the trees. After weaving in and around for several minutes, they suddenly came upon the victorious group, the bodies of their enemy already being piled in front of them, and too many of the honored dead beside them.

Reading stepped toward them, dirty but unharmed as Kinti rushed past them and into his arms, saying something over and over that Acton echoed the sentiments of.

"Thank God you're okay!"

Rio Negro, Northern Amazon, Brazil

Command Master Sergeant Burt "Big Dog" Dawson pointed ahead, holding a finger up to his mouth. The motor of a high speed boat could be heard approaching. At the helm, his second-in-command, Master Sergeant Mike "Red" Belme, cut their speed and guided them toward the shore, out of the line of sight of the boat that should come around the bend in the river any moment.

"Prepare to engage if hostile," ordered Dawson, his men taking up position from stem to stern as he raised his night vision binoculars. An impressive high speed boat banked around the corner, empty lest its pilot.

Its pilot dressed head to toe in combat gear.

"Niner, take the shot!"

A round was immediately fired from Niner's M24A2 SWS Sniper Weapon System, the unit's best shot lying prone on the prow of the boat. The pilot of the oncoming craft immediately dropped, the dead man's switch dropping the boat into idle almost immediately. Red gunned the motor, taking them back into the flow of the river, spinning the wheel to bring them alongside. Sergeants Will "Spock" Lightman and Trip "Mickey" McDonald jumped aboard, Spock securing the controls, Mickey making certain the target was dead. He gave a thumbs up.

Dawson checked the GPS. They were only a couple of miles from the coordinates provided and either this boat had just dropped off an assault team, or it was fleeing a failed assault. He was betting on the latter. If it had just dropped off a team it would have not been at full throttle, potentially giving away the element of surprise, the motor loud enough to probably be heard back at the native village these coordinates apparently represented.

He pointed to the shore. "Secure the boat there then get back onboard."

Spock nodded, gunning the engine and expertly bringing it to the shore, Mickey jumping to the ground, lashing the boat to two trees, fore and aft, as Red brought their CIA provided boat alongside. Spock and Mickey climbed back in and Dawson was about to give the order to get underway when he heard something.

"Cut the engine!"

Red complied and they all listened.

"Sounds like gunfire, BD," said Sergeant Leon "Atlas" James, his impossibly deep voice almost a whisper.

"Definitely," concurred Spock.

"Punch it, Chewie!" ordered Dawson, Red immediately firing the engine up and pointing them downriver. "Gear up, we're going in hot!" As he prepped himself along with the men, he kept a keen eye on the shore, and when done, smacked Red on the back and took over the controls, allowing his second-in-command and best friend to prep. A glow among the trees became visible and he wondered if it were a controlled campfire or a torched village, it impossible to tell, the glow seeming very large.

He spotted an inlet, almost hidden by low hanging tree branches and cut the power, bringing them along the shoreline as the gunfire, now loud, continued to fill the night. Red jumped to the shore and tied the boat to a tree, Spock doing the same aft, then all twelve Bravo Team members jumped ashore, Dawson splitting them into two teams. His six heading along the shoreline of the inlet, the other team led by Red sweeping from the south.

As they advanced, Team Two double-timing it using the noise from the gunfire as not only an indicator as to where the parties were, but cover for any noise they might make, Dawson's expert ears began to dissect the battle. He could hear three distinct weapons. MP5's, Type 79's and Glocks.

He would expect the MP5's were Leather's ex-SAS men, the Type 79's the hostiles—presumed Chinese for the moment—and the Glocks could be anybody's guess, but he was presuming the good guys or perhaps a mixture of both.

Suddenly everything went silent, then cheers erupted along with hooting reminiscent of an old John Wayne western, coming from the far side of the village they had just gained sight of. He spotted a group of half a dozen men cautiously rise from their positions as one of them spoke into his comm.

"This is Team Lead, say again?"

A transmission was repeated and the man whom Dawson recognized from the desert in Egypt, retired Lt. Colonel Cameron Leather motioned for his men to advance. They rushed the tree line, weapons at the ready, but no gunfire was heard as they disappeared into the dense forest.

Dawson activated his comm. "Bravo Two, Bravo One. Sweep right, over."

"Bravo One, Bravo Two, sweeping right, over."

Dawson and his team maintained their cover, each behind a good size tree, friendly fire still deadly. He hesitated to call the satellite phone number he had been given just in case it might give away someone's position, or worse, startle someone who might just shoot the poor bastard holding the device. They waited for several minutes for someone to emerge from the jungle, but no one did.

Clever man.

"This is Sergeant Major Dawson, United States Military! Is Colonel Leather there?" he shouted as loud as he could toward the village.

"Right behind you, Sergeant Major."

Dawson grinned as he turned to see Leather and his men approaching from the rear, guns raised but now lowering. "Good thing you identified yourselves."

Dawson smiled, pointing behind him. Leather turned and laughed, Red's team behind them. His orders to sweep right had Red's team doubling back while sweeping the jungle for another group of attackers. He had suspected that with the north side of the village apparently secure, any further attack would come from the south where they were.

And with the delay in anyone appearing, not even a celebrant, he had suspected Leather had ordered everyone to stay in the trees while they investigated the new arrivals.

"How'd you know we were here?" he asked as his men rose, exchanging greetings with the other team.

Leather motioned toward the opening of the inlet. "Saw your boat go by, assumed it was a third wave. Hoofed it around the inlet, across the opening then came up behind you."

"I had a feeling. Your celebration got too quiet."

"Yeah, well, no explaining things to the locals."

"Everything secure?"

Leather nodded. "Yes. And now I have to go retrieve my man."

Dawson frowned. "You lost one?"

"Chester. He was our spotter. It sounds like he got jumped by the second squad."

"I'm sorry to hear that. We'll secure the area so you guys can take care of business then get some well-deserved rack time."

"I appreciate that, Sergeant Major." Leather walked away with several of his men, a solemn procession if Dawson had ever seen one. He pointed at Red.

"Team Two, set up camp then get some sleep, we'll wake you in four hours." He turned to Niner. "You and Mickey bring the boat in and unload the gear, then retrieve the hostile's transport and bring it back here. Search it thoroughly. I want to know if there's any indication as to where they came from."

Niner clicked his heels. "Yes'm!" Dawson raised his MP5 and Niner ran away, magic fingers on display, Mickey in pursuit, hands up in surrender as Red's team helped Leather's salvage what they could from their camp while waiting for their gear to arrive.

"Good to see you, Sergeant Major."

Dawson turned and saw the two professors approaching. Handshakes were exchanged, a hug received from Professor Palmer. "Glad to see you two made it in one piece." Dawson motioned toward the bodies of the attacking force now being dragged into the open by the natives. "How many, you figure?"

"About two dozen," replied Acton, "in two separate forces."

"You got lucky."

Acton nodded. "Damned lucky. If it weren't for the help of the natives, I don't know if we'd have been able to hold back the second squad."

"And we have no idea how many more there are, and whether or not they're on their way."

Acton seemed to pale slightly at his assessment. "You don't think it's over?"

Dawson shook his head as he walked toward the bodies. "Two dozen men were just killed. Someone is going to want to know how. If I were them, and I had the resources available, I'd be sending a larger force to investigate. If they sent this many men, they were expecting to slaughter everyone. They are determined to keep whatever operation they have going secret."

"This is definitely not illegal loggers," said Acton as Dawson knelt and peeled back the facemask on one of the dead men. "Chinese?"

Dawson nodded. "Based on their equipment, I'd say yes. Whether or not they were Special Forces or not, I'd doubt it. A head on assault on the inlet was stupid. My guess is they're PLA or former PLA with money behind them that gives them access to some good equipment."

"So we might be dealing with the Chinese military here?"

Dawson shrugged. "Could be, but I doubt it. My guess is they wouldn't risk the international incident if they were found out. My guess is a private Chinese company, tacitly or secretly supported by the Chinese government, and most likely the Venezuelans, has set up shop just across the border, doing something seriously illegal, and seriously profitable."

"So now what do we do?" asked Laura. "If we're not safe because we know too much, how far will they go to pursue us?"

"That's the sixty-four-thousand dollar question, isn't it? My unsanctioned job, since none of us is actually here, is to get you two, the Dean and Agent Reading to safety."

"What about Terrence and Jenny? And that Turnbull guy?" Acton paused. "In fact, what about Parker? Did you encounter the Brazilian rescue team?"

Dawson shook his head. "Negative. We did find some debris that suggested at least one boat, maybe two, had been recently destroyed, but no bodies. They probably floated right by this place."

"Jesus," murmured Acton. "They'll stop at nothing."

"So what about my students and the environmentalists?" asked Laura, not letting the subject be changed.

"We have to assume they're being held at the GPS coordinates we have for the plane disappearing from radar. If we assume that's their base of operations, I can only suggest one course of action that will have the highest chance of retrieving your people, and perhaps ending this entire situation."

"What's that?" asked Acton.

"Take the fight to them."

Illegal Rare Earth Element Strip Mine, Northern Amazon, Venezuela

"I understand, comrade. And when can we expect reinforcements?"

"Tomorrow, midday. We've sent five platoons, over one hundred men. That will bring you to company strength."

Dr. Chen was pleased with the number of men being sent, but the arrival time was problematic. It was dawn now and that meant perhaps thirty-six hours before their arrival, with an unknown sized force as close as a few hours away. "We have only a platoon left, along with a platoon of Venezuelans who are nearly useless. Should whoever eliminated our men decide to attack, we may not be able to hold."

"That is your problem to deal with. Should the mine fall, we will liberate it once the reinforcements arrive." There was a pause on the other end of the secure line. "You need to hold until tomorrow. Do not fail us, Doctor."

Chen felt a shiver race up his spine. "I have no intention of failing, comrade." The line went dead, the conversation over. He hung up the phone and leaned back in his chair, looking out the window at the morning sun as it began to rise, signaling the start to another day of mining.

Only one had apparently survived the initial attack on the village, he having been left with the transport boat. He had radioed in, reporting heavy gunfire then the loss of contact with both squads. Then contact was lost with him as well.

Two dozen highly trained soldiers of the People's Liberation Army, dead.

It had been the most difficult report of his career. Not because he had any feelings for these men or their families, but because it signified failure. If he were on the other end of the line, he'd already be arranging for his successor to arrive with the new troops, and then his execution.

He wondered if his contact was as strict as he was? Chen knew that when the day came for him to occupy such a position, he wouldn't hesitate to eliminate someone like himself who had failed so miserably in dealing with this problem.

And now the question was how to deal with the problem. He didn't have the men to go on the offensive again, so he'd have to take a defensive posture until the reinforcements arrived. He found it almost impossible to believe that their opponents would stage an attack on the mine. First they'd have to find it, then get here and fight unknown numbers. It would be suicide with what their numbers were. Half a dozen private security, a few academics and an ex-police officer. He also knew the natives wouldn't come near the place, too terrified thanks to the intimidation tactics he had his teams employing.

This place was cursed, anyone who dared approach never to return.

But somehow this small ragtag group had managed to wipe out two dozen of his country's best. Obviously they had somehow known they were coming and laid a trap. That was the only way they could have beaten such overwhelming odds.

But this time things would be different. This was *his* territory. They had heavy weapons and defensive positions surrounding the mine and the command area in the event the natives did attempt an uprising. Hardened machine gun nests worked equally well against ex-Special Air Services men as they did restless natives.

And no matter what happened, victory would be assured when a company sized group of reinforcements arrived.

We just need to hold for less than 36 hours.

His only concerns now were the Western hostages. He snapped his fingers and his assistant leapt into his office.

"Get me Ling."

Terrence Mitchell sat on a cot holding Jenny. Their cell was a decent size for two inmates, bunk beds against one wall, a small sink and toilet at the rear wall, the opposing wall had a barred window to the outside with an awning that let no direct sunlight in, and the front wall was merely bars providing no privacy.

It was, though, a good size for two.

But not for the seven it now contained. Besides them and Turnbull, it also contained the other four environmentalists who had been captured the previous week. They had told of a pretty much solitary existence since then. They were fed regularly, allowed to bathe in a communal shower, and given fresh clothes and bed linens twice a week. They slept in shifts of two, which now included two more shifts due to the new arrivals.

No one dared complain.

It was the Mitchells' turn on the beds, but neither could sleep, both too frightened. Mitchell was still trembling, still not believing what was going on. "What do you think they'll do to us?"

John Tinmouth, the leader of the PAN expedition shrugged. "I don't know, but the fact they haven't put us to work in the mines like they have the natives means they have some other purpose in mind."

"What kind of mine is it?" asked Jenny. "Gold? Silver? It would have to be pretty valuable to go to all this trouble."

Tinmouth laughed. "If it were just gold or silver, nobody would bother. No, this is definitely a rare earth element mine of some type. The rarer it is, the more its worth. Why do you think rappers wear platinum now? It's worth more than gold per ounce. And that's barely classified as one of the rare elements. And it's not just the price, it's the *rare* part. Most rare earth elements were deposited here by asteroid and meteor impacts over billions of years. Once we run out, we're out. We'll need to find alternatives or go to outer space to find it. Right now it's much cheaper to find it here, environmental laws be damned." His head drooped between his knees as he pulled at his hair in frustration. "This is one of the worst I've ever seen though. And it makes me wonder how many more are out there."

As the morning light began to get brighter, the sounds of activity outside could be heard as the mine began operations for the day, the cries and wails of the terrified natives heartbreaking, tears rolling down many of the cheeks in the room.

"We have to stop this."

Heads bobbed in agreement to Mitchell's statement. "But how?" asked Tinmouth. "We're locked up in here, and the only times were allowed out they have guns trained on us."

Mitchell nodded toward the other side of the gate. "They don't seem to be watching us."

"There's a camera on the wall aimed directly at us."

Mitchell leaned forward and frowned as the camera came into view. "Didn't see that." He looked about. "Let's assume the camera wasn't there. What would—what could—we do to get ourselves out?"

"Pick the lock?" suggested Jenny.

"Dig our way out?" suggested another man named Lincoln.

Jenny pointed to the window. "File away the bars?"

Somebody chuckled from the other side of the cell door, the sound of slowly clapping hands as they approached reverberating through their cell. Mitchell felt Jenny grip his arm tighter as his own heart began to race.

"Very amusing," said a voice before the man it belonged to came into view. He was Chinese, very white, and as tall as any of the men in the room. His Asian features seemed muted somehow, and he had no trace of an accent.

Could he be half-Caucasian?

245

"My name is Steven Ling. For those of you wondering, yes, I am half-American—on my mother's side. But when the country of my grandparents needed my help, I was happy to oblige. You see, my old home, the United States, frowned upon my particular talent. But my new home, China, the home of my ancestors, does not let little things like international law and the Geneva Convention get in the way of what is best for the people."

Mitchell gulped. *He must be some sort of torturer!* He resisted the urge to look at Jenny, not wanting to give any indication of a bond between them that could be used against him. Then again, the circulation-killing grip she had on his left arm was probably giving away their connection.

And they seemed to know exactly who they were, regardless.

Probably courtesy of the Chinese CIA, whatever they're called.

"And today, what's best for the people of China is to make this little mess you've created, go away. I will not suggest you cooperate. I actually encourage you not to, otherwise my job is too easy, and I love my job, but only when it's difficult.

"Please don't cooperate, please resist. You will make my day." Half a smile crept on his face. He pointed to Turnbull. "Mr. Robert Turnbull. Please step forward. You will be first."

Turnbull didn't budge, his skin so pale he appeared as if he might faint. Ling motioned to the camera and the cell unlocked.

That settles the question of whether or not it works.

Ling stepped inside, no apparent concerns over the fact he was outnumbered seven to one. He stopped in front of Turnbull, Ling's boots so shiny they reflected the pale grayness of the terrified prisoner.

"You will rise."

The voice wasn't any louder than normal, but it was firm. It wasn't a request, nor a barked order. It was merely a statement of fact. Turnbull shifted slightly, then rose, his knees a little wobbly. Jenny reached up and steadied him with a hand on his back. It startled the poor bastard as he trembled more noticeably.

"Very good. Follow me without delay."

Ling exited the cell then turned right. Turnbull followed as if in a trance, not looking at anyone until he turned and made eye contact with Mitchell. Mitchell felt himself waver, never having seen true fear before in his life. It was unlike anything he had ever pictured, Hollywood never having done it justice before.

"Have a seat."

"Oh no!" whispered Jenny as she buried her head in Mitchell's chest. Mitchell turned away from the cell door as it closed, its open iron bars doing nothing to block the sounds from the very next cell. And Mitchell knew they would be forced to listen to whatever was done to their poor companion.

"We shall now begin."

A blood curdling scream erupted from around the corner. Without being able to see what was causing Turnbull so much pain, Mitchell's imagination went wild, conjuring the most horrifying images the movies had ever suggested to him one human may be capable of doing to another.

But he knew it must be far worse, as he had never heard such a scream of terror or pain from any living creature before.

And he started to cry, as they all did, realizing one of them would be next.

TikTik held Tuk's Mother tight as they all looked up at the strange lodges where their captors seemed to dwell. A scream of horror and pain, so intense it was released unashamedly, had them all scared, those in the belly of the beast with her looking at each other, wondering, she knew, if that might be their fate too some day. She looked at Mother but there was nothing there, no fear, no life. Just resignation that her life was over. TikTik placed a gentle kiss on Mother's cheek, patting the other, then held her even tighter, trying to provide some sense of humanity in the horrifying reality they now found themselves in.

Their night had been thankfully uneventful, though there had been little joy. They were kept behind a strange wall made of incredibly strong spider webbing. They had been shown how to get water from a magical hollowed out log where you turned a round knot on it and water came out. Turn the knot the other way, the water stopped. There were several of them at one end of where they were being held. Food had been waiting for them, strange looking food she had never experienced before, but it was warm and filling, and she was grateful. They each had what to her felt like the most comfortable bed she had ever slept on, though their quarters were more cramped than the lodge, and cover from the elements was provided by a strange large, shiny thin blanket that covered the entire area overtop the spider webbing.

Once inside, they had been left alone and were free to move around. The latrine facilities were extremely odd, some sort of raised hole that you sat on. One of the other women, who didn't even speak a language she understood, had demonstrated for her. It had been odd but not having to burry your waste afterward quite nice.

She had taken care of Mother, getting her food and water, then shown her too how to use the latrine, then those of Tuk's tribe were shown an area of beds that the others indicated were for them.

The most wondrous part of the experience however had been the next morning when they were shown to an area with a hard floor and a long log that stretched from one end to the other that could produce rain. Everyone was given this strange white ball and as she watched, she was amazed to see it produced a cleaning product like she was able to make with some effort from some of the plants from the forest, but nothing like this.

It smelled incredible.

She found it the first pleasurable experience since she had arrived, bathing herself like she never had before, but as she did, her tribe's colors washed away, leaving her skin completely bare, her face devoid of the markings identifying her family.

It had devastated her when it appeared there would be no way for her to reapply the mud mixture used to give her the reddish tint she was so used to seeing. And seeing all the others, their naked bodies truly naked, was something she hadn't experienced since she was a child playing in the river, before the colorings were applied after the Womanhood Ceremony.

The final humiliation, as she now thought of it, was to be given coverings like their captors wore. Strange skins that covered them from their necks to their ankles, then a pair of skins with hard bottoms for their feet. After her short stint in the rocks yesterday without these coverings, she realized it might just be a good thing, the rocks sharp, many of her people already complaining of cut feet.

But why today, and not yesterday? Why let us injure ourselves then?

Perhaps it was to show them why they needed these coverings.

An act of kindness?

That she doubted. She could tell by the way they were treated that their captors had no respect for them though intended to keep them strong and healthy if possible. They obviously wanted them to work for them, to slave away among their rocks.

For a *very* long time.

Her chest tightened and she placed her head on Mother's shoulder and began to cry quietly, tears rolling down her bare cheeks. She felt Mother's hand touch her face, her thumb gently wiping away the tears.

249

"Don't worry, little one. My son will save us."

Oh, if only that were true!

Barasana Village on the Rio Negro, Northern Amazon, Brazil

"You take care of yourself now," Acton said, shaking Milton's hand. He knew his friend was in pain when he didn't get out of his chair for their customary thumping hug. "Take it easy and get that back looked at. Laura has arranged for her plane to take you home as soon as you arrive."

Milton shook his head. "No, that's a waste of money. I can wait for the rest of you."

Acton pointed his finger at him. "Don't be stupid. You know you've overextended yourself. Get your ass on that plane, get home, and rest up. We'll see you as soon as we're done here. Understood?"

Milton shook his head, a slight smile breaking out. "Yes, mom."

"Good. Now hug Daddy Laura then get your ass home."

Laura bent down and gave Milton a hug and a kiss, then while still bent over, said, "Take the plane right away. It barely costs me any more whether it's in the air or on the runway waiting. You need to take care of yourself so you can come to the next World Cup."

Milton nodded and with a wry grin, said, "Not exactly the incentive to get better I was looking for, but I'll take it."

They laughed and disembarked as the boat's mooring lines were freed. It had been decided that it was safe now for the boat to travel back to Manaus now that they knew their enemy was based in the opposite direction. More help was on the way, and had been since yesterday when contact was lost with Colombo's boat, so it was hoped they might meet-up by tomorrow morning. Acton was just happy to get Milton heading back toward civilization where he could tend to his back and not have to be worried about him being helplessly shot during an attack.

251

Leather's man, Trent, would also be making the journey back. He wasn't a hundred percent yet and Leather wanted him to act as security for Milton should anything untoward happen and to file reports with the appropriate authorities should they not return.

He was also accompanying Chester's remains.

Acton had left Reading to suggest Laura go with them then smiled as she shot the idea down quite abruptly. Reading himself hadn't offered to leave, he fully intending to stay with his friends and, Acton was sure, happy to extend his time with Kinti, they spending the night together on the boat, enough noise made that he had turned bright red this morning as the Bravo Team gave him fist bumps and high fives until he finally told them to 'bugger off!'.

Which merely elicited a huge round of laughter.

The Juliana pulled out of the inlet, everyone waving, and as soon as it was out of sight the loading of the two remaining boats resumed. Leather's team along with Acton, Laura and Reading would take the captured boat, the Delta Team the boat they had arrived in. The villagers were moving inland to join several other villages until they received word it would be safe to return. Tuk and a group of the warriors were determined to help, and with Kinti translating it had been determined he intended to return to his village then track the enemy back to wherever they had taken his family.

There was room on the boats for some of the warriors but they had all refused, the very thought terrifying them, which Acton thought was probably for the best. After all, they were going up against guns and body armor and all they had were spears and darts.

By the time they reached their destination Acton was hoping everything would be long settled.

He climbed aboard with Laura then watched out of the corner of his eye as Reading gave Kinti a long kiss goodbye, then with an obviously heavy heart, joined the others as she waved, calling his name the entire time the boat left the inlet.

Acton joined his friend at the rear of the boat as he stared back toward the inlet. "You okay?" he asked quietly.

Reading grunted. "Yeah, I guess. I just hope that Tuk and his group don't make it before we've mopped up this operation. I'd hate to see anything happen to her."

"I hear ya. This has been one hell of a vacation."

Reading sighed. "Best damned one I've ever had."

Acton chuckled. "Not the characterization I would have chosen, but from your perspective, I'd wholeheartedly agree. She's a beautiful woman."

"Smart too! She came up with the idea for making the rope glow so Leather's team could see it. She speaks multiple languages. Great cook."

"She'll make someone a great mate someday."

"Yeah, somebody. Somebody other than me."

"You had to know going in there never was a future."

"Oh, I knew that. I just didn't know how quickly and how strongly these damned feelings would develop."

"It's called love, my friend, and there's no explaining it. Look at Laura and me. We were in love after less than twenty-four hours together, and most of that was under heavy fire. We didn't get to spend hardly any alone time like you and Kinti. After several days together, I couldn't imagine being without her."

"You're not helping."

Acton laughed. "No, I guess not. My point is that there's nothing wrong with feeling the way you do about her. But when we leave, it's going to be one of the most necessary and hardest things you've ever done in your life. There's no way she can come with us."

"I know." He sucked in a deep breath. "Let's go kill some bad guys so I can feel better."

Acton slapped him on the back as they turned to join the others. On the open water they were making excellent time north and in less than two hours were at the coordinates marked on a map Niner had found when he searched the captured boat.

As they approached the coordinates Dawson, from the helm of the lead boat, motioned for both boats to go to the shore south of the position marked on the map. Acton held onto the rail with one hand, the other around Laura's waist as the boat banked sharply, the engines cut. The two boats were quickly lashed to the shore and everyone disembarked in silence, heading inland about a hundred feet then turning north, Bravo Team taking point while Leather's team, codenamed Charlie Team for the mission, covered their rear while protecting the three civilians.

As they advanced, Acton began to see evidence of modern man among the trees, pointing it out silently to the others. Discarded cans, water bottles, wrappers. All signs of the wasteful modern ways.

Would it kill you to put your garbage in your pack and dispose of it later?

One good thing about the garbage however was that it left little doubt they were getting close to whatever it was they were looking for. Dawson froze as clenched fists shot up. Dawson was pointing at his eyes then ahead. He motioned for everyone to take a knee as he and Niner advanced.

The jungle seemed quiet, as if whatever had lived here had been scared away at some point, the stench of fear keeping away new arrivals. Acton could feel his heart slamming against his chest as they waited, the breath held in his chest beginning to burn.

He exhaled, slowly, making it worse as he then needed half a dozen breaths to get back to normal, all sounding extremely loud to him.

No one seemed to notice.

The rest of Bravo Team suddenly rose, advancing, Leather touching his earpiece.

"Charlie Team hold," he whispered.

Acton looked down at the Glock 22 in his hand, his trigger finger resting along the barrel as he prepped himself for whatever lay ahead. He heard Laura breathing to his left, slightly faster than normal, Reading to his right, his breathing heavier though from exertion rather than fear. They had all been fairly sedentary the past month, though Acton and Laura had hit the treadmill daily during the World Cup. Reading had said a vacation meant a vacation from everything, including the treadmill. A month later he was complaining about the ten pounds he had gained and the fact he was winded after a flight of stairs.

Now he was paying the price.

Acton knew Reading hated being a burden, and when he wasn't able to keep up with Acton when chasing after Laura, Acton knew the man had been embarrassed and humiliated. He had no doubt the gym was in Reading's future as soon as he was back home in London.

If I know him he'll shape up after this.

"All clear," said Leather, everyone rising and walking toward the Bravo Team position. They still walked cautiously, all examining the ground and trees overhead. As they pushed through some brush Laura gasped.

A large dirt road, hidden from above by the tree canopy, extended from the river to as far as the eye could see to the east, a near perfectly straight line. It was wide enough for two good sized trucks to pass each other, albeit carefully, and seemed well maintained, the foliage not allowed to creep back.

"How would they have made this?" asked Reading.

"Some sort of Jungle Cutter like from Indiana Jones Four," replied Acton. "That was based on a T-55 tank and fictional but the basic premise is sound. They basically have large spinning saws that cut at an angle so anything they cut drops off to the sides. Look." He pointed to the previously unnoticed logs at near 45 degree angles along the path the road took. "A secondary set of blades on the same vehicle saws off any remaining stumps low enough so vehicles can pass without getting caught on them, an integrated wood chipper breaks down the stumps and spits it out to the side"—he pointed at the obvious debris—"then a final vehicle comes along with a grinding bit that tears apart the remainder of the stumps at ground level to make the ride smoother. They then fill in the holes with concrete and gravel where they find it too rough to drive on. Unfortunately human beings became far too efficient at knocking out roads in a hurry during the mid-twentieth century."

Reading frowned. "It looks like the techniques haven't been lost to time."

Dawson strode over to Leather's team surrounding the civilians. He pointed back toward the river. "There's a landing there. I'd like to leave one of your men behind as a lookout, just in case we get some unwelcome guests."

Leather turned to his team, pointing at one of his men. "Donny, you're up."

Another man stepped forward. "Sir, if you don't mind, perhaps I better take it. I twisted my ankle back there a bit and it's pretty tender."

Leather nodded. "Okay, Potts, you're up. If you see anything, radio it in and get your ass out of there. Make your way back to where the boats are moored and if you're able to, take one and get back to civilization. I don't want you trying to reach us on that ankle."

"Yes, sir!"

Potts headed for the shore, Dawson looking at the GPS. "We've got about three hours to those coordinates at a good pace. Let's move while we've got daylight to burn." He turned back to his team. "Niner, Mickey, you're on point. Get about a mile ahead and maintain radio contact."

"Roger that, BD." Niner and Mickey took off at a good jog, carefully watching the sides of the road for any signs of the enemy, while everyone else got in a staggered column with Acton, Laura and Reading in the middle. The pace was brisk but reasonable, the conversation light, and Acton soon forgot they were on their way to possibly die when Dawson held up his fist and everyone dropped to a knee, turning toward the jungle on either side. Acton shoved the earpiece that had fallen out unnoticed back into place.

"Bravo Leader, Bravo One-One. We've spotted some sort of hardened checkpoint about half a klick ahead, over."

Dawson's voice came over the earpiece, replying to Niner's report. "Bravo One-One, Bravo Leader. Any sign of activity, over?"

"Negative Bravo Leader. We're in the bush, approaching the position. It appears…no, wait. I've got eyes on two hostiles. Doesn't look like they've spotted us, over."

"Do you have a clear shot on both targets, over?"

"Affirmative, Bravo Leader. Permission to engage, over?"

"Permission granted. Take out the targets, over."

Two shots rang out from down the road, and only two shots.

"Targets eliminated, outpost secure. They've got a radio here, BD. They're probably supposed to check in at some point, over."

"Hold your position until we arrive, out."

Dawson looked at Leather. "I think we've lost our element of surprise."

Leather grimaced then shrugged. "Story of our lives?"

Dawson chuckled. "Too true." He circled his hand over his head. "Double-time!"

Acton started to jog with the others, Laura in front of him, Reading behind, muttering to himself.

"I should've gone with Greg, the lucky bastard."

Tuk looked over his shoulder and was impressed to see Kinti right beside him, the warriors of her tribe, along with several others, behind them. When they had delivered the women, children and elders to a neighboring village and told them of what was happening, the warriors there had been enraged as well and were determined to join them. Word was spreading as messengers were sent throughout the forest and at each point where they would rest, they were joined by an ever growing group of men determined to help the Spirit People who were going to fight on their behalf to free their imprisoned neighbors.

Tuk had nearly cried when the first village's warriors had asked to join them. To think that complete strangers who had never even heard of his tribe would be willing to fight the Panther People, who he knew now were merely Spirit People in strange coverings, warmed his heart and gave him hope. He just prayed that his family and friends were still alive.

He also knew, from Kinti, that the Spirit People weren't spirits, but men just like him from very far away. They spoke different languages than the tribes, they had different ways and different tools, but underneath their coverings they were human just like he was, therefore just as vulnerable.

Which meant they could die in their attempt to help his village.

"We should rest here," he said, noticing Kinti beginning to tire. "It will give others time to join us."

Kinti nodded as they came to a halt, calling out the order in the languages she knew, it being spread amongst the hundreds now with them. Food and water was broken out, and the ragtag army sat in silence, catching their breaths as they had been running at a near sprint, some of them, like

Tuk and Kinti's people, for most of the day. The sun was getting low in the horizon, but Tuk was determined to travel through the night if necessary. They were making excellent time and should be at TikTik's village not too long after nightfall where they could rest for a few hours then continue to his village where they would track the Panther People at the crack of dawn.

Somebody said something and Tuk looked up, not understanding the words. He rose as an imposing warrior approached with several others from his tribe, their markings not familiar. Kinti greeted them in several languages, their leader stopping her at her third attempt, clearly understanding. She translated for Tuk.

"Is *this* your leader?" Even without the translation Tuk could hear the shock in the man's voice that someone as pathetic and weak as he could be leading such a group. And in his mind, he *wasn't* the leader. He had said he was going to go to his village and track the Panther People, then the others decided to join him. Everyone here he felt was merely following him through the forest, not following *him*.

Kinti nodded. "Yes." That word he at least understood without translating. And it shocked him. Others from her tribe gathered, all standing behind Tuk, as if supporting him. One of their warriors, Skip, spoke to the new warrior and Kinti translated for Tuk.

"Yes, he is our leader."

"*This*, this small, puny man?"

"His name is Tuk, and you would do well to show some respect," said Skip, stepping forward and baring his teeth slightly as he gave a single shake of his spear. He held out his free hand, palm open toward Tuk. "This mighty warrior survived an attack by the Panther People, even managing to nearly pierce the skin of one with a perfectly thrown spear. He then was able to escape them, despite their magic, and find us!"

Skip was telling a story now, a story that might well become legend, and Tuk could tell by the way Skip was holding himself, his voice raised for all to hear, that Tuk's life would never be the same from this moment forward. Even if the tale being spun was exaggerated, he could feel his own chest swell as the words poured from this man's mouth, a man who didn't know him until yesterday, and a man who was now at his side, willing to die to help his family and friends, people who he had never even heard of before.

"*This* mighty warrior, singlehandedly battled a *female* yakumama snake…and won!"

Cheers erupted around them and spears were shaken in the air as the hundreds gathered, most hearing the stories for the first time, were emboldened with the courage of their new leader. Tuk muttered to Kinti about Lau-ra being of great help but she merely squeezed his hand, signaling silence.

"And for those who doubt this deed, I saw the carcass with my own eyes! Opened down the middle, its head cut off! Not only did he kill the beast himself, he then fed on it, sharing his kill with one of the Spirit People!"

More cheers, even the new arrivals beginning to be infected.

"And if this is not enough proof of his courage as a warrior, three days ago he captured and won the heart of a Spirit Woman, and took her to be his mate, then when he discovered his village had been destroyed, his people taken by the Panther People, he asked her people's help, and they granted it!"

Skip had to wait for the cheers to die, the crowd enraptured at the tale of bravery of this small warrior, Skip's storytelling abilities even having Tuk convinced in the truth of the tale, at times forgetting it was his own exploits that were being embellished.

"Right now, the Spirit People, who many of us have feared, and now know, thanks to the mighty Tuk, are human just like us, but from a land so far away they know not our ways, even right now, they are going into battle to help us. To help stop those who would destroy our villages, who would kill the great forest the Mother has provided us, who would enslave our people! Even right now they are going to fight, because this"—he grabbed Tuk's hand and shoved it in the air—"this great warrior demanded it!"

Tuk fought back the tears of pride he now felt, every fiber of his being wishing his mother and father could see him now, the elders who always insulted him, Pol and TikTik who could see the faith they had in him hadn't been misplaced. But he knew tears right now would be the wrong thing to show. Strength was what was needed.

And a show of contrition.

He stepped toward the mighty warrior, who he knew with one swipe of his hand could probably fell him with ease, and extended both hands as a sign of friendship, Kinti at his side to translate.

"I would be honored if the mighty warriors of your tribe would join us in our fight, a fight that we partake in not just for ourselves and our loved ones, but for the great Mother Herself!"

His wrists were clasped firmly by the other warrior, his face grim, but impressed. And as he announced his decision, Kinti translating for him, he felt another surge of ecstasy spread through his body.

"I and my warriors are honored to fight for the great Mother and Her children. And we are equally honored to fight alongside such a great warrior as stands before me know. Let any man who would ever doubt him, answer to me!"

The cheers were deafening as Tuk suddenly found himself embraced by the massive man, he returning it as strongly as he could. More greetings were exchanged with the new arrivals, and with the pleasantries, if one could call them that, over, Tuk gave the word to move on.

And by the time it spread, nearly a thousand warriors were behind him, all following the great Tuk.

Illegal Rare Earth Element Strip Mine, Northern Amazon, Venezuela

Jenny gasped as the gate to their cell opened and two men dragged the barely conscious body of Bob Turnbull inside. They dropped him on the floor, Mitchell and one of the others leaping forward to catch him before he fell. They carried him to the bed, laying him down, Jenny propping his head up with a pillow as he moaned in agony.

"Water!" ordered Jenny, one of the other environmentalists jumping at the sink to fulfill her orders. Water was quickly brought, repeatedly, there only one small tin cup, and a pillowcase was repurposed as a cloth to begin cleaning his body.

"They barely touched his face," observed Mitchell. "It sounded like he took quite a beating over there, I'm surprised."

Jenny unbuttoned Turnbull's shirt and gasped as his chest and stomach were revealed to be pockmarked with angry bruises and welts, as if he had been beaten mercilessly, his skin pinched and twisted repeatedly with some sort of tool for the past several hours. The sight almost made Mitchell vomit as he realized now the cause of the poor man's screams they had been subjected to from the next room, the only words his begging for his life, then eventually, begging for them to kill him.

Anything to end the pain.

All of the hell Turnbull had put them through was forgiven as Mitchell watched his wife try to clean up the man, to provide him some modicum of comfort, his pain still excruciating as he writhed on the cot. Jenny simply kept applying the cool cloth to his face and neck, careful not to touch any of his wounds, instead simply cooing softly to him, he eventually drifting into a restless sleep.

The metal gates of their cell suddenly slammed open, waking Turnbull who saw Steven Ling standing there again with a smile. He began to cry, curling into a ball, turning toward the wall, away from his torturer. But it wasn't to matter.

Ling pointed at Mitchell.

"Come with me."

Mitchell felt his vision narrow into a dark tunnel, his knees giving out as he collapsed to the floor. His world became blurs and echoes, nothing distinct, until his mind suddenly forced him back to reality, a warning being sent by his brain that if he didn't come to, he would have no opportunity to defend himself against what was about to happen.

As he snapped back to reality he felt his arms being gripped tightly, his feet dragging on the ground, then his surroundings suddenly came into focus and he realized it was too late—he was already out of his cell, Jenny's voice screaming for them to let him go, no one else saying anything.

They sat him in a chair, clamped his wrists to the arms, his ankles to the legs. His shirt was ripped open and he prepared himself for the first blow, his eyes wincing, his head turning away.

"I think we'll try something different."

He opened his eyes and gasped as Ling motioned toward a nearby table upon which sat among other things a car battery and jumper cables, along with some sort of crude device that looked like it came out of the fifties, knobs and dials on its surface.

What the hell are they going to do with that?

One of the men who had carried him in clamped the jumper cables to Mitchell's nipples and he cried out in pain.

A waste of energy on his part.

For the true pain was only about to begin.

Dawson lay prone on his stomach, just within the tree line, Niner at his side. They had arrived about an hour ago and after scouting the area had determined they were facing about forty hostiles, half well-disciplined Chinese, the other half undisciplined Venezuelans. And they had confirmed it wasn't a logging operation at all, but some sort of massive strip mine.

The mine's perimeter appeared relatively unguarded, theft and safety not a concern. It was the central compound that was well guarded by the Chinese, with five machine gun nests at the edge of the cleared area, camouflage netting extending over the entire zone, hiding it from overhead.

It was incredible.

The mine was huge, at least compared to anything he had seen in person. It was deep, hundreds of feet, a long, winding road corkscrewing down into the pit. Within they could hear heavy vehicles and humans toiling away miserably, along with the shouts of the mostly Venezuelans working the slaves.

The airstrip was just north of them, it too covered, a hangar with a single plane the only structure. Leather's men had cleared it then set up position surrounding the mine, their orders to protect the native prisoners should it become necessary.

The final confirmation came in over his comm, the last team of two in position, each machine gun nest covered. If they were going to succeed, surprise was the key. The sun was just starting to set, it low in the horizon, the trees casting long shadows, the netting obstructing the sun even more.

"Bravo Team, Bravo One. Execute in three, two, one, execute!"

His voice was barely a whisper, he too close to his targets to risk them hearing him give the orders that would mean their deaths. As he and Niner both rose to a knee, taking aim with their suppressed Glocks, their two targets, sitting comfortably in their dugout position stopped their idle chatter and jumped for the machinegun mounted behind the sandbags.

Dawson squeezed the trigger, as did Niner, both targets down in heaps, dead. "Team One clear, over," he reported as he and Niner crawled on their bellies toward the position so they wouldn't be seen.

"Team Four clear, over," reported Spock, followed by reports from each of the other teams. Dawson and Niner poured themselves into their enemy's foxhole, confirming the kills then moving the bodies out of the way.

Screams of agony erupted from the compound, someone begging for mercy as he wailed at the top of his lungs. Dawson surveyed the scene and was about to signal the next phase when trouble erupted from the trees, a patrol they hadn't known about charging Red's position from behind, Red and Mickey momentarily distracted by the sounds of torture.

He activated his comm.

"Red, check your six!"

Leather was positioned near the road leading into the mine, the compound about fifty yards away, the wails of the poor bastard being tortured sending shivers up and down his spine. For he recognized the voice.

Terrence Mitchell.

Suddenly four men charged out of the forest, Venezuelan uniforms barely visible, rushing one of the Delta positions. As they were about to open fire, they began to shout a warning to the camp.

Leather jumped to his feet and squeezed off four rounds from his MP5, taking down all four men, silencing their warning, but too late. His men advanced from their positions, covering the short distance to the pit of the mine, aiming their weapons into the depths, the MP5's effective firing range of 200 meters more than enough to reach the bottom with accuracy should it become necessary.

266

As he hit the deck, taking aim into the pit, he saw the Delta Operators move in on the central compound just as the entire area was flooded with light.

So much for the element of surprise.

Dr. Chen hit the alarm, the shots heard outside clearly not from his men's weapons, his own training while in the People's Liberation Army enough to familiarize himself with the sound of an MP5. He entered a code into his computer that immediately began to wipe the entire network, there no paperwork here that needed destroying. He stepped out of his office as several of his men rushed by, weapons ready, the blood curdling screams of one of their prisoners suddenly stopping.

He grabbed one of the Venezuelans as they rushed by. "Kill the prisoners."

The man snapped a salute then exited the building, shouting for some of the other men to help him. Chen unlocked a door revealing a set of stairs descending into darkness. The lights automatically came on as he entered the stairwell, closing the door behind him. Without rushing, he calmly descended the stairs then began his escape through the secret passage that would open several hundred meters into the forest, where he'd be able to await the arrival of the reinforcements that would be here in less than 24 hours.

Any victory you achieve here today will be short lived.

Acton, Laura and Reading were at a safe distance down the road when the all clear on the machine gun nests had been announced and barely seconds later gunfire had erupted, then an alarm. Instinct had Acton on his feet, sprinting toward the battle, his Glock at the ready, spare body armor brought by Bravo Team protecting much of his body.

As he came around the bend, Laura and a cursing Reading a close distance behind him, he saw the compound to the right, the Bravo Team advancing rapidly, Leather's team already in position around the pit. Acton noticed the rear of the breezeway connected buildings wasn't covered yet and decided to take up position near the north side while the Bravo Team members swept around the south side toward the rear.

"Kill the prisoners!" somebody yelled in Spanish, running into the building next to him.

"Christ!" he exclaimed, sprinting toward the door closest him. "They're going to kill the prisoners!"

Mitchell was almost deaf to his own screams, and when the electricity was shut off, his body, every muscle and fiber tensed, suddenly relaxed, the relief almost overwhelming, causing adrenaline to rush through his system that set off a panic attack. As his eyes focused he saw shapes moving around him, then suddenly a siren sounded. Footfalls faded into the distance and as his eyes focused, he found he was alone, still strapped to his chair.

With the jumper cables still attached to his nipples.

More footfalls and his heart sank as he realized his torture was about to resume. Several sets of the footfalls faded to the left, suggesting some of those running had stopped in front of Jenny's cell, then suddenly one man appeared in front of him wearing a green army uniform, distinctly Hispanic features rather than Chinese.

The man raised his weapon to fire and Mitchell squeezed his eyes shut, yelling, "I love you, Jenny!"

"Terrence!"

Shots cracked in the hallway and he waited for the pain, but none came, instead all he could hear were the screams from the next cell. He opened his eyes, straining against the clasps holding him in place as he cried out for Jenny. "You bastards! I'll kill you all! I'll kill you all!" he cried, hope drained from him completely.

That was when he noticed the soldier who was about to shoot him was lying in a heap on the floor and Professor Acton was rushing by, his weapon raised, Special Agent Reading right behind him.

Then a sight almost as beautiful as his wife on their wedding day appeared in the door, crying his name.

"Terrence!"

Professor Laura Palmer rushed into his cell and dropped to her knees, surveying him without touching, her eyes filled with tears. "You poor dear," she whispered over and over as she carefully removed the jumper cables, tossing them aside. As she unscrewed the clasps Jenny burst into the room, her arms extended in front of her the entire way as she raced toward him, grabbing him and hugging him as hard as she could, and with his first hand freed, he returned the hug, thanking God and the Professors for having saved his beloved wife.

The gunfire was sporadic and controlled, the vast majority of resistance eliminated during the initial attack on the machine gun nests. They were clearly shorthanded, the two squads Leather's team had eliminated the night before critical to their overall security.

They probably never expected to actually have to defend against anybody but natives with spears.

As he cleared another room in the complex with Niner at his side, more all clears were announced over his comm, and within minutes the entire complex was secured.

"Bravo Team Two, Bravo One. Begin room by room search for intel. Team One, secure the exterior, over."

Team Two Leader, Red, acknowledged the orders as Dawson exited the compound, sending two men to cover the road and the landing strip, two at the rear of the compound to take over machine gun emplacements, then he and Niner headed for the pit.

Leather's men suddenly began to take fire, several rolling back from their positions, the others returning fire.

TikTik grabbed Mother and pulled her toward the massive rock wall, hiding behind a pile of stone as the others scattered in every direction, their guards, these co-conspirators of the Panther People, aiming their spears at the top of the pit they were in, the oddly shaped sticks making loud sounds unlike anything she had ever heard. She saw small puffs of smoke erupt from the rock face overhead then noticed there were men with their own odd spears, pointing them down into the pit.

The odd loud cracking or snapping sounds echoed through the pit, her fellow prisoners screaming in terror as some of the guards turned their strange spears and began pointing at those fleeing. One closest to her suddenly dropped to the ground, blood rushing from his chest as if hit by an invisible spear. She pushed Mother behind the rock farther, keeping both their heads down as more and more of their captors fell.

Within minutes the strange sounds stopped and the cries and wails of her people grew quiet. She slowly emerged from behind the rock and gasped. Almost all of the guards were dead, those that remained alive had their hands in the air, their spears tossed away on the ground.

She motioned to Mother. "Come out now, Mother. It's safe."

But as she and the others watched her heart sank as the figures running down the long path toward the bottom were black from head to toe. She began to cry, the others realizing as she did, everyone slowly backing away toward the walls, not sure what to do.

For approaching them with their strange spears were more Panther People.

Leather's team along with four of the Bravo Team members quickly ran down the corkscrew road, it taking almost fifteen minutes to reach the bottom. Two Bravo Team snipers were on either side of the pit just in case any of the surrendering guards decided to change their minds but in reaching the bottom with no incident, it appeared the fight had been drummed out of them.

"Does anybody speak Portuguese?"

His man, Graham Norton, a former Captain under his command before he left the SAS, and an avid footballer, was fluent in both Spanish and Portuguese, and when no one responded to his first query, Norton repeated it in Spanish.

Several voices responded.

"We are here to help you," said Norton, slinging his weapon and holding his empty hands out. "You are safe now. Those who can understand me, please tell your people."

As Norton tried to calm the quickly gathering throng of natives, Leather and the others loaded the half dozen remaining Venezuelan guards and the more than two dozen workers onto an old yellow school bus. The Delta team took them up to the top, the entire imprisoned population cowering in fear at the sound of the engine.

These poor bastards have probably never seen a vehicle before.

He looked at the massive dozers and dump trucks, wondering what these primitive people must have thought of them.

Probably like we'd think of dinosaurs.

His heart went out to them as they continued to emerge from their hiding places. Leather walked over to Norton. "How many do you figure?"

Norton shook his head. "I'm guessing about two or three hundred at this point."

"Okay, there's some cages with facilities up top that it looks like they were being kept in. I suggest we move them there, but explain that they are no longer prisoners and are free to leave if they want."

"I'll try, sir, but these people are terrified. They think we're the Panther People."

"What the hell is that?"

Norton shrugged. "No idea, but they're scared of us. I think we should get them out of here, fed, and show them we're human."

"Human?"

"And not Panthers."

"Good luck with that." He turned as the bus returned, Norton turning back to the gathered natives, asking them to get on the bus. Many appeared reluctant, but with much coaxing from Norton, and smiles from the Delta team, the bus was eventually filled with the sun already getting low in the sky.

This is going to take all bloody night!

Leather's comm squawked. "Charlie One, Charlie Four. Sir, we've got a problem, over."

"Charlie Four, Charlie One. What kind of problem?"

"The natives, sir. As soon as they got off the bus they ran into the forest."

Leather smiled, their problem suddenly solving itself. "I fail to see how that's a problem, Lieutenant."

"But I thought we were going to keep them in the cages?"

"Out of necessity, not choice. If they feel better off in the forest, then fantastic. Perhaps they know their way home and are simply returning to their villages. Either way, they're no longer our problem. Charlie One, out."

Maybe we'll be out of here by morning!

"Everyone okay in here?"

Dawson strode down the hallway of the building the civilians had taken refuge in, pleased to see the two students safe, though Mitchell looked like he'd been put through the ringer. He looked into a cell and found one of the civilians lying on a bed, his shirt open, his body a mess.

"Jesus Christ, what the hell happened to him?"

"He was tortured for hours." Mitchell's wife, Jenny, answered, her voice cracking as she looked at the poor bastard.

"What did they want?"

"Nothing! They asked him nothing!" she cried. "It was all so pointless." She threw her arms out. "All of this! So pointless! Why did any of this have to happen?"

"Greed."

Acton's answer was simple and probably the truth. That and strategic defense. Dawson knew from briefings that the Chinese, who controlled almost the entire market in rare earth elements were already beginning to hold back the sale of these elements to other countries so they could supply their rapidly expanding economy. Off the book supplies like these were of massive strategic importance and could give them the edge in the future should sanctions or other means be used to try and force them to sell their known supplies on the open market.

Supplies no one knew about? Those could be kept by the Chinese with none the wiser.

It made him wonder how many of these mines might be scattered across the globe, the Chinese never known for caring about environmental laws.

They build a coal fired power plant every two weeks and the environmentalists criticize America?

273

"What's the status, Sergeant Major?"

Dawson turned to Reading. "All the Chinese troops are dead, half a dozen Venezuelan regulars captured along with a support staff of about a dozen—cooks and the like. Another few dozen workers. We're holding them in one of the cages they were keeping the natives in except for the support staff. They're cooking food right now for everyone."

"Good, I'm starving," replied Mitchell from the chair he was sitting in. "Getting fried with a car battery works up an appetite, I guess."

Jenny smiled, squeezing his shoulders.

"And the natives?" asked Laura.

"Most are fleeing into the jungle, but a few aren't leaving. We're not sure why, but they're the ones we can't communicate with. The others we were able to communicate with through translators, some having members that could speak Spanish. But this remaining group, about twenty, don't speak Spanish or Portuguese, and they seem terrified."

"They're probably one of the uncontacted tribes. Perhaps James and I should go see what we can do."

Dawson nodded. "Sounds like a good idea to me. We're going to hole up here the night then head out at first light after we destroy this place."

"Can you?" asked Acton.

"Absolutely. We found a large store of dynamite for the mine, plus we've got lots of C4 and detonators."

"And the prisoners?"

"We'll leave them in their cage with provisions, then notify the authorities after we cross the border." He looked at the other civilians milling around. "Are you the PAN environmentalists?"

One nodded. "John Tinmouth. Thanks for coming."

"You're welcome." He pointed to a bunch of camera and video equipment sitting on a table. "Is that your stuff?"

Tinmouth nodded. "Yeah, they confiscated it when they captured us."

"Then I suggest you get outside and document as much of what you can now. There might not be time in the morning, and most of the natives are gone."

Tinmouth's eyes opened slightly wider. "My God, I'd forgotten why we were here!" He paused. "Is it safe outside?"

"Yes. Just stick within sight of my men. And make sure none of them get on tape."

Tinmouth and two of the others geared up and left, one remaining behind with the tortured man.

"I'll have Niner come in and give him a look. Might not be much we can do for him now, but we can at least give him some painkillers."

"Yeah man, painkillers," whispered the man with a smile on his face, his thumb in the air.

Acton turned to Dawson. "Sergeant Major?"

"Yes."

"What do we do with the natives that won't leave?"

Dawson sighed.

"That's the elephant in the room, isn't it?"

TikTik fed Mother who seemed to be coming around from the shock of everything now that the prison they were in had been opened, and their new jailors seemed much friendlier. The Panther People—the new ones— had removed much of their coverings to reveal that they were human, like her, but not like her.

They're so pale!

They all looked quite ill to her, but they were friendly though their smiles sometimes turned challenging, though when they did, they never seemed angry. She wondered if perhaps they just smiled differently than her people.

And they weren't all pale. One was as dark as the ground she stood on, another with strange eyes had the same color skin as her almost. It was all very confusing.

Everyone was gone except her people. Their small group of about twenty had been isolated from the beginning. No one spoke their language and the new jailors couldn't seem to communicate with them either. They had been too terrified to leave without permission, and after a quick discussion no one really knew what to do, so the decision had been made to stay and placate their new captors until it was clear what was going on.

One thing that was good about their new captors was none appeared intoxicated. In the short time she had been here she had seen some of the men enter the cage and take women away, raping them all night, returning them broken in body and spirit, only to force them to work in the stone pit the next morning.

She had always kept her face hidden, for she knew she was pretty and didn't want to attract any attention.

But now for some reason she felt safe. She knew their old captors were evil and these new ones had killed most of them, those that remained now in another spider web prison nearby, quiet, sullen, defeated.

With their prisons closed, men with the strange spears guarding them.

She gave Mother her last spoonful then quickly finished her own meal, not sure when they would eat again. Curling up on her bed beside Mother, she closed her eyes, her thoughts turning to Tuk, wondering if he were still alive somewhere, thinking of her.

"So what do you think?"

Dawson surveyed the natives just settling down for the night, Leather at his side. "I'm not sure. We can't waste time in the morning trying to convince them to go. We need to evac ASAP before more hostiles arrive. Something tells me the Chinese know they've lost their mine."

"What makes you say that?"

"The civilians were mentioning the leader seemed to be a guy called Dr. Chen. We haven't found him or his body. Nor have we found the torturer, Ling. I'm guessing some sort of escape tunnel."

Leather's eyebrows climbed slightly. "Interesting. We should find that. Might prove handy."

"Might also be a weakness if new arrivals know about it. I'm thinking we blow it in the morning. I've got some men looking for it now."

"You're probably right. I sent one of my men with a vehicle to the river to supplement our lookout. They should be able to provide us with some warning should anyone attempt to land."

"Good thinking." Dawson turned back to the two dozen natives. "What are we going to do with you?"

TikTik's Village, Northern Amazon, Venezuela

"Tuk! Thank the Mother you are alive!"

TikTik's mother rushed toward him as he entered the village with Kinti and some of the warriors. He hugged her tight, the familiar sight of the woman who would keep him and TikTik apart still welcome. "The village was attacked by the Panther People," he explained.

"Some of our men went to the village yesterday and found it empty."

"No bodies?"

"No."

"Not even Bruk's?"

Her eyes narrowed. "Why? What do you know? What happened?"

"I saw them drag Bruk's body into the village, and—" His voice cracked, tears filling his eyes and she knew without him saying what had happened.

"TikTik?" she whispered, her hand over her mouth.

He nodded, his head dropping to his chest. "I saw them kill her too."

TikTik's father arrived just as the words were uttered and the proud warrior's shoulders slumped as all life seemed to drain from his face. He said nothing as he held his sobbing wife and led her away. The villagers gathered to hear the story repeated, then some began to get nervous as more and more warriors began to ring the village.

"Who are all these people?" asked one of the elders.

"They are warriors from many tribes who are following me into battle. We are going to fight the Panther People, and take our people back!" announced Tuk with pride, his chest swelling as jaws dropped in shock.

"They're following *you*? *You* who can barely hold a spear?"

278

Tuk was suddenly thankful only Kinti was able to speak his language, and she stepped forward and gave a speech almost as rousing as Skip had earlier, the warriors surrounding the village thick now, and when she was done, she turned to the gathered crowd, and in the language of her village, shouted, "And we follow Tuk into battle!"

"Tuk! Tuk! Tuk!" erupted as a thousand voices chanted his name from every direction. His arms sprouted goose bumps as pride with a hint of embarrassment surged through his being, and as TikTik's villagers looked on in awe, some still getting Kinti's story translated as not all spoke Tuk's language, some of them couldn't help but be overwhelmed, joining in the chanting, some rushing to their lodges to get their weapons.

Tuk held up his hands, quieting the crowd, smiling. He turned to the elder. "Honored Elder, we ask nothing of you except permission to rest in the forest for the night. At dawn we will go to my village then track the Panther People to their lair, where we will crush them and free our people."

The elder, overwhelmed, nodded. "You are our honored guests." Kinti translated and a cheer rang out from the weary warriors who had been running all day. "We cannot provide for so many, but the Mother can, and they are welcome to partake of Her bounty."

Tuk grasped the man's wrists. "Thank you, Elder."

He let go and turned to the mass. "We will rest here tonight. Eat and drink whatever the Mother provides, and get your rest. For tomorrow, we fight!"

Rio Negro Landing, Northern Amazon, Venezuela

Potts woke to find Donny, his relief, shaking him by the shoulder. "Wake up, mate, we've got company!" A shot of adrenaline surged through his system making him immediately alert as he quickly checked himself, readying his weapon as he looked in the direction Donny was pointing.

"Bloody hell!" he exclaimed as he spotted several large transport boats coming their way, another coming around the bend. "These guys are serious. What's the count?"

"Looks like about a platoon on each and there's three, four—no, make that five of them. Each with a transport vehicle."

"Christ, radio it in, I'll get the vehicle started."

"Charlie One, Charlie Lookout, come in, over."

Potts scrambled up the embankment toward the road, jumping into the old Toyota truck and turning the key that had been left in the ignition. The engine roared to life as Donny jumped in the passenger side.

"I can't reach base! Nothing but static!"

"They must be jamming us!" Potts put the vehicle in gear, pulling away as quietly as he could, slowly building speed so their engine wouldn't be heard and dust wouldn't be kicked up that might be spotted from the river. A gentle rain overnight was helping as the ground was still damp, and soon he was able to hit about 30 mph before it became too rough to go any faster. He tried his comm and found it too was jammed. "We'll just have to deliver the message personally."

Two men stepped out of the trees, handguns raised, opening fire. Potts swerved toward them rather than away, causing them both to dive to the ground. As Potts gunned it, the gunfire continued and Donny cried out, grabbing his shoulder as the distance between the shooters increased. Soon out of range, Potts sat back up, slowing down to smooth out the ride. He looked at Donny. "Are you okay?"

Donny held his shoulder, looking at it, and nodded. "Lucky ricochet, I think. Just a deep scratch."

"Do you need me to stop and patch you up or are you going to survive until we reach the mine?"

"Just fowkin' drive! If we stop I'm dead anyway!"

Potts nodded, continuing forward, the rearview mirror showing their attackers as mere specs now. Suddenly a light came on in the dash and he cursed, the fuel light on. He looked at the gauge and the needle was quickly bottoming out.

"They must have hit the fuel tank. We're about to run out!"

Donny grimaced. "Well, this is just turning out to be a bloody wonderful day!"

Tuk's Village, Northern Amazon, Venezuela

Kinti held Tuk's hand, trying to comfort the poor man as he surveyed the sight in front of them. His village had been levelled, every building, every structure, destroyed, shredded by some type of beast, the logs barely recognizable. Tracks of the beast that Tuk had described were everywhere, strange, not spaced out paw marks like most animals, but continuous lines, almost like a slithering snake.

It was pure evil, whatever it was.

And the elder was right. There were no bodies to be seen. It was as if someone had wanted to wipe the village from existence. Not finding Bruk's or TikTik's bodies was concerning though. It meant that the others might be dead too, the bodies simply vanished by some magic possessed by the Panther People, or perhaps simply taken with them as food for their beast.

"Be strong," she said as she noticed his eyes fill with tears. "The others are scared with what they see. You must be strong for them."

Tuk nodded, quickly blinking back the tears.

"Let it turn to anger. Look what they did to the Mother's people, to Her precious bounty. Let it turn to anger and share that anger with the warriors."

She felt Tuk's grip on her hand tighten, then his head shot backward and a roar erupted from him the likes of which she never would have believed him possible. It sent shivers down her spine as he let go of her hand, his becoming fists as he dropped his head back down, glaring at the sights around him.

"Look what these evil beasts have done to my home!" he shouted, Kinti quickly translating to the gathered throng. "Look what they have done to the Mother's people! Look what they have done to the Mother's bounty!" Tuk slowly turned, his arms outstretched as he spoke. "*This* is the destructive power we are facing. A power unlike anything we have ever seen, but I know they can be killed. I have seen it with my own eyes, as have the Barasana people. We saw them killed by the Spirit People with their strange weapons, but *we*, people like you and I, killed them as well. With nothing more than this!" He shoved his spear high into the air as the warriors roared, their bravado returning. "Today we will find these Panther People and destroy them once and for all, so they can no longer harm the bounty of the great Mother, and they no longer haunt the dreams of our children!"

Kinti shouted the last of the translation, others translating her words, but it was clear the message had been delivered even if most hadn't heard it. The warriors were enraged, whipped into a frenzy ready to battle anything that might be found ahead.

Then Tuk, raising his spear, rushed into the forest, in the direction the beast had clearly laid out for them, its path of destruction self-defeating as they sprinted, unhindered by the jungle.

Illegal Rare Earth Element Strip Mine, Northern Amazon, Venezuela

"Fire in the hole!"

Dawson ducked, turning away from the pit as Niner hit the detonator. A series of massive explosions ripped down the first few hundred feet of the road carved in the side of the steep rock wall, and as Dawson held his breath, a wall of dust rolling past him, he headed toward the edge to see Niner's handiwork.

A stiff breeze cleared the dust away from the surface fairly quickly, but inside the pit was another story. It would take a long while for the dust to settle there, but already it was clear a large portion of the far side of the pit had collapsed, taking the road with it.

"Good work!" he yelled, giving a thumbs up.

"That should set them back a few weeks," agreed Red, approaching from the runway. He held his hands up to his mouth. "Clear the area!" He pointed toward a vehicle approaching, Mickey at the wheel, dragging the netting that had covered the runway behind it. The plane had been disabled earlier, the flimsy hangar knocked down with a shove from the massive Atlas, and now the final piece of camouflage from this makeshift airport was about to disappear.

Mickey stepped out just at the edge of the pit then stepped over to the passenger side, opposite the hook dragging the netting, and pushed the vehicle the few feet it needed to teeter over the edge, then momentum and gravity took over as Mickey raced away, the massive netting gaining speed as the vehicle dropped to the pit floor, the final couple hundred feet whipping by fast enough to tear someone's arm off.

Dawson was pleased with the speed at which things were progressing. Everyone had been up before dawn, all had been fed and the prisoners locked in their cage with extra provisions. The school bus had been brought around and was ready for their evac to the river as soon as they were done, which should be within the next few minutes.

"Ready for the pit netting!" announced Niner, waving the detonator.

Dawson activated his comm. "Confirm everyone is out from under the netting or inside a building or cage. Charlie Team check the civilians, Bravo Team sound off by the numbers, over."

Confirmations quickly came through as he, along with Mickey, headed into the main complex, Niner inside the cage with the natives, its chain link cover hopefully all the protection they'd need. He could see from his vantage point that the professors had all the natives at the far edge, where the danger was lowest, and all huddled under mattresses. And he could tell from here they were terrified.

We're going to have to force them into the forest, I know it!

With the last all clear received, he activated his comm. "Proceed!"

"Fire in the hole!"

A series of explosions surrounded the entire facility as the poles holding the netting in place overhead were blasted in sequence, the net collapsing in the middle, dragging the couple of dozen poles with it, these twenty foot metal beams tearing across the ground, damaging anything they hit. The building he was in shook as a beam was dragged across the roof of the breezeway, tearing it apart, and he heard screams from the cage as a beam was dragged across the top of the chain link, it thankfully holding. Within seconds the entire netting and its infrastructure had been dragged into the pit, as if it had never existed.

The final explosives were for the compound buildings themselves and the runway, and would be detonated when everyone was safely away.

Which meant it was time to leave.

"There, see, everybody is okay, and it's all over now," said Laura calmly, removing the mattress she had been lying under and tossing it aside. James rose with her, piling his atop Laura's, then began to lift other mattresses off the terrified natives, natives who had probably never heard sounds that loud in their lives. Some were so terrified that as she tried to remove their mattresses, a small tug-of-war played out, she letting go after a second try to move onto the next, the more nervous she knew would come around as they saw their friends give up their cover.

"Very good," she said, smiling, careful not to show her teeth. "You are all very brave." She realized she was talking to them like children, but she could think of no other way to speak to them other than to be as calm, soothing and friendly as possible. "You are all as brave as my friend Tuk, and he was like you. Tuk had never seen people like us before, and now he's my friend."

A young woman rushed over to her, dragging an older woman with her, both with expressions of disbelief written over the faces. The young one grabbed Laura by the sleeve, a flurry of words erupting from her, none of which she could understand, followed by the one word she did. Tuk.

Did they know him, or was Tuk another word in their language?

"Tuk?" she asked, singling out the word.

The young one's head bobbed in excitement as the older woman grabbed at her heart, a smile spreading on her face. The girl pointed at her eyes, then at Laura's eyes, then said the single word again, "Tuk", her intonation questioning.

"Did I see, Tuk?" She nodded deliberately, pointing at her eyes. "Yes, Tuk, yes!"

She pulled out her phone and brought up a photo of her and Tuk that had been taken the morning before they went their separate ways. She held it up for them. "Tuk!"

The young girl looked at the photo and jumped back, scared. She then stepped forward and grabbed the phone out of her hand, talking to it, the word "Tuk" repeated several times, then she tried shaking the phone.

Laura laughed as she realized the poor girl thought Tuk was in the phone. She held out her hand, smiling, and the girl put the phone back in her hand. "Watch." She took a photo of James then showed them. Nods seemed to suggest they understood that Tuk wasn't in the phone, since James was still standing where he had been.

Instead, the girl and the older woman, who Laura was beginning to think might be Tuk's mother, hugged each other, crying with relief.

This must be Tuk's people!

Potts looked over his shoulder as the road widened into the mine site. The transport vehicles with the enemy troops were within sight, maybe five minutes behind them, the road too rough to go too fast on. Their vehicle had carried them half the way, but the rest they had covered on foot at a sprint, Donny's wounded shoulder and his recovering ankle holding out admirably. As they turned the corner they saw a completely changed site, none of the netting in place, sunlight pouring in.

"They're coming!" he shouted, waving his arms to get everyone's attention, their comms still not working on last check a few minutes ago. He spotted Dawson and Leather coming out of one of the buildings, running toward them.

"Report!" ordered Leather.

"Our vehicle broke down and our comms were jammed. They're not even five minutes behind us. Five transports, each carrying a platoon, about one hundred men. We took some fire from two individuals who came out of the forest, probably the missing men from last night. Donny here's been hit in the shoulder, but not bad. We've only got minutes, sir!"

Dawson was already walking away, trying his comm. "Jammed!" He shouted instead. "Man the machine guns! A company of the enemy is not even five minutes out!" Immediately Bravo and Charlie teams raced into position as Dawson ran toward the cage. "Professors, get the civilians and the natives out of here now. Head south as fast as you can. We'll delay them here as long as we can, then try to join you. Whatever you do don't wait for us, just keep running south, then head south-west. You should eventually hit the river. Use your satphone to call for help."

"Got it!" replied Acton as they began to urge the nearly panicking natives out of the cage. They didn't know what was going on, but he could tell they knew something bad was happening. Apparently though some sort of trust had been established as a young girl was urging the others to follow her and Professor Palmer.

Leather ran back from the road, binoculars in hand. "They're mobilizing about half a klick down the road, spreading out fast. They'll have us outflanked in minutes."

Today just might be a good day to die.

Acton took the lead, his gun out, Reading directly behind him to the right, Laura to the left, the natives and environmentalists behind them. Jenny was helping Terrence who seemed to have regained most of his strength, and Turnbull was being carried on a stretcher by his four friends. As they moved forward Acton kept glancing to his right, knowing the enemy was in that direction, then froze, raising his hand, bringing everyone to a stop. He pointed.

Dark figures could be seen spreading out rapidly, coming directly toward them and already ahead of their position, sweeping forward.

"Fall back!" he whispered harshly, motioning for everyone to turn around, the natives at first confused until one of them spotted the figures, warning the others.

They rushed back toward the camp and Acton tried his comm, afraid they might startle the defenders if they burst into the open, but there was nothing but static.

As they approached the edge of the cleared area he rushed ahead. "They're coming!" he shouted, but no one heard him as every machine gun nest opened up.

Niner squeezed the trigger for a second, firing off a burst from the confiscated Chinese machine gun, Jimmy at his side feeding him ammo. They had plenty, the Chinese well supplied, but he didn't want to waste it. They were outnumbered almost six to one and he had a funny feeling today was the day he was finally going to take a dirt nap.

But not without taking out my six!

He was sure he had easily accomplished that prerequisite already, and as he squeezed off another controlled burst, another shadowy figure in the forest dropping, he felt a tap on his shoulder. He looked to where Jimmy was pointing and cursed.

The civilians and the natives were coming out of the forest, obviously already outflanked.

He pointed at the buildings. "Take cover in there. Shoot through the windows if you have to!"

Acton nodded as they whipped by, yanking open the door to the building that had housed the prisoners. Niner squeezed off several more bursts, providing cover for the refugees.

289

If we die today with them still here, we'll have accomplished nothing.

The thought pissed him off.

He fired again.

Acton slammed the door shut as the last of their ragtag crew cleared the threshold, locking it behind him, knowing that a gun or a good shoulder would have it opened easily, but at least there would be some warning. Reading was already racing to the other end to lock the door there. Acton pointed at the dead Venezuelan soldiers from earlier. "Get their weapons and magazines, including knives. Anything we can use."

Laura and two of the environmentalists began to strip down the soldiers as Turnbull was placed on the floor near the rear wall and away from any windows. Acton turned to Mitchell. "Feel up for fighting?"

"Absolutely, sir!"

"You and Jenny, take two of the AK's and three clips each and cover that end," he said, pointing to where Reading was returning from. "Remember your training. Opposing fields of fire, watch out for grenades. These guys aren't coming to take prisoners."

"Yes, sir!" Mitchell and his wife tore ass toward the other end, Jenny covering the door, Mitchell the window in the cell facing out to the forest.

"Give me those knives," he said, bending over as Laura handed him three large knives taken from the belts of the dead soldiers. Acton turned to the natives and picked the strongest looking ones he could see, handing them the knives by the blade. The men smiled, nodding their understanding.

It's do or die, and these guys deserve a chance to defend themselves.

Acton turned to the environmentalists. "Who here knows how to use a Glock?"

All of them stepped forward and he chuckled.

Ask that in Britain and you'd probably be asked, "What's a bloody Glock?"

He handed his gun and ammo over, replacing it with the remaining AK-47, Laura handing out two handguns and some ammo taken from the soldiers. "Arm yourselves with whatever you can. Try to conserve your ammo."

"They're coming!" It was Mitchell's voice. Acton looked down the hall and saw Jenny joining her husband in the cell. Acton rushed to the already opened window, motioning for the natives to move farther inside the building. Laura directed them into two of the rooms facing the pit, motioning for them to all get low. The men with the knives positioned themselves at the door to the rooms as Acton took up position at the window, immediately spotting two of the enemy emerging from the trees.

"Hold your fire!" he whispered to Laura, who passed the message down to Reading, who again passed it down to the Mitchells.

Acton counted three, then four, then six, crouching, advancing cautiously. He remained just out of sight, barely a sliver of his head in view, the glare of the sun overhead, from the east obscuring their view, the awning over his window casting a shadow that hid him even more.

The last emerged into the open, out of sight of the machine gun nests.

He rose from his hiding place, squeezing the trigger, signaling the others to open fire.

Dawson checked left and saw half a dozen Chinese coming into sight, but before he could turn to engage they were all wiped out by he assumed the occupants of the building.

Good goin' Docs!

He returned his attention to the portion of the forest he was covering, just left of the road, squeezing off a few bursts at shadows, making sure to keep left of where Spock and Mickey were positioned. They were in depressions on either side of the road, taking out targets of opportunity while they could, but with orders to fall back as soon as the enemy got within fifty yards.

Speaking of…

Spock tore around the corner, Mickey on his heels as they sprinted toward his position. "Bring the rain!" shouted Spock, prompting Dawson to open fire on their former position. Screams could be heard as he made use of his precious ammo, but seconds later he was out.

"Reload!" he yelled as Mickey and Spock dove behind their hardened foxhole, Atlas reloading. He felt the slap on his back and opened fire as the cleared area between the road and airfield filled with dozens of troops. He took out at least a dozen before they hit the ground, returning fire, his sandbags taking some serious hits.

This could be it!

Tuk held up his hand and the entire procession came to a halt, quiet within seconds. He listened and frowned, the strange noises he had heard when his village was attacked occurring once again, not far from here. He turned to face the warriors, fear written on many of their faces, the sounds so alien to them. Kinti translated once again his words as he spoke them.

"Men! Warriors! Be not afraid! The strange sounds you hear are merely the Panther People's spears! They are fast, they can't be seen, but they are thrown in the direction they point the stick in their hands, so if you see one pointed at you, get down! Remember, the Spirit People are on our side so do not harm them! And should fear enter your heart, remember that the Mother is on our side! She will protect you! And should She feel it is your time to join Her in the afterlife, then embrace it! For today we fight for Her children and Her forest, Her bounty meant for us, not for the Panther

People who would steal it. So push the fear aside, hold your spear tight, and let's earn our honored place in the afterlife!"

The warriors roared and Tuk turned, yelling at the top of his lungs as he sprinted forward, Kinti at his side, and as each foot touched the ground, he swore he could feel the Mother herself vibrating with the courage of the thousand warriors he led.

Chen raised his hand.

"Cease fire!" he yelled. "Cease fire!"

His troops held their fire, keeping their weapons trained on the enemy positions, they themselves beginning to hold their fire. Chen motioned for a megaphone and was tossed one by one of his men.

"Colonel Leather and friends, this is Dr. Chen. You are surrounded by overwhelming numbers on all sides. There is no hope of winning this battle. I suggest you surrender now and save yourselves. I guarantee you will not be killed."

He heard several laughs from the opposing side.

"I give you sixty seconds."

Dawson took the opportunity to have Spock and Mickey redeploy to one of the machine gun nests that had been left unmanned when he saw Leather sprinting from his position, rolling into the foxhole with him and Atlas.

"What do you think?" asked Leather as Dawson took a bead on Chen as the cocky bastard strode out into the open, a dozen of his troops surrounding him on all sides but the all-important front.

"There's no way they're letting us live. This is too big a secret. Best case scenario they force us to work the mines."

"I'd rather be dead with honor than a slave like my great-granddaddy," said Atlas.

"Agreed," said Dawson.

Leather extended his hand. "It's been an honor and a privilege to fight by your side, Sergeant Major."

Dawson shook the man's hand, his face grim. "Who dares, wins, Colonel."

Leather smiled at the citation of the SAS motto. "Then let us dare."

He raised his weapon, taking aim at the troops in front of them, but before any shots were fired, a dull roar began to the south, spreading around the entire area, getting louder as it did so.

"What the hell is that?" asked Dawson.

Atlas looked to the trees. "Sounds like we're in the middle of a football stadium."

Dawson's eyes narrowed. "Could Tuk's people have got here already?"

Leather shrugged. "If they sprinted and travelled at night, absolutely. But they were barely fifty if that. That sounds like hundreds, if not more."

Atlas looked around nervously. "Then who the hell is it?"

Dawson frowned. "Whoever or whatever it is, let's just hope it's on our side."

Chen looked around, as did his men. The sound was getting louder and now surrounded them from all sides it seemed, except for the road, though that gap he had the sense was closing quickly. His men were nervous, looking about and slowly backing away from the mine site, even he having to resist the urge to move.

As he listened it became quite clear it was the shouting of people, hundreds of people, thousands of people. How many he had no idea. The one thing he was sure of was that they were natives, which meant spears and darts.

And he had body armor.

"They're merely natives with nothing but spears!" he shouted to his men. "Prepare to teach them a lesson!"

His men stopped retreating, turning their attention to the forest, slowly moving out of the line of fire of the defenders when everything stopped.

Chen looked at the far side of the compound, where a single, small native stood, a woman approaching from his right.

TikTik gasped, jumping up excitedly as she pointed out the window at the lone warrior who had appeared from the forest, soon accompanied by a woman. "It's Tuk!" she cried, the rest of the villagers pushing to get a look through the two windows available to them. She felt a flush of jealousy as the beautiful woman stood by his side, and she wondered if he had taken a mate.

Her chest tightened, sadness gripping her as she realized what she had wished for her friend had come true, her guilty heart aching as it tried to reconcile the fact she was now available again and he wasn't. But she also knew her mother and father, especially her mother, would never let her mate with him, that much they had made abundantly clear.

She felt a hand grip her arm and she turned to see Mother smiling at her, tears filling her eyes as if she knew exactly what she was thinking. She turned back to the window, looking at Tuk simply standing there, spear in hand, nobody doing anything, defenders or aggressors. It was as if the Mother Herself had held her breath, waiting to see what this lone, weak man would, or even could, do against the magic of the Panther People.

And then he spoke, with a confidence and volume she had never heard from him in all her years. It gave her goose bumps as she swelled with pride, knowing in an instant that this was no longer the Tuk of several days ago, but a new Tuk, a Tuk worthy of being the mate to any woman he should so desire.

"I am Tuk! Warrior for the great Mother! In Her name, I demand you surrender your spears or die!"

The woman with him was shouting in a different language, one she didn't recognize, but as she finished, the entire forest surrounding them erupted in, "Tuk! Tuk! Tuk!"

Tears rolled down her cheeks as she looked at Mother in awe, a look of pride on the old woman's face she had never seen before. They hugged each other as those in the room patted them on the back.

"That's my boy!" cried Mother, the pride and shame of not feeling it until now evident in her voice.

Suddenly the strange sounds of the Panther People's spears erupted and TikTik jumped back to the window to see Tuk dive to the side, rolling back to his feet and with incredible speed, hurl his spear through the air. TikTik expected it to fall short, far short, as did they all, but as they watched it continued to gain height, to travel forward straight and true, and when it became clear it might just have enough distance to reach the enemy, she began to cheer, joining the hundreds of voices chanting her girlhood crush's name.

Then cried for joy when it impaled the leader through the chest, his expression one of stunned disbelief before he crumpled to the ground.

Tuk dropped to the ground almost immediately after he loosed the spear, rolling over to Kinti as he watched it sail through the air. It was as if every set of eyes in this strange place were watching his throw, the Panther People even stopping aiming their strange spears, and when the throw proved true, he smiled, grabbing Kinti by the shoulder and shaking her.

"Did you see that?" he cried, it the most incredible throw he had ever seen from anyone. The strange sounds erupted from all over as he heard his warriors storm forward, filled with confidence now that they had seen one of their enemy felled by their leader.

Kinti gasped.

Tuk's eyes narrowed, then he cried out, "No!" as he rolled her over to see blood oozing from her stomach. He didn't know anything to say, no one else speaking his language. He jumped up, facing the strange shelters, and yelled the only word he could.

"Help!"

And almost immediately, the man he presumed was Kinti's mate burst from one of the lodges, racing toward them as spears darkened the sky.

Dawson opened fire, killing everything he could as hundreds of spears began to strike the ground, many impaling the Chinese unfortunate enough to be occupying the same spot of earth. Dozens upon dozens died within the first minute as hundreds of natives poured from the tree line and into the open. Dawson continued to fire until it was no longer safe to do so, the natives about to become intermingled with the surviving Chinese.

The lines were broken and it was evident all command structure had collapsed, the troops retreating in an orderly manner down the road, firing coordinated bursts at the advancing natives, then when the numbers proved simply too overwhelming, turning tail and sprinting toward their transports.

Dawson simply sat back, his hands in the open as natives overwhelmed their positions, spears and stone knives threatening them, but not killing them.

"Just stay calm, smile, but don't show any teeth," muttered Leather under his breath.

Dawson smiled, his teeth covered tightly by his lips, his hands out as he slowly looked around to see the same thing happening at the other nests. As the screams of the Chinese became more distant, their gunfire more sporadic, he realized the immediate danger here was over, and slowly rose when he spotted Tuk coming toward them with a strut in his step he hadn't thought possible in the simple, diminutive man.

He said something, waving his hand and the spears were immediately lifted. Dawson stepped out of the foxhole and approached Tuk. The young native held out both arms and Dawson grasped them by the wrists as the young man smiled, saying something.

But there was no one to translate and Dawson wondered where Kinti was.

"Tuk!" cried a woman's voice. Dawson turned to see one of the young native girls who had been hiding in the compound buildings jump from the door, racing toward them, the rest of the natives inside streaming after her.

"Tuk!"

Tuk spun to see TikTik running toward him. He cried out in joy as he rushed through the crowd of warriors toward her. But rather than greet her with the traditional two arm grasp of friends, he grabbed around her body, lifting her into the air like he would his mate, and held her tight as tears rolled down his cheeks.

"I thought you were dead!"

She shook her head. "No, only Bruk."

Tuk pushed back slightly in deference to his dead friend, and TikTik's dead mate. But she held onto him, tight. "I'm so sorry for your loss, TikTik."

"As am I. And I will mourn him, but move on. For I know now that I will be mated to the man, to the warrior I always wanted to be mated to my entire life."

Tuk felt his chest tighten slightly as his eyes narrowed. "Who?" he finally asked, his voice almost cracking at the thought of there being even more competition for the beautiful TikTik's heart.

"You, of course!"

Tuk took a moment to process what she had said, then when it finally clicked, he smiled, pulling her closer and kissing her.

The warriors a thousand strong erupted in cheers, eventually turning into chants of "Tuk! Tuk! Tuk!" once gain as Tuk, the once terrified young man respected by no one, reveled in the glory deserved of the greatest leader the people of the northern Amazon had ever known.

More than worthy to be the mate of the beautiful TikTik.

Dawson backed away from the public display of affection, happy for the scrawny guy, as Niner and Jimmy ran up.

"They're gone boss. What remained of them took one of the transports to the river. My guess is they're scramming."

"For how long is the question," replied Dawson. "Casualties?" he asked Red.

Red shook his head. "Negative. Everyone made it, including Charlie Team and the civilians."

Dawson shook his head. "Not everybody."

All around them warriors were picking up their dead and wounded, carrying them over their heads into the forest, their numbers quickly dwindling.

"Oh shit," muttered Dawson as he saw Acton running toward where Tuk had thrown the spear from that changed the tide of the battle. They all turned to see the young woman that Reading was head over heels for, lying on the ground, Reading kneeling over her body.

"Not everybody at all."

"You'll be okay, you'll be okay," cried Reading, tears rolling down his cheeks as he repeated the comforting words to her, over and over, knowing she couldn't understand them, and knowing he was lying for her benefit. He could see the life draining from her face, her eyes barely open, but her smile still there as she whispered his name, holding his cheek.

"Kinti love Hugh."

A gasp erupted from his chest as he kissed her, holding her head in his hand as he caressed her cheek.

"Hugh loves Kinti," he whispered, her smile spreading as she closed her eyes, her last breath escaping her lungs with a sigh that seemed to echo through the forest, bringing silence with it as all watched the grief and pain caused by wars the world over, no matter the size or side.

Reading grabbed her, lifting her up, hugging her hard as he cried harder than he had ever cried, not giving a damn about British reserve, cultural norms, or what others thought. He had lost friends before, family before, but never someone he had loved and cared for so intensely, in such short a period of time, and though the words exchanged between them could probably be counted on two hands, his heart felt like it had lived a lifetime with this young woman, and he had no idea how he could possibly recover from this loss.

He had known he'd have to leave her behind, and had prepared himself for the temporary pain it would cause, but he would be leaving knowing she was alive and well and would eventually move on to live a long, happy life.

But now she was dead. Because of him. If he had never spotted the inlet, they never would have set up camp there. Tuk would never have kidnapped Laura, and he would have never met Kinti.

She would be alive.

"It's my fault," he whispered.

He sensed Acton kneel beside him, then felt his friend's hand on his shoulder.

"You know that's not true," he said gently.

"I'm the one who spotted the inlet," he said, repeating his twisted logic.

Acton squeezed his shoulder. "You were merely the *first* to spot it. Fabricio would have spotted it if you hadn't. It was the perfect place to set up camp and it was nearly sunset."

Reading sniffed, knowing that Acton was right, though knowing made it no less painful.

"But she's dead, Jim. She's dead!" he sobbed again, his chest heaving several times before he could get control. "She's dead," his voice barely a whisper.

"But she died with the man she loved, knowing that he loved her. She could have died tomorrow from a snake bite, but she died today helping save this entire forest of people, fighting alongside the man she loved, and dying in his arms. I saw her face when you told her you loved her. That was the happiest woman I've ever seen. You have to remember that."

Reading nodded and looked up as Skip and several of the others from Kinti's tribe stepped forward. Skip said something in Portuguese, and Leather's man translated. "They need to take her now."

Reading gently lay her body down on the ground and kissed her forehead one last time, then stood up, stepping back as her family and friends picked up her body, carrying her over their heads into the forest.

"Give me a moment," he said, his back to the others, as he watched the procession slowly disappear into the trees. He heard the others leave, and as the tears began to subside, control exerted once again over his emotions, he wiped his face dry, then swore to never love again.

Acton Residence, St. Paul, Maryland

Acton squeezed Laura's hand as they sat on the couch, Reading on the TV's Skype app, Milton sitting in the La-Z-boy in a state of bliss as it massaged him from head to toe.

"I definitely have to get one of these," he said, his voice monotone as he exaggerated the vibrations going through his body. "Maybe my health insurance will cover it."

Acton laughed, as did Reading, one of the few he had heard from him in the two weeks since they had left the Amazon behind them. Milton's back was nearly fully recovered, it just needing some rest and physiotherapy. It was Reading they were all concerned about, he refusing to talk about Kinti or what had happened.

"The past is the past," was all he would say, but they knew he was hurting, and in true Reading style, was keeping it bottled inside.

"I assume you've heard the news," said Reading. "It broke yesterday."

"Yup, watched the report on the BBC last night," said Acton. "Great coverage. Looks like everybody is picking up on it." The environmentalists had broken the story on the Internet, posting all the footage they had taken, plus taped interviews they had done with each other, making sure there was no way the evidence could be hidden, it shared thousands of times on social media long before they went to the press.

And once they had, the story caught on like wildfire, the public loving good villains like the Chinese and Venezuelans, and heroes like the natives who had fought back and won. No mention was made of the help from the Delta Force or the ex-SAS operators, and any rumors to that effect were sloughed off as just that, rumors. The important thing was that the mine was officially closed, the Venezuelans denying all knowledge of it and imprisoning a few patsies. The Chinese simply ignored questions.

Acton was still left to wonder how many other secret mines were out there in the world, or even in the Amazon itself.

He hoped if they were there, they weren't exploiting the natives like this one did.

"So, have you two made a decision?"

Acton's eyebrows popped. "About what?"

Reading shook his head. "About where you're going to live? You said within two weeks of being back you'd decide."

Acton blushed, realizing they hadn't really made the decision. They'd talked about it a bit, but they both kept saying they were willing to live where the other one wanted.

"How would you feel about living in England?" asked Reading.

Acton shrugged. "Perfectly fine. The only problem I think I'd have is learning the language. You guys can't seem to make up your mind on what words you actually use. Some of you swear you never use the word 'daft' or 'guv' yet every night on your television you've got people saying those very words! I'm afraid to try and use any of your slang when I'm there for fear somebody jumps down my throat who thinks their colloquialisms and only theirs extend to the entire Empire!"

Reading laughed, tossing his head back and Acton exchanged a wink with Laura who was happy as well to see their friend finally having a good time. "Nobody here speaks the same bloody language. Just make sure you keep that damned accent of yours, and you'll be forgiven every time."

"I wouldn't be so sure of that," laughed Acton. "But I'll just keep plugging along, doing my bloody best even if I sound like a daft nutter if that's okay with you, guv."

Reading pissed himself laughing as Milton vibrated out his own laugh, Laura's head resting on Acton's shoulder as she giggled.

"Well, I have a little tidbit to contribute to this conversation," said Laura, turning in her seat to face Acton. I was offered a job in Washington, and I'm thinking of taking it."

Acton's smile spread from ear to ear. "That's only an hour from here!"

She nodded. "What do you think? Decision made?"

He grabbed her by the shoulders, beginning to pull her in for a hug then stopped. "Is it a good job? I mean, will you be happy doing it like you're happy in London?"

She nodded. "It's a great job. And I've arranged for it to be only part time, and London has agreed to let me keep the dig going in Egypt, as long as I fund it, which I was doing anyway. But it means I get to keep my students!"

Acton pulled her in, hugging her hard.

"Decision made!"

Tuk's Village, Northern Amazon, Venezuela

Tuk strode through the forest, his hunting party behind him, a large boar he himself had taken down draped between the shoulders of two men far larger than him. As he had discovered at the Battle of Tuk versus the Panther People, as it had become known, he realized the weakness he thought he had for throwing the spear was something from his childhood. As an adult he had become quite strong, but simply had never learned to put the power into his throw until it had become necessary.

His throw had felled a yakumama snake and the leader of the Panther People. One had been seen only by Lau-ra, the Woman of Light, the other seen by a thousand men throughout the forest, the story now legend.

He stepped into the clearing that was their rebuilt village, the neighboring tribes helping them after the complete destruction left behind. It had been almost two seasons since the battle, and sometimes it seemed like a dream, but the constant reminder that it wasn't rose to greet him as he came into sight.

TikTik.

Round with child, his child, she was now his mate, enthusiastically endorsed by her parents, it impossible to refuse the great Tuk his desires.

"Tuk!" she cried as she ran up to him, embracing him hard, kissing him with a passion that still fired him up every time. Many had died that day, including the precious Kinti and his friend Bruk days before, but he had travelled to the pit in the earth several times since to see it abandoned, now merely a scar on the great Mother's surface.

He was happy. More happy than he could have ever imagined possible. He had TikTik to thank for that, for agreeing to be his mate, and for always having loved him.

And he had the great Mother, who had sent him a messenger, a messenger that had sent him down a path he could never have imagined for himself, turning a small, insignificant man, full of self-pity and self-loathing, into a respected hunter, warrior, father and husband.

He looked up at the sky overhead and thanked the Mother's messenger with a silent prayer.

Lau-ra-pal-mer.

THE END

ACKNOWLEDGEMENTS

As I watched the World Cup, rediscovering my love of soccer (yes, soccer!), I began to think of the Amazon and the proverbial fish out of water. I lived in West Germany for seven years from the ages eight to fifteen while my father was stationed there. We lived on what was called "the economy", which meant we lived among the Germans, rather than on base, my parents wisely wanting to embrace the culture rather than live in some microcosm of our own behind a fence.

From my bedroom window there was a beautiful soccer field within sight, kids playing on it all the time, soccer fields in Europe like baseball diamonds in America—everywhere.

In our small town of Hugsweier there were pretty much only German kids there, so if I wanted to have any fun, I'd need to learn the language and play with the German kids.

When in Rome.

The German kids were fantastic, and I learned to play soccer, learned the language, and quite quickly I was fairly fluent in German, and a damned good soccer player. I had my favorite team (Bayern München) and my favorite player (Karl-Heinz Rummenigge) and learned to love soccer while making friends, learning a language and discovering a culture.

All because a small English speaking kid had the courage to step out onto a soccer field and ask in broken German if he could play.

While thinking of the World Cup, Brazil and the Amazon (yes, this is going somewhere!), I thought of the uncontacted tribes, and the kernel of a story began. What would happen if some lonely member of one of these tribes were to step out of the forest and ask for help like that little boy asking to play?

What is remarkable about this novel is that after I was about half way finished, news broke about an uncontacted tribe actually making contact due to a massacre at their village committed by Peruvian illegal loggers. As has proven true far too often, once again one of my books had been "torn from the headlines" but before the headlines were even written (remember The Arab Fall where I predicted the return of the military to power in Egypt? It happened about two weeks after I published.)

Then of course I have to torture my characters. What would happen if Laura were kidnapped by one of these natives? How would our heroes manage when their technology couldn't help them?

I think it turned out to be a lot of fun, and I'm hoping you agree.

While writing this a great sadness occurred that as a writer, I helped deal with through my writing. My best friend of over twenty years, Paul Conway, succumbed to complications from non-Hodgkin lymphoma and died. He was my first boss when I arrived here fresh out of university, and we became friends very quickly, talking to or seeing each other four or five times a week for those decades, until he became quite sick. His death less than two months ago still haunts me, and I miss him dearly.

The character Pol in this book is a small tribute to him, he always being there for me during the good times and the bad, just as he was for Tuk. And to this day I am still haunted by the fact I missed his last phone call to me, when he knew he was dying, just as Tuk missed Pol's last request to talk to him. I never did get to talk to my friend again. Part of me is devastated by this, but I cling to the memory of our last conversation. He was too sick to see me, but he sounded healthy—he was having a good day. We talked for over forty minutes about anything but his illness. It was a perfectly normal conversation like the old days, discussing things like political correctness gone mad, and whether or not we'd still find Eddie Murphy's Delirious funny today now that so much of it would now be considered politically incorrect. That conversation is what I will try to remember, rather than the one I missed. I love you buddy, and you'll never be forgotten.

As always people need to be thanked. My father once again for the research, Brent Richards for some military lingo and weapons info, Fred Newton for some nautical terms and boat info, and Sherrie Men for some Chinese cultural info.

And as per usual, one final thing as a reminder to those who have not already done so, please visit my website at www.jrobertkennedy.com then sign up for the Insiders Club. You'll get emails about new book releases, new collections, sales, etc. Only an email or two a month tops, I promise! And don't forget to join me on Facebook, Twitter and Goodreads.

And as always, to my wife, daughter, parents and friends, thank you once again for your support. And to you the readers, thank you! You've all made this possible.

ABOUT THE AUTHOR

J. Robert Kennedy is the author of over one dozen international best sellers, including the smash hit James Acton Thrillers series, the first installment of which, The Protocol, has been on the best sellers list since its release, including a three month run at number one. In addition to the other novels from this series, Brass Monkey, Broken Dove, The Templar's Relic (also a number one best seller), Flags of Sin, The Arab Fall (also #1), The Circle of Eight (also #1) and The Venice Code (also #1), he has written the international best sellers Rogue Operator, Containment Failure, Cold Warriors, Depraved Difference, Tick Tock, The Redeemer and The Turned. Robert spends his time in Ontario, Canada with his family.

Visit Robert's website at www.jrobertkennedy.com for the latest news and contact information.

The Protocol

A James Acton Thriller, Book #1

For two thousand years the Triarii have protected us, influencing history from the crusades to the discovery of America. Descendent from the Roman Empire, they pervade every level of society, and are now in a race with our own government to retrieve an ancient artifact thought to have been lost forever.

Caught in the middle is archaeology professor James Acton, relentlessly hunted by the elite Delta Force, under orders to stop at nothing to possess what he has found, and the Triarii, equally determined to prevent the discovery from falling into the wrong hands.

With his students and friends dying around him, Acton flees to find the one person who might be able to help him, but little does he know he may actually be racing directly into the hands of an organization he knows nothing about...

Brass Monkey

A James Acton Thriller, Book #2

A nuclear missile, lost during the Cold War, is now in play--the most public spy swap in history, with a gorgeous agent the center of international attention, triggers the end-game of a corrupt Soviet Colonel's twenty five year plan. Pursued across the globe by the Russian authorities, including a brutal Spetsnaz unit, those involved will stop at nothing to deliver their weapon, and ensure their pay day, regardless of the terrifying consequences.

When Laura Palmer confronts a UNICEF group for trespassing on her Egyptian archaeological dig site, she unwittingly stumbles upon the ultimate weapons deal, and becomes entangled in an international conspiracy that sends her lover, archeology Professor James Acton, racing to Egypt with the most unlikely of allies, not only to rescue her, but to prevent the start of a holy war that could result in Islam and Christianity wiping each other out.

From the bestselling author of Depraved Difference and The Protocol comes Brass Monkey, a thriller international in scope, certain to offend some, and stimulate debate in others. Brass Monkey pulls no punches in confronting the conflict between two of the world's most powerful, and divergent, religions, and the terrifying possibilities the future may hold if left unchecked.

Broken Dove

A James Acton Thriller, Book #3

With the Triarii in control of the Roman Catholic Church, an organization founded by Saint Peter himself takes action, murdering one of the new Pope's operatives. Detective Chaney, called in by the Pope to investigate, disappears, and, to the horror of the Papal staff sent to inform His Holiness, they find him missing too, the only clue a secret chest, presented to each new pope on the eve of their election, since the beginning of the Church.

Interpol Agent Reading, determined to find his friend, calls Professors James Acton and Laura Palmer to Rome to examine the chest and its forbidden contents, but before they can arrive, they are intercepted by an organization older than the Church, demanding the professors retrieve an item stolen in ancient Judea in exchange for the lives of their friends.

All of your favorite characters from The Protocol return to solve the most infamous kidnapping in history, against the backdrop of a two thousand year old battle pitting ancient foes with diametrically opposed agendas.

From the internationally bestselling author of Depraved Difference and The Protocol comes Broken Dove, the third entry in the smash hit James Acton Thrillers series, where J. Robert Kennedy reveals a secret concealed by the Church for almost 1200 years, and a fascinating interpretation of what the real reason behind the denials might be.

The Templar's Relic

A James Acton Thriller, Book #4

**THE CHURCH HELPED DESTROY THE TEMPLARS.
WILL A TWIST OF FATE LET THEM GET THEIR
REVENGE 700 YEARS LATER?**

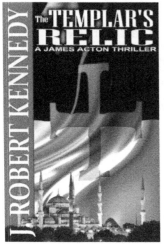

The Vault must be sealed, but a construction accident leads to a miraculous discovery--an ancient tomb containing four Templar Knights, long forgotten, on the grounds of the Vatican. Not knowing who they can trust, the Vatican requests Professors James Acton and Laura Palmer examine the find, but what they discover, a precious Islamic relic, lost during the Crusades, triggers a set of events that shake the entire world, pitting the two greatest religions against each other.

Join Professors James Acton and Laura Palmer, INTERPOL Agent Hugh Reading, Scotland Yard DI Martin Chaney, and the Delta Force Bravo Team as they race against time to defuse a worldwide crisis that could quickly devolve into all-out war.

At risk is nothing less than the Vatican itself, and the rock upon which it was built.

From J. Robert Kennedy, the author of six international bestsellers including Depraved Difference and The Protocol, comes The Templar's Relic, the fourth entry in the smash hit James Acton Thrillers series, where once again Kennedy takes history and twists it to his own ends, resulting in a heart pounding thrill ride filled with action, suspense, humor and heartbreak.

Flags of Sin

A James Acton Thriller, Book #5

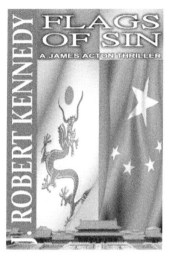

Archaeology Professor James Acton simply wants to get away from everything, and relax. A trip to China seems just the answer, and he and his fiancée, Professor Laura Palmer, are soon on a flight to Beijing.

But while boarding, they bump into an old friend, Delta Force Command Sergeant Major Burt Dawson, who surreptitiously delivers a message that they must meet the next day, for Dawson knows something they don't.

China is about to erupt into chaos.

Foreign tourists and diplomats are being targeted by unknown forces, and if they don't get out of China in time, they could be caught up in events no one had seen coming.

J. Robert Kennedy, the author of eight international best sellers, including the smash hit James Acton Thrillers, takes history once again and turns it on its head, sending his reluctant heroes James Acton and Laura Palmer into harm's way, to not only save themselves, but to try and save a country from a century old conspiracy it knew nothing about.

The Arab Fall

A James Acton Thriller, Book #6

**THE GREATEST ARCHEOLOGICAL DISCOVERY SINCE
KING TUT'S TOMB IS ABOUT TO BE DESTROYED!**

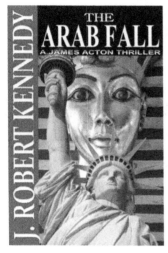

The Arab Spring has happened and Egypt has yet to calm down, but with the dig site on the edge of the Nubian Desert, a thousand miles from the excitement, Professor Laura Palmer and her fiancé Professor James Acton return with a group of students, and two friends: Interpol Special Agent Hugh Reading, and Scotland Yard DI Martin Chaney.

But an accidental find by Chaney may lead to the greatest archaeological discovery since the tomb of King Tutankhamen, perhaps even greater. And when news of it spreads, it reaches the ears of a group hell-bent on the destruction of all idols and icons, their mere existence considered blasphemous to Islam.

As chaos hits the major cities of the world in a coordinated attack, unbeknownst to the professors, students and friends, they are about to be faced with one of the most difficult decisions of their lives. Stay and protect the greatest archaeological find of our times, or save themselves and their students from harm, leaving the find to be destroyed by fanatics determined to wipe it from the history books.

From J. Robert Kennedy, the author of eleven international bestsellers including Rogue Operator and The Protocol, comes The Arab Fall, the sixth entry in the smash hit James Acton Thrillers series, where Kennedy once again takes events from history and today's headlines, and twists them into a heart pounding adventure filled with humor and heartbreak, as one of their own is left severely wounded, fighting for their life.

The Circle of Eight

A James Acton Thriller, Book #7

ABANDONED BY THEIR GOVERNMENT, DELTA TEAM BRAVO FIGHTS TO NOT ONLY SAVE THEMSELVES AND THEIR FAMILIES, BUT HUMANITY AS WELL.

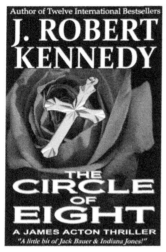

The Bravo Team is targeted by a madman after one of their own intervenes in a rape. Little do they know this internationally well-respected banker is also a senior member of an organization long thought extinct, whose stated goals for a reshaped world are not only terrifying, but with today's globalization, totally achievable.

As the Bravo Team fights for its very survival, they are suspended, left adrift without their support network. To save themselves and their families, markers are called in, former members volunteer their services, favors are asked for past services, and the expertise of two professors, James Acton and his fiancée Laura Palmer, is requested.

It is a race around the globe to save what remains of the Bravo Team, abandoned by their government, alone in their mission, with only their friends to rely upon, as an organization over six centuries old works in the background to destroy them and all who help them, as it moves forward with plans that could see the world population decimated in an attempt to recreate Eden.

In The Circle of Eight J. Robert Kennedy, author of over a dozen international best sellers, is at his best, weaving a tale spanning centuries and delivering a taut thriller that will keep you on the edge of your seat from page one until the breathtaking conclusion.

The Venice Code

A James Acton Thriller, Book #8

A SEVEN HUNDRED YEAR OLD MYSTERY IS ABOUT TO BE SOLVED.

BUT HOW MANY MUST DIE FIRST?

A former President's son is kidnapped in a brazen attack on the streets of Potomac by the very ancient organization that murdered his father, convinced he knows the location of an item stolen from them by the late president.

A close friend awakes from a coma with a message for archeology Professor James Acton from the same organization, sending him along with his fiancée Professor Laura Palmer on a quest to find an object only rumored to exist, while trying desperately to keep one step ahead of a foe hell-bent on possessing it.

And seven hundred years ago, the Mongol Empire threatens to fracture into civil war as the northern capital devolves into idol worship, the Khan sending in a trusted family to save the empire--two brothers and a son, Marco Polo, whose actions have ramifications that resonate to this day.

From J. Robert Kennedy, the author of fourteen international best sellers comes The Venice Code, the latest installment of the hit James Acton Thrillers series. Join James Acton and his friends, including Delta Team Bravo and CIA Special Agent Dylan Kane in their greatest adventure yet, an adventure seven hundred years in the making.

Pompeii's Ghosts

A James Acton Thriller, Book #9

POMPEII IS ABOUT TO CLAIM ITS FINAL VICTIMS—TWO THOUSAND YEARS LATER!

Two thousand years ago Roman Emperor Vespasian tries to preserve an empire by hiding a massive treasure in the quiet town of Pompeii should someone challenge his throne. Unbeknownst to him nature is about to unleash its wrath upon the Empire during which the best and worst of Rome's citizens will be revealed during a time when duty and honor were more than words, they were ideals worth dying for.

Professor James Acton has just arrived in Egypt to visit his fiancée Professor Laura Palmer at her dig site when a United Nations helicopter arrives carrying representatives with an urgent demand that they come to Eritrea to authenticate an odd find that threatens to start a war—an ancient Roman vessel with over one billion dollars of gold in its hold.

It is a massive amount of wealth found in the world's poorest region, and everyone wants it. Nobody can be trusted, not even closest friends or even family. Greed, lust and heroism are the orders of the day as the citizens of Pompeii try to survive nature's fury, and James Acton tries to survive man's greed while risking his own life to protect those around him.

Pompeii's Ghosts delivers the historical drama and modern day action that best selling author J. Robert Kennedy's fans have come to expect. Pompeii's Ghosts opens with a shocker that will keep you on the edge of your seat until the thrilling conclusion in a story torn from the headlines.

Amazon Burning

A James Acton Thriller, Book #10

IN THE DEPTHS OF THE AMAZON,
ONE OF THEIR OWN HAS BEEN TAKEN!

Days from any form of modern civilization, archeology Professor James Acton awakes to gunshots. Finding his wife missing, taken by a member of one of the uncontacted tribes, he and his friend INTERPOL Special Agent Hugh Reading try desperately to find her in the dark of the jungle, but quickly realize there is no hope without help.

And with help three days away, he knows the longer they wait, the farther away she'll be.

And the less hope there will be of ever finding the woman he loves.

Amazon Burning is the tenth installment of the James Acton Thrillers series in which the author of seventeen international bestsellers, J. Robert Kennedy, reunites James and his wife Laura Palmer with Hugh Reading, CIA Special Agent Dylan Kane, Delta Team-Bravo and others in a race against time to save one of their own, while behind the scenes a far darker, sinister force is at play, determined to keep its existence a secret from the world. The stakes are high, the action is full-throttle, and hearts will be broken as lives are changed forever in another James Acton adventure ripped from the headlines.

Rogue Operator

A Special Agent Dylan Kane Thriller, Book #1

**TO SAVE THE COUNTRY HE LOVES, SPECIAL AGENT
DYLAN KANE MIGHT HAVE TO BETRAY IT.**

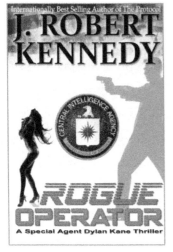

Three top secret research scientists are presumed dead in a boating accident, but the kidnapping of their families the same day raises questions the FBI and local police can't answer, leaving them waiting for a ransom demand that will never come.

Central Intelligence Agency Analyst Chris Leroux stumbles upon the story, and finds a phone conversation that was never supposed to happen. When he reports it to his boss, the National Clandestine Services Chief, he is uncharacteristically reprimanded for conducting an unauthorized investigation and told to leave it to the FBI.

But he can't let it go.

For he knows something the FBI doesn't.

One of the scientists is alive.

Chris makes a call to his childhood friend, CIA Special Agent Dylan Kane, leading to a race across the globe to stop a conspiracy reaching the highest levels of political and corporate America, that if not stopped, could lead to war with an enemy armed with a weapon far worse than anything in the American arsenal, with the potential to not only destroy the world, but consume it.

J. Robert Kennedy, the author of nine international best sellers, including the smash hit James Acton Thrillers, introduces Rogue Operator, the first installment of his newest series, The Special Agent Dylan Kane Thrillers, promising to bring all of the action and intrigue of the James Acton Thrillers with a hero who lives below the radar, waiting for his country to call when it most desperately needs him.

Containment Failure

A Special Agent Dylan Kane Thriller, Book #2

THE BLACK DEATH KILLED ALMOST HALF OF EUROPE'S POPULATION. THIS TIME BILLIONS ARE AT RISK.

New Orleans has been quarantined, an unknown virus sweeping the city, killing one hundred percent of those infected. The Centers for Disease Control, desperate to find a cure, is approached by BioDyne Pharma who reveal a former employee has turned a cutting edge medical treatment capable of targeting specific genetic sequences into a weapon, and released it.

CIA Special Agent Dylan Kane has been given one guideline from his boss: consider yourself unleashed, leaving Kane and New Orleans Police Detective Isabelle Laprise battling to stay alive as an insidious disease and terrified mobs spread through the city while they desperately seek those behind the greatest crime ever perpetrated.

The stakes have never been higher as Kane battles to save not only his friends and the country he loves, but all of mankind.

In Containment Failure, eleven times internationally bestselling author J. Robert Kennedy delivers a terrifying tale of what could happen when science goes mad, with enough sorrow, heartbreak, laughs and passion to keep readers on the edge of their seats until the chilling conclusion.

Cold Warriors

A Special Agent Dylan Kane Thriller, Book #3

THE COUNTRY'S BEST HOPE IN DEFEATING A FORGOTTEN SOVIET WEAPON LIES WITH DYLAN KANE AND THE COLD WARRIORS WHO ORIGINALLY DISCOVERED IT.

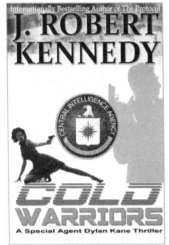

While in Chechnya CIA Special Agent Dylan Kane stumbles upon a meeting between a known Chechen drug lord and a retired General once responsible for the entire Soviet nuclear arsenal. Money is exchanged for a data stick and the resulting transmission begins a race across the globe to discover just what was sold, the only clue a reference to a top secret Soviet weapon called Crimson Rush.

Unknown to Kane, this isn't the first time America has faced this threat and he soon receives a mysterious message, relayed through his friend and CIA analyst Chris Leroux, arranging a meeting with perhaps the one man alive today who can help answer the questions the nation's entire intelligence apparatus is asking--the Cold Warrior who had discovered the threat the first time.

Over thirty years ago.

In Cold Warriors, the third installment of the hit Special Agent Dylan Kane Thrillers series, J. Robert Kennedy, the author of thirteen international bestsellers including The Protocol and Rogue Operator, weaves a tale spanning two generations and three continents with all the heart pounding, edge of your seat action his readers have come to expect. Take a journey back in time as the unsung heroes of a war forgotten try to protect our way of life against our greatest enemy, and see how their war never really ended, the horrors of decades ago still a very real threat today.

The Turned

Zander Varga, Vampire Detective, Book #1

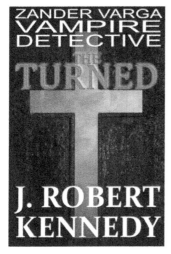

Zander has relived his wife's death at the hands of vampires every day for almost three hundred years, his perfect memory a curse of becoming one of The Turned—infecting him their final heinous act after her murder.

Nineteen year-old Sydney Winter knows Zander's secret, a secret preserved by the women in her family for four generations. But with her mother in a coma, she's thrust into the front lines, ahead of her time, to fight side-by-side with Zander.

And she wouldn't change a thing. She loves the excitement, she loves the danger. And she loves Zander. But it's a love that will have to go unrequited, because Zander has only one thing on his mind. And it's been the same thing for over two hundred years. Revenge.

But today, revenge will have to wait, because Zander Varga, Private Detective, has a new case. A woman's husband is missing. The police aren't interested. But Zander is. Something doesn't smell right, and he's determined to find out why.

From J. Robert Kennedy, the internationally bestselling author of The Protocol and Depraved Difference, comes his sixth novel, The Turned, a terrifying story that in true Kennedy fashion takes a completely new twist on the origin of vampires, tying it directly to a well-known moment in history. Told from the perspective of Zander Varga and his assistant, Sydney Winter, The Turned is loaded with action, humor, terror and a centuries long love that must eventually be let go.

Depraved Difference

A Detective Shakespeare Mystery, Book #1

WOULD YOU HELP, WOULD YOU RUN,
OR WOULD YOU JUST WATCH?

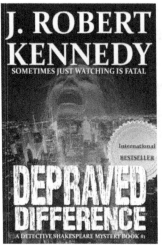

When a young woman is brutally assaulted by two men on the subway, her cries for help fall on the deaf ears of onlookers too terrified to get involved, her misery ended with the crushing stomp of a steel-toed boot. A cellphone video of her vicious murder, callously released on the Internet, its popularity a testament to today's depraved society, serves as a trigger, pulled a year later, for a killer.

Emailed a video documenting the final moments of a woman's life, entertainment reporter Aynslee Kai, rather than ask why the killer chose her to tell the story, decides to capitalize on the opportunity to further her career. Assigned to the case is Hayden Eldridge, a detective left to learn the ropes by a disgraced partner, and as videos continue to follow victims, he discovers they were all witnesses to the vicious subway murder a year earlier, proving sometimes just watching is fatal.

From the author of The Protocol and Brass Monkey, Depraved Difference is a fast-paced murder suspense novel with enough laughs, heartbreak, terror and twists to keep you on the edge of your seat, then knock you flat on the floor with an ending so shocking, you'll read it again just to pick up the clues.

Tick Tock

A Detective Shakespeare Mystery, Book #2

SOMETIMES HELL IS OTHER PEOPLE

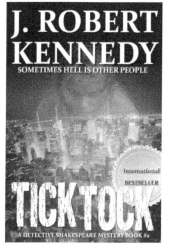

Crime Scene tech Frank Brata digs deep and finds the courage to ask his colleague, Sarah, out for coffee after work. Their good time turns into a nightmare when Frank wakes up the next morning covered in blood, with no recollection of what happened, and Sarah's body floating in the tub.

Billionaire Richard Tate is the toast of the town, loved by everyone but his wife. His plans for a romantic weekend with his mistress ends in disaster, waking the next morning to find her murdered, floating in the tub. After fleeing in a panic, he returns to find the hotel room spotless, and no sign of the body. An envelope found at the scene contains not the expected blackmail note, but something far more sinister.

Two murders, with the same MO, targeting both the average working man, and the richest of society, sets a rejuvenated Detective Shakespeare, and his new reluctant partner, Amber Trace, after a murderer whose motivations are a mystery, and who appears to be aided by the very people they would least expect—their own.

Tick Tock, Book #2 in the internationally bestselling Detective Shakespeare Mysteries series, picks up right where Depraved Difference left off, and asks a simple question: What would you do? What would you do if you couldn't prove your innocence, but knew you weren't capable of murder? Would you hide the very evidence that might clear you, or would you turn yourself in and trust the system to work?

J. ROBERT KENNEDY

The Redeemer

A Detective Shakespeare Mystery, Book #3

SOMETIMES LIFE GIVES MURDER A SECOND CHANCE

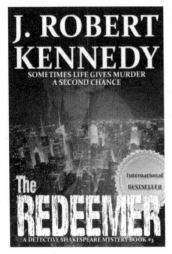

It was the case that destroyed Detective Justin Shakespeare's career, beginning a downward spiral of self-loathing and self-destruction lasting half a decade. And today things are only going to get worse. The Widow Rapist is free on a technicality, and it is up to Detective Shakespeare and his partner Amber Trace to find the evidence, five years cold, to put him back in prison before he strikes again.

But Shakespeare and Trace aren't alone in their desire for justice. The Seven are the survivors, avowed to not let the memories of their loved ones be forgotten. And with the release of the Widow Rapist, they are determined to take justice into their own hands, restoring balance to a flawed system.

At stake is a second chance, a chance at redemption, a chance to salvage a career destroyed, a reputation tarnished, and a life diminished.

A chance brought to Detective Shakespeare whether he wants it or not.

A chance brought to him by The Redeemer.

From J. Robert Kennedy, the author of seven international bestsellers including Depraved Difference and The Protocol, comes the third entry in the acclaimed Detective Shakespeare Mysteries series, The Redeemer, a dark tale exploring the psyches of the serial killer, the victim, and the police, as they all try to achieve the same goals.

Balance. And redemption.

Made in the USA
Las Vegas, NV
14 August 2022